THE DAISY PATCH

Peggy Williams

PublishAmerica
Baltimore

First printing

ISBN: 1-59286-862-2
PUBLISHED BY
PUBLISHAMERICA, LLLP.
www.publishamerica.com
Baltimore

Printed in the United States of America

*Dedicated to
my father, Gordon,
who taught me to love reading and to my beloved Christian.
Heaven's gain is my loss.*

Acknowledgements

I would like to thank all the people who encouraged or helped. There are a few, however, who stand out and should be given either credit or blame for bringing this book to publication. Bea Jakubowski, who read an early draft, and survived it. Patricia Lothian, my first reader who told me to keep going. My son, Christopher, and Dr. John Shea, who encouraged me. Jo Lane Thomas, the editor who worked on this long and hard, thanks. Matt Connolly, my medical man on call, who emailed me some sound advice. But sometimes I just made it up as I went along, sorry, Matt. Thanks to Scott Blevins at overstock.com and Carl Rosendorf at SmartBargains.com for allowing me to mention their wonderful websites in this book. I want to thank Dee Johnson for her wonderful design work on *The Daisy Patch* website. And last, but not least, my friend, Diana Pierce, a talented writer herself, she gave me pointers, and encouragement. Her email advice was priceless. Any mistakes are mine, not theirs.

Chapter 1

Thoughts of dinner flew out of Kurt Van Doren's head as he watched the trauma team fight for the man in ER. They were hooking up fluids and blood, nurses were cutting off clothes, and techs were taking blood samples. Don Schuler, the ER guy on duty, was snapping out orders. He looked up with relief as Kurt waded in. The gaping wound from the knife fight was momentarily packed and stabilized so Kurt, with a team of techs, started for surgery on a gallop.

They took the corner to the elevators at top speed and promptly collided with another gurney parked right outside of radiology. The collision pushed Kurt sideways and off balance and he steadied himself by grabbing the lady on the stretcher. Embarrassed, he hesitated then apologized. "Oh, sorry, we're in a hurry here, hope I didn't hurt you?"

I was taking a quiet catnap while waiting for my x-rays, when this team in full flight rammed my stretcher. It gave me a fright, but no harm done that I could see. I heard muffled noises as they steadied the patient and his swaying IV. Hands reached out and grabbed my shoulder. I twisted in time to see a green blur bounce away from me, steady my oxygen equipment, and apologize. I shot a look at the bloody patient and yelled back, "Hey! Watch out there! I'll live, which is more than I can say for that poor man, keep going." As they moved on, I got a better look at the green blur and realized he certainly was good-looking and his face was vaguely familiar.

While waiting for the elevator the familiar face looked back and called out. "You're a trooper! Thanks."

Suddenly remembering a name, I called out, figuring if I was right he would react, if I was wrong no harm done. "Hey, Stretch, you're Donna's friend."

He looked surprised, and as the doors started to close said, "I'll see you later."

A bit of excitement as I lay in the hall waiting for the third or fourth set of x-rays scheduled for that day. I was losing count, and that's a sure sign I had been here too long.

The green blur was good-looking, and I'm sure he was the man my friend, Donna, dragged in to pose for pictures for our firm's most recent website—this one was on mental illness. I told her we needed a tall guy, a volunteer, to stand around in a white coat wearing a stethoscope and look professional. I'll have to check with her, but I think she recruited a real nurse or doctor for the part. As I remembered, he was very good-looking, polite, funny, and I figured him for a professional actor. All of us ladies enjoyed having the guy on the set for a couple of hours.

Doctor, nurse, orderly, what does it matter? I dismissed the man and concentrated on reading the bulletin board I was parked against—great material there on lunch schedules, phone protocol, giving blood, everything you always wanted to know about hand washing and disposal of contaminated material.

I had long given up any thought of good-looking men in my life, dating or romance. I always told myself a middle-aged blonde who falls in love hasn't got much of a chance in a world full of size 2 Barbie dolls all looking for Mr. Right. And for a woman like me, who has spent the past 2 months in and out of hospitals, it's just plain too crazy to contemplate. I'm certainly no Barbie doll…not even close.

Last year I would have described myself as middle 40s, to be honest I'm 47. My eyes are blue, I have a round face, and I'm told rather good features. I'm one of those women who hear, "you have such a pretty face," from people who really mean, "you're not bad looking but lose the lard, sweetie." I have a satisfying job, a functioning family, and up until a few months ago, my health. Now, after a long-undiagnosed illness that resulted in heart surgery, I'm a much thinner blue-eyed blonde with a face not quiet so round, and I'm in desperate need of work on my roots. I know life will get better again, the eternal optimist, that's me. My positive attitude was being sorely tested, however, by this latest hospital trip.

Two days of endless tests for my chest and my leg kept me busy and left me exhausted. The view out my hospital room window was of a boiler room roof and the television service in the District Hospital Center was limited. So I had just straightened myself up to read a few chapters of the latest thriller my daughter, Holly, had brought to me.

A tap on my door and a masculine voice said, "Mrs. Suit?"

8

In walked the klutzy guy from the radiology crash that I knew as Stretch. He was way over 6 feet, had a study build, and tousled brown hair. He was dressed in rumpled surgical greens, and a badge hung crookedly from the pocket of his long white lab coat. It was partially hidden by the standard neckwear of so many doctors and nurses, a stethoscope. On closer inspection, I could see green eyes with long lashes. My mother used to call those bedroom eyes. He smiled at me, and when I smiled back I noticed a dimple in one cheek and a chin that could do with a shave.

My God I'm in love! My heart gave a thud, and I could hear my new artificial valve clicking away in my chest. Dr. Gorgeous has walked in and I look like Wanda the Witch, I thought to myself as he took my hand, smiled, and looked in my eyes. I was now positive he was the guy who posed for our website pictures back in March.

"Mrs. Suit, I'm Dr. Kurt Van Doren, alias Stretch, Donna's friend. Again, forgive me for bumping into you but it was sort of an emergency. You're right, I did the group scene for her website back in March. How did you recognize me, were you there?"

"I was supervising the shoot, Stretch. I had no idea you were a real doctor. All I said to Donna was we needed a tall guy to wear a white coat and look professional. She dragged you in and introduced you to us simply as Stretch. I thought you were an actor of some kind."

"Nope, just a guy on his day off. I should explain that Donna's an old family friend. She's known me since I was a kid, so she didn't have a hard time digging up a tall guy. How's she doing in retirement? I haven't heard from her in months?"

"She's fine. She loves Florida from her emails. I'm glad you stopped back up to see me."

"Actually I'm from vascular surgery and, as you know, we're going to do something about that aneurysm in your leg. I'm here to answer any questions you may have concerning your surgery. Dr. Rainey and the rest of the team will be up in a few minutes. Meanwhile, if you have any questions fire away."

Since I had just fallen for the guy I was naturally aware of how bad I looked. My appearance could be compared to that of a junkyard Ford. The faded blue hospital gown competed for attention with my pasty complexion. As I mentioned before, my hair was a mess, and although I had it cut at the therapy center, I needed a good blonde rinse and special attention to my roots. My arms were bruised from elbow to wrist from daily lab tests, and to top it off, my contacts were at home. Love struck, I removed my old owl-eyed glasses and stared at him. Dr. Gorgeous took hold of my hand; the warmth in his touch was very distracting.

I guess I must have looked a little stunned because the good doctor continued, "Mrs. Suit, do you understand me? I said we're going to fix that spot on your leg, the aneurysm. Didn't anyone tell you we were coming?"

"Tell me what?" I asked, still suffering from the effects of cupid's arrow. "No one came in and said be prepared for surgery. No one even comes into my room except to weigh me and bring horrible food several times a day. My daughter, Holly, visits regularly, and the President of the United States swung through the ward, I was told, but somehow he managed to skip me. No, I had no idea you were coming." I need to shut up, smile, and act reasonably intelligent, I thought. He was quite the distraction last March at our shoot, and a bigger hit today.

Dr. Van Doren looked at me and flashed a dazzling professional smile. He continued to pat my hand in the absent manner people use when dealing with the feeble minded. Considering my stammering and babbling, I'm sure he would soon start to talk slowly and use only one-syllable words.

"No one came up? The nurses didn't tell you we were coming in to talk to you about your surgery?"

I turned my head and looked him square in the eye, which was tough because it meant I would blush and say something stupid again. "Doctor, I'm not senile, I don't forget things. Like I just said, no one told me anything. I'm sorry if this makes you uncomfortable, but that's the way it is. However, I know this thing is dangerous, so if the work needs to be done, it's going to be in my best interest to listen to you and get it over with."

He released my hand. "I'm sorry they didn't tell you."

He sighed and sat down in the low armchair next to my bed, closed his eyes for a second, and rubbed the bridge of his nose. He continued in a tired, exasperated voice, "I guess the nurses must have overlooked it." He smiled at me and patted my hand unconsciously.

I was enjoying the touching a little too much, so I slowly pulled my hand away from the distracting doctor. I knew the mix-up was not his fault, and remembering the warmth of his touch, I smiled over at him from my rumpled bed. He seemed tired and rather worn down. Poor man is almost as bad off as me. I need to brighten his mood.

"I really don't have any questions that can't wait and you look tired, Doc. Relax until Superman, Lois and the rest of the Daily Planet staff show up with the full story. I'll pretend you're not here. Take a quick break."

I don't know why or where the boldness came from, possibly because I was bored, but I winked and gave the man a slight smile; love or lust can do that to you, I suppose. He sat there rubbing the bridge of his nose like he had

10

a headache. We were both quiet for a short time. I needed some small talk, something light and fun to distract the poor man and just to make conversation. A small piece of trivia. I pulled one out now to calm myself and charm this poor tired guy. I wanted to make sure he knew I didn't blame him for the communication gap.

"Hey, just tell me if I am right or wrong here. At some point your people, your ancestors, all came from Upstate New York or New England, am I right?"

"No, gotcha, they're all from Chicago." He stood, arms still crossed, he rocked forward on his feet and looked thoughtful. "I remember my grandmother telling me when I was a kid that my father's people came from Upstate New York originally. My mother and her family came to this country from Holland in the 1930s, I do know that. But you don't know my family. You're a mind reader, a what do you call it?" He snapped his fingers as he tried to remember. "I've got it, a psychic, a mind reader?" He seemed amused at my rather on-target guess.

Trying for charm, since beauty was out of the question, I said, "It's hard to call you Dr. Van Doren. I'm used to your other name from the website shoot."

"Donna's really the only person who ever called me Stretch."

"Good. I won't call you that then.

"Anyway, to get back to your name and history. Most of the Dutch and Germans who settled this country in the early days settled in Pennsylvania, New York, and the rest of New England. You know about New York City and New Amsterdam, all kids learn about it in school, you just forgot it. A lot of the Dutch people had that prefix Van and the Germans, Von, so it follows your ancestors probably started out in this country up there. I was a history major in school. I also read Irving's *Legend of Sleepy Hollow*, or I could be psychic."

I was shocked to realize I was flirting with this man in the rumpled surgical greens. This is crazy, flirting at my age and with a younger man, probably a married younger man, what was I thinking here? But then I rationalized it as—who the hell cares? It was a flirtation on my part, and I was probably one of 50 adoring women he sees each day.

Together we waited for his chief. We talked about why I was here. What had happened to me this past summer. He explained to me exactly how they were going to repair my aneurysm the following Monday.

A rap on the door announced Dr. Rainey with the rest of his team. The main man was a slight but handsome light-skinned black man with the palest blue eyes I have ever seen. They were almost colorless, like ice. His fine-boned features and straight black hair gave him a striking hawk-like appearance.

The team fanned out around the end of my bed like birds of prey around a carcass. Rainey, in a soft monotone, explained exactly what Kurt had told me. I must give credit to my new friend, he explained the procedure in greater detail and made it simple enough so that I, as a layperson, could understand. I just kept glancing at those lovely green eyes and that cute crooked smile as Dr. Rainey continued his monologue.

The whole appearance of the main man took about 2 minutes. The team, including my interesting doctor, flew out of the little room. In the rush of their departure, their white coats billowed out, so they looked like a flock of swans floating down the hall.

Kurt Van Doren walked between Dr. Rainey and the other surgical resident, Pat Sewell, thinking: What an interesting and funny lady. She's been through hell and still gutsy. Got to hand it to her, she not only keeps smiling, she had me smiling, too. She was aware of how tired I was, and kind enough to be concerned. She's the patient, and yet she kept telling me to take it easy. Think I'll read up on her a bit.

He broke off from the team and strode into the ward clerk's office, picking up the Suit chart. He settled in and read it from beginning to end.

I again picked up the new mystery and tried to read, but after watching those green eyes and shamelessly flirting with Dr. Van Doren, I was bored. Later, as I lay in a light sleep, I heard.

"Psst, are you sleeping?" The nice doctor again tapped on the open door and walked in smiling. He took my hand in what I could tell was an automatic gesture. I was definitely enjoying the hand-holding part. "I've been reading your chart. It's been a damn hard summer for you, Mrs. Suit."

"Doc, as long as I get to hold your hand it was all worth it." I was flirting with him again. I simply could not help myself. Between the boredom and falling in love, I was shameless.

He moved his hand away from mine. It was as if he realized what a bold hussy I was. "How can you be so flip after all you have been through?"

"To tell you the truth, what's happened scares hell out of me, so I just ignore it and live for now."

He sat down in the chair next to my bed and stretched tired muscles in his arms by flexing. I suspect that for him it had been a long shift. Even I know residents are expected to pull them.

"You were on target about my folks, you know. I remembered things my

12

mother told me. And yes, they were originally from New York and moved to Chicago many years ago."

"Don't tell me you called your mom to ask her about that after our talk this morning?"

"No, Mrs. Suit. She died when I was 13. One of the reasons I think I am here today is I remember the doctors, hospitals, smells, sounds, it was fearful and exciting. Sort of stuck with me I guess."

"I'm so sorry I brought the subject up. It must've been hard for you at that age to lose your mom. By the way, call me Maggie, or whatever, not Mrs. Suit. Makes me sound like my own dear, departed mother-in-law."

"Good, you can call me Kurt.

"You married, Maggie?"

"No, divorced about a thousand years ago. Raised the kids by myself. It's just that Mrs. Suit sounds so formal and *old* and I hate the idea of both right now. What about you, got a wife and family?"

"Nah, not for me. I tried it but it's over about 4 years now. Never again. I think I'm not the domestic type. Got a nice daughter though, I'll show you her picture sometime. She's got a ton of curls the same color as mine."

Looking at the man, I figured he must be hell on the nurses—a girl on every floor. I could see why he's divorced. He probably liked the swinging bachelor life, but still he loves his kid, that you can tell.

The noise and smell of the food trays coming up both alerted and sickened me. Food turned my stomach. Unfortunately, the food at this hospital was enough to turn a healthy person's stomach. A young girl, dressed in a brown shirt with yellow collar and wearing a hairnet, brought in my tray, smiled mechanically, and put it down on my bed stand. I struggled to sit up, and put on my robe. Kurt helped and I snapped the top closed. "Thanks, you're pretty handy with a robe. Do you do that for all the ladies around here?"

"Lots of robes in this place, lady, you get used to it. I only help the wicked ones, the ones who can read my fortune." He smiled down at me as I sat there. The smell of the food made me nauseated.

I lifted the lid, put the top back on and pushed it away. "What do they do to perfectly good food to make it so awful? Yuk!"

He picked up the lid, took my fork, and prodded the limp shape that was masquerading as a chicken breast.

Handing the fork back to me with a piece of the mystery mass speared on it, he answered my question. "To be honest, all the food here is disgusting. You can sometimes get better stuff in the cafeteria downstairs if you're careful. Here, you better eat something, according to your chart you're very anemic and malnourished."

I looked at the speared piece of chicken, shook my head, and shivered in disgust.

He shoved the stray fork, meat and all, on the tray. He moved the stand to the foot of my bed and said, "Look, I've got an idea, forget this crap. I haven't eaten yet. I'm clear for a bit, why don't I go down, get my food, and bring you something back, too? Now, what do you want? Has to be within reason as I only have about ten bucks in my locker."

"Oh, that's nice of you, but you don't have to do that."

"Don't have to but I want you to have something to enjoy. Anything? Come on, what do you fancy, lady?"

"They have these fruit bars down there, frozen juice bars, and it's one of the things I can truly say I like eating right now. Tell you what. If you get me one I'll owe you. While you're gone, I'll try to get some of this chicken thing and a vegetable down and then I'll have my fruit bar for dessert."

He carefully moved the stand containing the food tray closer to me.

"What flavor, or don't you care?" He tossed over his shoulder as he walked out.

"Better red color than anything, cherry, strawberry, raspberry."

"Gotcha." He disappeared.

Kurt left her room humming an old Elvis tune, he nodded and smiled as he went past the nurse's station. The cafeteria was crowded with folks all trying to get lunch. He grabbed a burger and trimmings and as he left he picked up a cherry-flavored juice pop for his new friend up on 3 East. He waited to pay for the food and thought about the gutsy blonde who could not walk. Not very nutritional but at least she'll get some sugar into her. I'm going to ask Fred Kelly if I can write in a nutritional supplement to be taken at meals, that should help her a little, he thought. He threaded his way through the throng and headed back upstairs to Maggie's tiny room on 3 East.

Chapter 2

I did not expect to see him again. But about 20 minutes later he was back, carrying a covered dish with a frozen fruit bar balanced on top and a drink of some kind. He put the food down, inspected my tray, shook the milk carton and noted I had eaten some of the disgusting chicken and drank the milk. He nodded in approval. Sitting down, he took one of the napkins off my tray (he had forgotten to get some) and a towel from my nightstand. He balanced the meal on his knees and tucked into a huge hamburger, fries, and coleslaw, all the worst carbs and fats you can pack onto a plate.

"This making you sick to see me eat?"

"Heck no, anyone can eat, I just can't eat myself. I don't want to deny anyone else the pleasure. You look like a growing boy who needs his strength."

"At my age all my growing is out not up, I'm afraid. Middle age is fast approaching."

"Oh hell, I did middle age, still doing it in fact, and it's not so bad, believe me. You're what, 35 or 36?"

"Guess again, a lot older than that. I did a full 12 years in the Army before deciding to go on to college and med school. I got a late start, you might say. I'm closer to your age than I am to most of the other residents around here."

We ate and talked and forgot about the time.

"Hey, what's going on in here, girlfriend?" Sally, the chubby night nurse came to check on me. She glanced over at Kurt as he sat with his empty plate.

"Now what are you doing in here, Dr.V? You're not supposed to be fooling around with the patients like this, eatin' together, and laughin' all over the place. We heard you way down the hall in the nurse's station. You keep this up and Nora will catch you. And you know how much she loves ya, Doc."

Getting up and taking his plate and napkins and my pop stick, he dumped them in the waste can just as his beeper went off.

"Who's Nora?" I asked as she stood there chuckling with the man I thought of as Doctor Gorgeous.

Kurt smiled at both of us in a sheepish manner and said, "Got to go, see you later, uh, Aunt Maggie." He pointed to Sally. "She can explain Nora better than me, I think." He turned and flew out the door and down the hall.

"What does he mean, Aunt Maggie? He's your relative or something, sweetie?"

"Yes, but we didn't want to make a big deal out of it. He's my nephew, I'm from Chicago originally."

I was glad the man had mentioned that town. This way I could get this lie straight. I realized he set me up, that rat.

I pushed myself up, moving into a more comfortable position, I asked, "Now, tell me about Nora. You two have me curious?"

She seemed to ignore the question. "He should have said you were his aunt and not let us wonder what was going on. We thought you both had lost your minds down here—all that laughin'." She was holding my wrist and checking my pulse while the aide wheeled in the hated blood pressure machine.

"Oh, come on, Sally, it wasn't that much noise. Face it, you guys were just curious why he was in here and brought food. Not much gets past that bunch up there, I'm sure. Now come on, what's with this Nora, is she an old girlfriend of his?"

Dropping my wrist and strapping on the pressure cuff she laughed and answered, "At least you answered our curious minds. Remember, 'inquirin' minds want to know,' to quote that supermarket rag my mother loves so much."

While the pressure machine was squeezing the life out of my arm, Sally told me about Nora. "Darlin', our Nora has it in for the good doctor, big time. Word has it that he's some kind of rich kid who got through medical school on his daddy's money. Now I've seen the man in action, and no matter what money there is he works hard, and it shows." She wrote down the diastolic and systolic numbers from the machine and then my pulse rate.

She continued as the cuff was removed. "The man is just plain good. He covers for others on leave. He's not too social but he's very kind to everyone on staff. Always ready to pitch in when anything is too much for us to handle and he's nearby. I've worked with him for the past 4 years." She looked at me and bent her head knowingly. "Girl, the man knows what he's doing."

The aide moved the pressure machine out and Sally stood by the doorway.

16

"Our Nora, she's the night supervisor. She's been here for 20 years now, I guess. Fine nurse but has a blind spot about what she sees as privilege. Most of the men and women residents aren't like your nephew. They're not making much money; some of them get paid less than we do. They work long hours, and their idea of a good time is a movie, or burger and Coke at the local bar. Nora found out that Dr. Van Doren drives a little sports car, and he owns an apartment he shares downtown. I don't know where she got her information, but it makes the doc look like a guy with money and that puts her nose out of joint big time. There's more to it, I guess, but I don't know what that part is."

Sally looked up and said almost to herself, "Must be that Sewell mess that really set her off a while back, too."

She looked back at me remembering I was there. "So whenever she can find fault, or put blame somewhere she puts it on him. It's a shame, he works hard and seems like a decent guy, money or no money, and Dr. Rainey relies on him a lot."

"She sounds like a sour old witch. You sure she just doesn't have the hots for the doc and he can't tolerate her? Hey, you don't think he'll get into trouble for visiting with his own aunt, do you?" I was curious about this woman now.

"Nah, you're family and that's different. But old Nora would light a fire under his chair if she found out you were just a friend not family." She fussed with my covers and unwound the tangled phone cord on my bed. "And as for having feelings, she's been married to some old cop in D.C. for a hundred years. She has a grown kid or two somewhere." She picked up my tray and started out the door. "Look, girl, I have to get back, but if you need anything, holler, you hear?" She walked out with my cold tray.

Interesting information, I thought to myself. I think this man who seemed so at home in my presence was a fun diversion. Probably same thing for him, too. I figured he was probably between conquests and needed amusement. For me, hell, I was still in love but it was obvious it would not last. Such is life for middle-aged blondes, like I said before, we're no competition for the young blood out there in this town.

Back to my mystery. The book was good but my mind kept wandering to how nice it felt to have my hand held and to have someone fuss over me a bit.

I kept looking out the window and wishing he would come back. It was plain obvious I had a huge crush on this guy.

After visiting hours, at around 9, a head peeked in my door. Back came Kurt with another fruit bar from the cafeteria. "Hungry yet?" he said as he held out the frozen bar to me.

I nodded, gave him a smile and reached for it, tearing off the paper. "You're a rat, you know, leaving me holding the bag with the Aunt Maggie story for the whole nurse's station to chatter about. And then hearing about that fearsome old bat Nora from Sally. Good thing I'm your dear auntie or your butt would be up the creek on some kind of charges I'm sure."

He took the fruit bar paper and dropped it in the trash and laughed, nodding his head. "Figured you were quick enough on the uptake to think of something. Actually Nora's not all that bad, she just seems to resent the fact that I have it a bit easier than some. Not my fault is all I can say, *Aunt Maggie.*" He emphasized the last two words with obvious delight.

He dropped into the lounge chair in my room. Looking at me he shook his head and said quietly, "Poor Auntie, alone here in the strange city, sick, and all she has are a daughter and her dear nephew."

I ignored his comment and bit into my treat. "How did you get this fruit bar? They close at around 7, don't they? At least to the public they do. Holly has missed it a couple of times."

"Got it earlier before they closed and kept it frozen at the nurse's station until I could get back here. Do you want to sleep?" He looked concerned.

I shifted in the bed. "All I do is sleep, or watch TV. Now that's a thrill. I can learn how to wash babies, inject insulin, or change my colostomy bag. Or for a rapid change of pace I can always count ceiling tiles. No, just talk to me until you're called again. How long do you work anyway? You were in here around 10 this morning, it's now almost 9 at night?"

"We all pull long shifts. I'm used to it, don't worry. Not staying on your account or anything, *Aunt Maggie.*" He laughed as he again emphasized my new status as his relative.

He looked into her eyes as he realized he was not telling the truth. He had arranged to stay later than he planned so he could spend time with her. Something about her laughter, her guts, was so refreshing. Her condition hasn't spoiled her or made her demanding as it does so many patients. Instead, she reaches out to people, the nurses all like her, the aides all know her, and she knows every one of them by name. She treats me like a friend, not just some suit that visits and charges.

We ate. Me with my fruit bar and Kurt ate his junk food: a candy bar, Pepsi, and a fruit bar like mine. The night nurse came in and I was introduced to her as his "Aunt Maggie."

He sat there relaxed and casually lied, "She's my Uncle Charlie's widow and she's a pretty good old girl."

18

"That's nice, Doc, but don't let Nora catch you. Aunt or no aunt, she'll skin you if she hears about you visiting."

She patted my bed, nodded her head in my direction and left.

I looked at him. "So glad you really like this 'old girl.' Poor old Aunt Maggie my eye! From my calculations I can tell you, *nephew dear*, I'm not that much older than you." I fluffed the covers and gave him a sharp look. We exploded in a conspiratorial laugh.

"You're what, about 2 or 3 years older than me? Hard to tell with your hospital pallor." He stretched and yawned. "We make a pretty good pair of liars, don't we? You know if I had an aunt or a cousin, I would like her to be like you. So for now, you're my Aunt Maggie, and I've known you for years and years, even though I only met you today."

"We're old souls, Kurt, old souls," I told him as I flipped the Popsicle stick in the trashcan.

Kurt smiled to himself going past the nurse's station at 3 East thinking: She's strong and upbeat. It's amazing how some patients seem to get to you more than others.

Chapter 3

Friday was not a good day. Around 11 a.m. a pleasant guy, who looked to be about 12 years old, introduced himself as Dr. Hildebrand. They get younger and younger, just like the cops. He stood at the end of my bed and explained how he planned to do a fluid removal (thorocentesis) on both of my lungs. Holly came down to be with me during this procedure. They hauled in some equipment and a nurse stood by as it started. Holly took one look and flew out the door.

"Try to hold very still, Mrs. Suit. It won't be long now."

"Call me Maggie, Dr. Hildebrand, I don't feel as old as a Mrs. Suit, yet."

"Sure, Maggie. I heard you're related to Kurt Van Doren on the surgical team, is that true?"

"Word does get around in this small city within a city, doesn't it?" I answered back noncommittally, or as noncommittally as I thought I could.

Dr. Hildebrand kept up the pressure on my back and said, "It's nice to know he has relatives. Man is a complete blank to most of us here. Never speaks about his life or family, never comes to hospital functions. Everyone speculates about him. He's good, takes a lot of work on himself and acts as Rainey's right-hand man. You can be quite proud of your nephew. Glad to know he has family outside the hospital here; he practically lives in this place."

"Oh, he has contacts and family right here in town. Me, for one, and his cousin Holly, who's right outside the door. But don't discuss Kurt with Holly as they are on the outs right now for some reason," I blithely lied to this nice doctor pulling who knows what out of my right lung.

Wait until I get hold of that sneaky rat later today, I thought. He'll pay for this with another fruit bar for sure. I'm not above a little social lying at times. *"Oh, the baby is soooo cute."* When truthfully you don't know whether to give it a banana or a bottle. But this was becoming a little too much. Also, I didn't want him to get into trouble with old Nasty Nora the night nurse. I was becoming a possessive aunt, defending her nephew.

"All finished, Maggie, you were a good patient. I'll get your daughter to come back in now." Hildebrand took his equipment, his nurse and exited my room. Holly marched back in.

After both the doctor and Holly left, I dozed and watched more TV, then tried to read my book. I even visualized or tried to figure out a way to meet this Nora person who was dogging Kurt's heels all the time. The old defensive Aunt Maggie was at it. Every time I heard footsteps outside my door, I glanced up, hoping to see Kurt. But no sign of the hospital's best looking bachelor. Disappointed, I got ready for bed and had them turn off my light. I snuggled down without the oxygen to see if I could make it through the night.

Just as I was dozing off I heard a quiet tap on the door, it opened gently and someone came in. Figuring it was another nurse I just burrowed further under the cover and stuck my hand out. A large soft paw I immediately recognized clamped onto my wrist, checking my pulse. I have to get over the crush on this man but his green eyes and crooked smile were hard to forget.

Kurt bent down to see her, as she lay covered up from head to toe against the refrigerated air. He felt relieved to be back in her room and reassure himself she was holding her own against that damn tricky aneurysm. He saw on the chart that the daily lab work showed no improvement in the anemia. Got to get some decent food in her somehow, get that supplement ordered. I'll call Fred's office in the morning, I think. He saw two blue eyes peek out from deep inside the blanket.

He smiled at her and said, "Shhh, don't say anything. I just came to say hi and tell you I was off late last night and today. Just wanted to stop in and see how you were doing. Heard the good news you were off the oxygen."

The handsome face I had waited all day to see was now peering at me under the cover. I had to say something about the gossip going around. "Do you realize it's all over the hospital that I'm your Aunt Maggie and everyone's been asking about you all day? I've lied my fool head off to about 20 people. This thing is getting out of hand. Do something about it!"

Leaning in close and speaking softly so he was not overheard, he replied, "Like what? I guess I could kill you off, but they might suspect your nephew right away, so for better or worse, you're my Aunt Maggie till you get out of here. Come on, it's funny, we're not hurting anyone."

By this time I had pulled the covers half off, sat up, and put on my glasses. "It's not funny! I don't know a lot about you and these folks know even less, thank heaven. Hell, I know more about you than they do and I've only known you for 2 days. Actually, most of what I know I *made* up for heaven's sake."

He flopped down in the chair, and glancing at me with those lovely green eyes he asked, "What did you tell them about me? I have to know to keep the stories straight, now."

I got more comfortable in the bed, then turned and said in a low voice, "I told them the usual crap about a boy who joined the Army to get away from a motherless home with a couple of siblings and a stern father."

He whispered back, "Oh, Maggie, that's some story. That crappy childhood thing is so sad, it will get me lots of sympathy from now on, I guess. Sorry, not your fault. I started it, didn't I, *Aunt Maggie?*"

I leaned toward him and again in a soft voice said, "You bet your booties, Doc. Hey, it was the best I could do on short notice. I had to remember what I said so they didn't catch me. What a story, it just grew like Pinocchio's nose."

I threw my housecoat around me and continued, "I rather liked the fire at Christmas in the apartment where you all lived near the university. Only I don't know where the University is in Chicago?"

"Just be vague, don't elaborate, you'll be out of here early next week, and I'll take the heat. I really deserve it for getting you into this. But remember, we're not hurting anyone, so who cares? Hell, it gives them something new to chew on in the lunchroom. As far as I know, I've rarely been the object on their hot line before, live too quiet a life, I guess." He was actually enjoying this charade, I could tell.

He patted my hand as I lay back down, pulled the covers up over my shoulders, plucked the glasses off my nose, put them on the table, turned off the light, and walked out.

"Good night, *Aunt Maggie*," he called loudly over his shoulder as he went off down the hall.

The performance was for the nurse's station, I'm positive. The visit lasted all of 3 minutes but in a way it made my day. My impression of him as a swinging bachelor with a smooth line was wavering a bit, as his colleagues complemented me on having such a great nephew. He could charm the leaves off a tree, he has a breezy bedside manner, and the nurses like and respect him. I snuggled down in the bed and said to myself, "I simply can't believe you live too quiet a life, no gossip. Hah! I think there's lots of speculation about you, Dr. Gorgeous."

22

***

Down at the nurse's station, Kurt glanced at Maggie's chart and noted that Kelly had added a comment that the aneurysm was a little larger than they suspected at first. He turned to the night nurse. "This thing could be dangerous, you're going to have to get in there tonight and check on her. If that ruptures, she won't have much time for us to get to it. Make sure you check often and let her know to call if she feels any change in that leg at all."

"She's your aunt, why don't you just come and check on her, too? You're her nephew, and sometimes things get quiet around here at night. Bet you could take a break, and keep an eye on her at the same time. The thing is life-threatening, so you'd have a reason for sitting there."

"Not in the rules, you know that. Lurking around in a patient's room could get me in big trouble, but as you said, it's serious and she's my aunt after all, maybe I'll consider it. Thanks for the idea." He hurried downstairs to his office.

The sleeping pill kicked in and I drifted off. Sometime during the night I remember someone checking on me; I was out of it and don't remember much. I remember turning and seeing Kurt reading or resting, probably too exhausted to care.

The man was either busy or off because Saturday came and went with no appearances of the *lying rat nephew*. The curiosity of the staff was quickly passing. Several nurses came in and explained how I needed to call them if there was any change in my right leg at all, at any time. I prepared for the coming surgery by sleeping, reading, and being bored.

The handsome Dr. Rainey showed up Sunday with the big red-haired female resident and my nephew. Surgery for Monday was scheduled if my blood level was right. They had been reducing the blood thinner I was taking since Friday. Kurt smiled impersonally, patted my hand, and floated out with the team.

Sunday night, he showed up with his late dinner and a fruit bar for me.

I sat up and reached for the frozen bar, pulling the paper off the sticky treat. "They tell me you're the one who ordered the nutritional junk I have to drink now. That stuff is so sweet and cloying! Like my fruit bars better." I waved the red bar at him. He laughed.

I ate the fruit bar, then let him know the curiosity had started to let up. "If people keep asking, I'll have your father on death row and two sisters in a crack house somewhere. And since we are in this so deep, why don't you tell me about your real life instead of this fantasy crap we've been dishing out?"

He sat down, pulling a towel from my locker onto his lap so the food would not make a mess. Biting into his tuna sub, he raised one eyebrow in an offer for me to join him. I shook my head no. He proceeded to work on the 12-inch monster. I worked my way down the frozen juice bar, still whining about the sweet nutrition drink he was forcing me to take.

Between bites he explained, "Before I start my tale of woe, yes, I'm guilty of the nutrition glop, as you put it. I had the idea and discussed it with Dr. Kelly. He thought it was an inspiration and had me order it up. So I'm not entirely to blame since he agreed. Now, on to the juicy stuff you wanted to hear. Not much to tell really, Maggie. Grew up in the city. I was fortunate that my father owned his own small contracting firm and managed to make some good investments, so his assets were reinvested in real estate. We live on the top floor of a great old place built in the 1920s on the East Side. My father has apartments all up the six floors that he rents out mostly to faculty and students. We have the whole top, which is quite large. On the first floor are some businesses but they come and go with the years. Jewelry store, clothing stores, one time there was a guy who wanted to put in a restaurant but the old man thought the smell would be bad for the upstairs so he nixed it. Enough background for you?"

I noticed he stayed well away from his mom, marriage, and divorce and I was not about to pry. After his revelations I commented, "It's a start anyway. By the way, again, I'm sorry about your mom, Kurt. You don't say much about that time in your life, and if I seemed to be prying I don't mean to." I moved my covers and turned to face him while he ate and explained the real Kurt to me.

He finished the sandwich quietly. I felt bad, like I had opened up a sore spot and taken him to a place he didn't want to go. He wiped his hands with the napkin and my once pristine towel, draped it over the sink, tossed the balled up napkin into the trashcan, missed, bent over, picked it up, and tossed again.

"Actually, I've never discussed her much with anyone. My father was always distant and couldn't bring himself to talk about it. We both grieved, but alone, in our own way. He invited this priest friend of his over several times for meals. He knew he couldn't help me but sort of hoped the priest could."

This was an uncomfortable subject and Kurt moved and shifted in the chair as memories came back.

"This priest, Father John, and I talked a little. I was at the age and emotional level where I hated to let the feelings out. It didn't seem manly, I suppose. Anyway, he encouraged me to go to the Christian Brothers boarding school at least for a year. He said it would give me some distance from the memories. It seemed a good idea at the time, and I've always been grateful to him for suggesting it. Getting away isn't easy for a 13-year-old so it was the perfect answer. I stayed until I graduated and left for the Army."

I could see the relief by his body language as the story ended. If I wasn't in love with this big hunk before, I know I fell at least a little in love with him at this point. I had to look away for a second or I would have cried. I changed the subject as the atmosphere in the room seemed a little close and sad. Maybe he wasn't such a swinging bachelor as I had figured. Just a nice guy. But I was withholding judgment on that. Probably never know the answer, and I sure as hell was not sticking around this place long enough to find out.

Sitting up, I smiled a little as I said, "Your real story sure isn't anything like the bull we've been throwing around here lately."

He looked at me, shook his head slightly and said, "No, except for Nora, no one knows much about me here, I prefer it that way, and now you. You seem to pull confidences out of me like I pull Kleenex. I know Nora found out about my situation and has it in for me. She imagines I'm part of the spoiled selfish idle rich, I suppose. She has a husband who's a retired D.C. cop and now a PI, so I guess she had me checked out. I don't know what her reason is except to be nosy or nasty."

I looked at my coconspirator and felt sorry for him. "Kurt, the staff around here seem to think you're a pretty good guy, why doesn't she?"

He obviously didn't have an answer so he shrugged his shoulders, and shook his head, as he looked down at the worn sneakers on his feet.

"We have to stop lying about this auntie thing. I'm glad it's sort of died down, and let's hope the story does you no harm."

Standing up, he walked to the end of my bed, and stretched. He seemed tired, and I knew it was only the beginning of his shift. "Hey, you've been enjoying this as much as me. It's just a small diversion like that priest that came in today."

"He didn't seem too upset over you being a lapsed member of the fold, I take it? Nora's a Catholic, and I figured one time to start a conversation with her about the church, sort of to break the ice and try to make friends. She asked me if I go to church regularly. She attends daily Mass here in the chapel. I, on the other hand, make it to church at Christmas and Easter. Christmas Eve has always seemed to me a special magical night since I was a kid."

"I know exactly what you mean, not the whole Christmas thing, but that night is special."

"Could never quite explain it to anyone before. But you feel it, too, so there must be something to it, Maggie."

"Never told your dad?"

"Nah, he'd never understand; too practical and hardheaded."

"Hey, my friend, we all can't be dreamers or sensitive people. We need the practical folks out there to keep us loonies on an even course through life. I'm sure he's fine and obviously took great care of you.

He walked around the room apparently uncomfortable with the conversation, his beeper went off. He sat down and took his cell phone and answered the page. Questions, answers given, more questions. "Got to go. If you're awake I can come back. I have to work tonight, and so far it's quiet but that can change fast. And, don't fret about Nasty Nora, she's pretty harmless. She's tough on everyone on staff at one time or another, not just me."

"I won't, I promise. You can come back, you won't disturb me, all I do is sleep. I look forward to company as a matter of fact. I'll just read till you get here, but don't let Nora get you."

Hell, there was no way I was going back to sleep now. The thought of more company and decent conversation, especially with this dear man, was more than enough to keep me going all night if I had to.

Later, tapping her door and not getting a response, Kurt entered. "Maggie, sorry I'm so late," he said quietly as he went over to her bed. He saw she was asleep, glasses on, book fallen in her lap. Poor kid, sleep's good for her. He put the book on her nightstand, brushed a curl from her forehead, removed her glasses gently as she made a small noise, and turned when he covered her arms. She sighed and got more comfortable. He snapped off her bed lamp and left the room. Amazing how she seems to look right into my head and into my so-called soul. Wonder if I have one? Never thought much about having a soul before. Neat lady—gutsy, funny, and perceptive.

Kurt sent an email to his friend Steve back in Chicago that night. He was a friend of Kurt's from undergraduate days. He went off to law school and Kurt to med school but they remained close and kept in touch. Now, with email, they talked almost every day. Kurt, older by 10 years than Steve, with experience in a bad marriage and fatherhood, was able to help Steve cope at times. When he and Ginny fought, Kurt listened like an experienced older brother and told him what kind of flowers to buy or how to apologize.

Email from Kurt: *All is quiet and boring here. How's the new house shaping up? Hope to see it sometime this holiday season. Send more pictures of godson, they are great. Met the most interesting lady patient. She's been very ill but more concerned with others than herself. I have nicknamed her my Aunt Maggie.*

Reply to Kurt's email: *Busy... can't talk now but watch out for those little old ladies.*

Chapter 4

I fell asleep, I don't remember Kurt coming back. Had a restful night and woke up Monday bored and restless, sick of hospitals, doctors—fretful, cranky. Washed and ready for the day, I slammed the top on the disgusting breakfast they sent up, which consisted of two limp pieces of half raw bacon, one hardboiled egg colder than a witch's tit, cold toast, weak coffee. Food coming up meant no surgery. Disappointed, I was ready to fling the whole mess at the door to my room when a familiar face peeked in and tapped on the door.

"Mrs. Suit? I thought that was you on my list for this morning. I read your profile and knew for sure. How are you doing? My goodness it says here you're ambulatory, and that's a far cry from when I saw you last."

The chipper voice belonged to Murphy, the physical therapist that had tried, with limited success, in getting me up when I was on the fifth floor for my initial heart surgery. A rather petite girl with ginger hair, a heart shaped face and dark brown eyes, she was amazingly strong, but I never felt I could trust her with me alone. I felt so weak, I was afraid of falling.

She held out her hands beckoning to me and said, "Come on, lady, show me what you can do, now that I've caught up with you again."

I smiled and was so pleased to see a familiar face. I forgot all about being cranky and flinging the breakfast tray. I threw off the covers, pulled myself to a sitting position, trying not to show what an effort it was. I had gotten up and had taken a couple of steps when suddenly a familiar face popped in the door. Kurt grinned at Murphy and me and walked in.

"Hey, gang, having a party or going dancing? Can anyone join? Should I sign your dance card first?"

I slowly made my way out the door and pretended to growl at him. "Shut up, you big goof. Can't you see I'm concentrating here on getting to my

28

ballet lesson?" I glanced over at him, smiled and said in a mock southern accent. "Yes, ya'll have to sign my card before bein' so bold as to ask me to dance."

"Here goes then." He bolted back into my room grabbed the menu card off the disgusting food tray, whipped out a pen, and initialed the thing, handed it over, bowed slightly and held out his hand. "Now it's my turn to dance with the lady, Murphy."

He stood next to me and gently pulled the walker out of my hands. I panicked, standing there fighting for balance, alone in the hall without my trusty steed. He took my arm in a firm grip and proceeded to walk me, ever so slowly and gently, down the hall.

My knees were weak and I was sweating. I am sure it was not just from fatigue but also from being so close to this man. I deliberately moved in a bit and he held on with one hand, then put the other long arm around my back to steady me.

"Hold on, partner, don't go too fast, your balance ain't that good, so lean on me more."

I really was tired as the stroll had taken us up past the nurse's station and around in a wide circle in the hall. We started back down the hall to my little room. Murphy walked behind us and kept up a steady stream of encouragement and banter. I could tell she was pleased that I was doing so good.

"Hey, Mrs. S, you'll be back on your feet in no time, I can see that. When is your surgery? When do you go home?"

Kurt walked me back to my door and explained, "That's what I'm here to tell you, Maggie—not just to fill up your dance card. Your blood still isn't right—the clotting factor." He handed me off to Murphy at the door, did a quick bow to both of us, and was off.

He turned as if remembering something, came back, and quietly said, "I'll pop in later if I get a chance, Aunt Maggie. You did fine, but I can tell you're tired. Rest. I'll see you later." He gave me a friendly hug and winked at both of us before he hurried down the hall and into another room on the far left.

The day passed in boredom and gloom. Holly came to visit, full of the story of getting past the Secret Service before the President's next visit scheduled for that afternoon. My nephew must have been busy, he never came back that night.

Lights in the hall and the familiar sound of the blood pressure machine squeaking and rattling into my room, and the aide's voice woke me the next morning.

It was chilly at 5:45. I was stiff from a night's sleep and not quite awake from the sleeping pill. The lights were bright in the hall. Thankfully, they didn't turn on my light until I was sitting up on the side of my bed with my housecoat clutched around my shoulders, waiting to get checked.

The aide was jolly, chubby, and very kind. Morning people must love her, but for me it was much too early. The shift nurse was quiet but efficient and as they finished up with my weight and stats, she commented, "You're still not eating." She wrote down another loss for me.

"Have you tasted the crap they pass off as food around here?" I asked as I slid off the scale and struggled to get back on the bed. I sat, rocking back, I raised my feet and pulled myself back into the warm covers.

The little Asian lab technician came bustling into the room. She carried a lab tray almost as big as she was. "Ah, you're awake! Good, I start with you this morning, missy. We have order here to take early as possible. But you have bad vein, I remember. We look." With that, she pulled my arm out, rested it on a pillow, tied a tourniquet around and started feeling for a vein. Finding one, she readied the vials for the needle.

I looked down at the little woman and then at my bruised sore arm. "Damn that hurts! Can't you just skip it one day? I have so many bruises and holes in me. I look like a sieve."

She kept looking intently and decided it was worth a try. After three tries, she could not draw blood and shook her head. "If we get good reading, they do you late today or early tomorrow, missy. You need this done."

I said, "If you can't get blood, how the hell are they going to do surgery? Can't they just try cutting and be careful about the blood, or give me some more if I bleed too much?"

I withdrew my arms under the covers, pulling the tourniquet off myself. "That's it, three times and you're out, out! No more. You can't find it. I have no veins left to puncture. Go back to the lab and tell them go to hell. Tell the surgeon, what's his name, Rainey, to go to hell, I've had it. Please, please no more."

By this time I was in tears. The technician packed up her vicious little basket of needles and rubbed my hand in sympathy, this time not looking for veins.

"You need to have it done. I can't do it now. You rest. We figure out something later. You have many bruises and many sticks with our needles and you need to rest now." She kept patting my arm being so kind. I felt rotten as she comforted me.

"I'm so sorry I was such a brat just now." I looked at her, sniffing and feeling ashamed of myself.

"No, you not brat. You are sick lady and lot done to you. We just have problem. We fix and get blood later. Not to worry. Rest." With that, she patted my hand one last time, picked up her equipment and left me with a smile. I just bawled and sniffed and curled up in a fetal position and tried to go back to sleep.

Someone buzzed Kurt awake in the small on-call room. He sat up, stretched, and dialed the number on his pager. His heart gave a little shift as the floor nurse on 3 East said they were having trouble with Maggie Suit and could he come up. He flew out the door, thinking only that the damn aneurysm had ruptured. He arrived so quickly the floor nurse had barely hung up. She explained to him about the technician and the blood problem. He smiled and reassured her he would take care of it. "I'm a natural born vampire, my dear. I'll get that blood for them." He patted her shoulder as he started for Maggie's room.

He tapped on the door and walked in. She looked so pitiful and sad lying there sleeping. The back of each hand was black and blue. He noticed the large bruise marks, up and down each arm. Some areas had tiny scabs and her skin was dry and red. The sleeve of her gown was up, and he saw the ugly end of her hep-lock where the powerful antibiotics were fed into her each day to control the dangerous virus that had destroyed her heart valve. The tape was pulling on the soft flesh of her inner arm.

I must have dozed because a short time later a gentle hand touched my shoulder. "Maggie, it's Kurt. What's this I hear they can't get blood for the clotting level? We need it, Maggie, you have to cooperate."

He startled me and I whipped around in the bed, looked up at him and my heart melted. He looked tired and rumpled and sweet. His eyes were still soft from sleep, his chin looked scratchy and needed a shave. He must have been called about this difficult patient with bad veins. Realizing who it was, he came to check on me.

"You poor sleepy man, I'm so sorry. I can't help it. I'm just drawn dry, I guess. The lady came in and tried 3 times, and nothing. Damn it, those needles hurt a lot when they go over and over the same places. There are sore spots under the skin, bruises. Just look at me!" I held up my scarred and battered arms. Tears welled up in my eyes and I just let them spill over."

He handed me my glasses, and a tissue, then sat down and gave me a gentle lecture. "I know you're hurting but it'll be over soon. Now, I'm going to get cleaned up and shave. Then I'm coming back with a tray and I'll get the blood myself, is that okay? I promise you no more pain. I have a talent for this and can hit pay dirt with no trouble. I'm a vascular guy, remember? I promise no more pain."

He held my hand, caressing the back of it gently with his thumb. He turned and walked quickly out of the room.

Kurt hurried down the hall to get showered and changed, scolding himself. What's happening to me here? She's a patient, not your real Aunt Maggie, get hold of yourself. Problem is, I'm beginning to think of her more as a friend and less as a patient. Let's hope I don't make an ass of myself and can draw that blood. Me and my big mouth making promises I don't know I can keep.

I cried some more, but it was from relief. I believed him. I trusted him. And yes, I think I was more than half in love with the man. Not that it mattered, it was a silly hospital flirtation. But for now it was real to me. He was real and it was nice to know someone cared.

By 6:30 Kurt was back, cleaned up, wide-awake, dressed in fresh surgical scrubs and carrying a technician's tray. "Here," he said as he put it down on the bed, "just as I promised. Now I want you to relax and give me what you call your bad arm. It's not as bruised as you think and I'm sure I can find a vein. I'm going to put the tourniquet on over your gown sleeve so it won't pinch so much."

"Yes, that feels better than just on the skin, thanks." I looked down at my arm as he busied himself with the tray, the vials, and chose a butterfly needle. He pushed the sleeve of my gown up over the tourniquet.

"Make a fist," he said. His hands started to move carefully from my wrist up to my upper arm, his thumb pressing for the magical vein. I kept looking at him as he concentrated on the arm and at that point he could have amputated it, and I wouldn't have cared. Every nerve was aware of his movement. He was concentrating and completely unaware of my reaction. I was alert to feelings a lot of women my age have started to forget. I think my heart was beating double time.

Kurt explored her bad arm, moving along, checking for a spot to draw the blood. He had promised her he could do it and he was trying hard not to think of her as family or a friend but just as a patient, and right now just a damn elusive vein. Oh hell, she was looking up at him so trustingly; it was like he was working on his daughter or his mother. Have to stop this shit, get back your professional demeanor. Concentrate, damn it!

32

***

"You're so scared, Maggie. I can hear your new valve clicking this morning." He continued exploring my arm, rubbing, stopping, and pressing. "Here, I got it. A little deep but I think it's a good one. The needle will hurt but I'm going to stretch the skin a bit to see if this little butterfly can do the job."

He continued to rub for a few more seconds. He looked up and out the door, apparently deciding on something. "No, I'm going to have to use a larger needle. I don't want to have to do this twice, and I've found a good one. I'm sorry, I promised no pain, but it will be minimal."

With that, he pulled the skin on my upper arm taut, pushed the needle in and started drawing a vial with a blue top that indicated clotting level tests. He popped in another vial, drew more out in a purple one, then a third in red. Withdrawing the needle he held cotton in place and put a tape over the cotton. He gently took my arm and folded it toward me "There, hold that for a minute, all done, not too bad a job if I say so myself. Are you okay now? No more tears?"

He looked down at me and winked as I smiled back weakly. "No more pain for today. If it's not good I'll do this again tomorrow myself, that's a promise. Now a big smile for me, come on." He cocked his head to one side in a coaxing manner.

"Okay, I'm trying. No more tears, I promise." I looked at him in a haze of tears, lust, and embarrassment.

"Good. Got to run, see you later maybe. See if you're put on the schedule. If not, I'll come and tell you myself. No more tears now." He repeated and backed out the door forgetting the tray. "Oops, have to have that." He ran back in and grabbed the tray with the blood vials. "See ya, kid."

How could you not fall in love with such a dear, sweet, competent man?

Murphy showed up after breakfast and we had a repeat of the walk down the hall to the nurse's station. This time I took her arm and allowed her to guide me. She was amazingly strong. I was no longer afraid of falling; my balance was getting better each day and so was my confidence.

Later that morning, Dr. Rainey showed up and announced the blood was almost at the right level. They would definitely put me on the schedule for Wednesday. He then walked over to the door, shut it, and came back to stand next to my bed. He looked rather more serious than usual and I began to feel quite uneasy.

Chapter 5

It was going to be bad, so I steeled myself for anything from more surgery to a fatal disease. My heart started pounding, and if they had taken my blood pressure at that moment, it would have gone through the roof.

"Mrs. Suit, I don't know how to discuss this with you diplomatically, but there have been some rumors and now a charge has been made by our night supervisor that Dr. Van Doren has been harassing you."

I felt relief. I was not dying, but then anger took over. "Oh, for goodness sake, Dr. Rainey, Kurt hasn't…"

He held up his hands and leaned against the sink. His lips curved up in a thin smile.

"Let me finish, Mrs. Suit, please, before you say anything. Nora Feeney has been a night supervisor here for 20 years, and her judgment goes without question. Unfortunately, as you probably already know from Dr. Van Doren, she holds some type of animosity or grudge against him. Now, in my estimation he's a fine dedicated physician. I'm telling you all this so you understand where I'm coming from. Mrs. Feeney has been told that Dr. Van Doren has been coming into this room at all hours of the day and night, and possibly slept in a chair next to your bed one night. Is that true, Mrs. Suit, and if it is true, why would he possibly do such a thing?"

I looked at him, furious and ready to spring out of bed and slap his cold, handsome face. His insinuation was obvious and disgusting. I was angry—at Rainey, at Nora, the fiend, and the person who tattled on Kurt. I just knew this would happen, the man was being too free with his stories and now look where it got him. In a controlled voice and with white-hot anger barely contained, I drew myself up in the bed and defended Kurt with everything I could muster. Damn it, for right now he *was* my family and no one messes with my family without hearing from me.

34

"Dr. Rainey, my nephew is a good doctor and a credit to our family. His father is very proud of him, we all are. I was married to Charles, his uncle. I only have one daughter and Kurt living in this area. He popped up to see me when I had my original heart surgery and that did not stir up trouble. I suppose that woman never caught him up there or at least he was not turned in like a naughty school boy on that floor," I lied smoothly. "I think he's been very concerned about this aneurysm as a physician and as a my nephew. It's a damn dangerous thing and has us all concerned. I'm very sorry if it offends her highness that we're on good terms with one another. Please tell Nasty Nurse Feeney he can come into my room at any time of the day or night if he so pleases and that she should mind her own damn business!"

Dr. Rainey moved away from the sink and looked at me with those cold, colorless eyes of his. "I also found out from several of the day and night nurses that Kurt's your nephew. Of course I can understand that as a family member it would be of more concern to him. I just had to come in to check on the situation. I'll tell Nurse Feeney what you just related to me. I'm sorry if this angered you, but we do have a set of standards that we expect our staff to maintain. In this case, Kurt did only what anyone would do under the circumstances. I would do it myself if you were my family, Mrs. Suit. I'm sorry if this caused you any problem, but I had to get to the bottom of it. If it's any consolation to you, I believed him. He's worked with me for almost 5 years now and if I do say so myself, I've trained him to be the fine surgeon he is today. I'll speak to Nora about this as soon as I can."

He started out the door and I called after him, "Dr. Rainey, I take it he'll have permission from her highness and you to continue his visits to me, if they don't offend the nursing staff and it doesn't interfere with his work?"

He looked back, hesitated a moment and said, "Of course, Mrs. Suit. He's welcome to come see you any time he has free…good day."

And again I raised my voice. "Doctor, he promised to take my blood personally since the technicians have such a hard time. Remind him for me, please."

Not used to being given orders, no matter how slight, he again turned and looked at me over the top of his glasses and said, "Oh yes, since he's a relative of yours, if he has time he can do it, otherwise one of the technicians will have to."

I imitated his look over the top of my glasses and said firmly, "He promised to do it. He knows what he's doing. He does it, or it doesn't get done, get him up here."

"We'll see, Mrs. Suit. I understand you have problems with the veins in your arms. The lab people can use your feet or legs if necessary. Your nephew is a busy man and not always available for this type of work." He was a bit impatient—you could tell.

"Get him freed up, Doc. I figure he's on the clock and I'm on the surgical roster. He's getting paid to work like the rest of you, so to get this whole show on the road he might as well get paid for doing my blood work. See to it." Dismissing the good doctor, I turned back to my book shaking underneath.

He answered sharply, "I'm sure since he's family he can work you in, barring an emergency. Have a good day. We'll get back to you about your surgery schedule."

Upset at being ordered around, he fled. The man has an ego and is used to having his way. I chuckled to myself and slid back under the covers.

Chapter 6

Holly arrived in a rush, her red hair flying and the black power suit showing off her figure enough to turn a lot of heads at the hospital. She's truly a beautiful young woman.

She came in carrying a bag, a covered sandwich for herself and a frozen fruit bar for me. She put a clean gown in my closet, sat down, and proceeded to unwrap her sandwich.

While she ate, she asked about the surgery. I told her about the bloodletting this morning and how it made me feel.

She cut me off. "Mother, I don't want to hear about your imaginary sex life. The man came in, felt your arm up, took some blood and left. Stop making such a big deal out of it." She was tired, I could tell. After eating she seemed more relaxed and we had a better visit. When she was ready to leave I noticed a shadow at my door. It was Kurt I was sure. I called out but got no response. Holly frowned at me and shook her head.

She stood up abruptly. "I'm leaving. I'll call you early tomorrow to see if you're on the schedule and what time. Goodnight, Mom."

Later Kurt breezed in. "Good news, you're on for tomorrow, lady. Can only stay a second but will be here early to do your blood. You're definitely getting there, should be no problem. Busy night, see ya."

Never got a chance to find out if it had been him at the door when Holly was here. I took my pill and went to sleep from sheer boredom. I wanted to discuss Rainey's interesting visit but there seemed to be no time.

The big day arrived. Kurt and the lab tech both showed up at 7:30. He was shaved, dressed neatly in pants, shirt and tie, his lab coat was crisp, and his lapel pin was on straight. He took my blood with a minimum of fuss since he knew where to hit for the pay dirt, as he called it. I was hoping for more caressing.

He took the vials of blood one after the other, looked at me and said, "I came by last night but you had company and I didn't want to disturb you. I heard your daughter give you hell about something, figured I'd be intruding. Couldn't catch what the words were, but the tone sure was tough. Is she always like that with you?"

I squirmed a little at what he said as the needle was withdrawn. He pressed on the spot, holding it for a moment then proceeded to put cotton and firm tape on the area.

"She's had a hard time with me sick and when you came to the door, I called out, but she told me I was making a fool of myself. Did you know about the charge Nasty Nora placed with Rainey about you?"

He put the vials in the lab tray and looked at me and asked, "No, what happened and how did you get involved?"

"Rainey came up here yesterday and told me she lodged an informal complaint against you. He was sort of doing his own investigation and leveled with me about it. I told him flatly you *were* my nephew by marriage and you had my permission to come in here any time. I lied and told him that you visited me upstairs in August but no one was nasty enough to report to the administration that one relative was visiting another."

He shook his head. "That woman is such a crab, just like your Holly. We were causing no harm and hope we can stay friends after all this is over. It looks like you have a nephew whether you want it or not. Good thing I'm on your dead husband's side, so she can't run DNA, right?" He patted my covered knee and smiled at me. "I'm proud of the way you defended me. Thanks."

I looked over and commented, "Rainey is a strange fish, isn't he? You seem more outgoing and social. How do you get along with someone as cold and deliberate as him?"

"He's a great teacher and a friend. And you're right, he's a cold, calculating man, but it makes for a great surgical temperament I guess, less involved that way."

"Is he married? I mean I'd like to meet that man's wife. She must be something."

"Nah, not now. Story goes he was married years and years ago but it didn't work out. There was a kid, too. But he never has so much as said a word in my five years here about an ex or a kid. The rest of us bitch about our wives or ex's and brag about our kids but he's never mentioned anything. Believe me, several of us have tried to draw him out on the subject. Even took him out and had a few drinks with the man, but he was still quiet on that topic."

38

"It must have been very painful for him to clam up and become so distant. Divorces can do that to you sometimes. I should know."

Kurt glanced at me. We both understood that pain, I could tell. He went on. "Look, enough of this gossip. You still have to get through the surgery this afternoon. We have you scheduled for 3:30 barring emergencies." He took the lab tray in hand and started out the door, pausing, he turned and said, "I honestly didn't hear you call out last night or I would have come back and introduced myself. Sorry. See you later today for sure." He was gone.

I called Holly. "Kurt said he was sorry to have missed you, and you didn't see him because he went next door. You'll see him after surgery today, I guess. It's at 3:30 so if you get here around then I'm sure it will be fine. I'll call you if they postpone for any reason. So come if you don't hear from me by 3:00, no earlier, these things are always late."

"Yes, I'll be there, and for God's sake stop making a big deal out of this man, will you? He's a doctor. He's probably used to older women like you who slobber over him. How's your breathing? You sound a bit raspy. Have they checked that again?"

"My breathing's fine. The surgery is so minor you don't even have to come if you don't want to. Whether you know it or not, I have guts enough to do this by myself."

"Stop acting like a martyr. I'll be there. Bye." She hung up.

No disgusting food to deal with today, just water and pills. But the highlight of each monotonous day in a hospital is the arrival of food and arrival of visitors; no matter how bad the food and how sour the visitors. I've had plenty of both lately. If it weren't for making friends with Kurt, this whole hospital stay would have been a nightmare.

I washed and combed my hair and put on a bit of makeup. Kept watching the big clock in my room. Three-thirty came and went and around 4 my carriage arrived without the white horses—just an orderly. I slowly walked to the gurney, and it was lowered so I could get on with help. Off we went to the pre-op surgical area. I was almost giddy, the long wait was over, I would be getting my final problem fixed, then back to physical therapy at the rehab facility tomorrow. I was on my way to being independent and I desperately needed that more than food, or any man, including Kurt and his problems.

Holly arrived as they finished preparing me. "Holly, I'm down here. Look at this outfit they have on me, all I need is a red nose."

The staff looked at me and started to laugh. Holly took one look at me and started to laugh, too. She seemed relaxed and not wearing the usual haggard expression that's haunted her all summer since my illness.

"You're a clown at times, that's for sure," she said to me. "You doing okay, not scared or anything, are you?" she asked as she put a hand on my arm.

"Goodness, girl, you're touching me. I'm still splitting the estate 3 ways, so don't try to butter me up."

She withdrew her hand and laughed at me, "You clown, stop it. You aren't scared?"

"No, I have a friend in the OR who will take good care of me. I have you outside here to defend my honor if need be. I'll be fine, don't worry. I know it's been hard on you, but just think, when this is over, a couple more weeks at the PT place, and then I'll be walking again and able to annoy the hell out of you for a few days at your house."

"That's the plan. And I think it will be all right. You're really not as interfering as some mothers I hear tales about." She leaned in and whispered, "Just forget this doctor business, okay? You'll be fine with Coop and me."

I leaned toward her and whispered back, "Deal. I'll forget the doctor and just get back on my feet."

She patted me as they released the brakes on my gurney and started wheeling me down through the double doors to the OR suites.

Inside the room it was cold and they pulled me up next to a narrow operating table. "Can you slide over, Mrs. Suit?" the technician asked.

Suddenly a tall set of surgical greens wearing a cap and mask appeared at my side and strong hands grabbed mine. "Hey, promised you I'd see you later, so here goes. I want to move you, so I'm going to lean over and pull on this side of the sheet and you sort of roll toward me, okay, Maggie.

"Let's go then, start moving." He then helped me move and suddenly I was all set.

"Put your arm out here on this pad, kid, so we can start the anesthesia." I guess I was a bit dopey from medicine because I flung out my arm on what I thought was the armrest. "Oomph! Not so hard, that isn't the pad, that's me you're thumping."

He jumped back and bent slightly over as I had inadvertently flung out my hand and punched him in a tender manly area. "Hey, don't get so familiar, Aunt Maggie." He laughed, straightened up and started strapping my arm down.

"Oh, I'm sorry. I'm so embarrassed. I was teasing Holly out there about me looking like I was having a baby. Go out and meet with her after this is done, please."

"Sure enough, sugar, will do. Now it's nighty-nite for you."

I was gone in an instant.

In another instant I was back, awake, and very cold. I asked brightly, "Is it over, folks—is it a boy or girl?" The staff look startled and started laughing.

"Are you still full of anesthesia or just being silly?" a nurse asked.

I replied, "I am seriously silly but wide-awake and freezing."

"Here, honey, this will make you feel better." A nurse placed a warmed blanket on me.

"How can you be so awake and funny at a time like this?" the nurse asked as she helped me cover up.

"It's a real talent honed over the past three months, ladies." They moved me to the post surgical area. I was fine. The only sad thought I had was that I would probably never see my hospital flirtation, Van Doren, alias the nephew. But the thrill of having all the work done and my future in front of me was overshadowing even this thought. I was on a high from drugs and expectations.

Chapter 7

Back in my room, Holly was waiting, smiling and joking with me about it all being finished, going back to the physical therapy center and then home to her in a couple of weeks. I was really happy.

She said that since I had been walking over the past 10 days, we should try to get me home in her car. The plan was she would come in late afternoon, and we could actually go to a drive-in and get some fattening fast food to eat, then to Ye Olde Towne of Gaithersburg. She would call on her cell phone and alert them to have help at the rehab center when we got there. I was sure I could get out of the car and into a wheelchair with help. It was a bit scary because of the incision but I was excited, too. Feeling a bit overconfident with the anesthesia just wearing off, I immediately agreed to the plan.

"Mom, you're doing fine. I know it's going to be slow going but I think you're more than ready to try the car. The nurses here will help you." They agreed they would be there for me.

After Holly left, I got curious and asked Mike, the night nurse, "What do you know about this nephew of mine, Kurt? I mean, I didn't see him much growing up and only met the man briefly at family functions. Then I moved to this area. He's been here at the hospital a long time, what do you think of him?"

Mike fussed around my bed and stared out the window. "Your nephew is a good guy, Mrs. S, but he has made a couple of enemies. Nora, the night supervisor for one. She's never liked him from the beginning, from what I've been told. Her story is he's a spoiled rich kid only playing at doctor. For some reason she doesn't trust him or like him. He's never mentioned anything."

He straightened my covers and helped me scoot up towards the top of my bed so I could reach the nightlight better, then continued, "And there has been a running rivalry between Dr. Van Doren and the other two residents in Rainey's department, Patricia Sewell and Vince Packard. When Kurt was appointed chief, not only Nora Feeney, but Pat Sewell went ballistic. She thought she had the job sewed up. Both of them called administration, screaming discrimination, claimed they favored him because they wanted a man in the spot."

He smiled and hesitated at the door. "Hey, you don't want to hear this hospital gossip. Take it from me, he's a good guy and works hard. Patricia Sewell is just jealous of him. She has a great reputation here at the Center, and expected to get the job. She figured she was a shoo-in anyway." He shrugged and continued, "Thought maybe it would give her a better chance in the boyfriend department, who knows? Problem is the lady is way over 200 lbs, she needs to start thinking diets not romance." His smile crinkled up around his eyes as he left.

I waited until the early evening and asked the same question of some of the night staff. Only one person, Milly Prentice, a little surgical nurse who came to check on me from downstairs, would share the standard gossip with me. I asked about this other guy, Vince Packard.

She was a small and sturdy brunette with short brown hair, bad skin but twinkling eyes. She came in and sat in my room with the door shut. "I'll give you the lowdown on that lowlife but I really don't want to get in trouble. Since Dr. Van Doren's your nephew, I'll tell you what I heard."

She crossed her legs and leaned toward me. "First of all, Vince Packard is married, has been for years, and there's a kid, I think. He never brings her or the kid around to hospital functions. Out of curiosity, someone checked his records and sure enough a Mrs. Packard is listed as his next of kin."

She uncrossed her legs, got comfortable, and continued, "Packard's been playing around with one or the other females in this hospital for several years. First it was Myra Greenbaum from obstetrics. Then there was talk of Nora Feeney's niece, Shelly, falling for his charms. I think that was a lie. Anyway, that would be an awful match up if Nora got pissed about it. I can see her going after Packard, Old Ironsides versus Mr. Hands."

"Old Ironsides? I have to meet this woman. I've heard quite a bit about her and her bitterness. But Mr. Hands? I love it, what a title. Is he one of those touchy-feely creeps you just know is getting his jollies when he touches or brushes up against you?"

She nodded her head and agreed. "Yup, you've got him in one. He was busy pursuing some gal in the administration office this past year and disappearing on his shifts. Word has it that Kurt, your nephew, Dr. Van

Doren, I should say, talked to him a couple of times about missing pages. When it kept up, Dr. Van Doren took the entire problem to Rainey, his surgical chief. Packard was pulled up on charges of negligence and unprofessional conduct. He blamed your nephew and I understand there was quite a blowup ending in Kurt, err, Dr. Van Doren getting a black eye and Dr. Packard ended up with a broken nose."

"That sounds pretty rough. Those charges must have been pretty serious for the man to attack Kurt."

"They were, and it was supposed to go in his file and all that, possibly a personnel report, administrative stuff I guess." She glanced nervously at the door as if expecting someone to come running in looking for her.

"His broken nose healed but he feels Dr. Van Doren was unfair to report him and that he deliberately hit him there to ruin his looks. He blames your nephew for the entire thing. Felt Dr. Van Doren shouldn't have tattled to Rainey, and now this may be on his record somewhere and it won't help his chances of getting a fellowship or position next year. The man is vain as a cat and can really hold a grudge. He still holds hard feelings about his so-called looks being spoiled."

"I haven't noticed any good-looking resident with a funny nose around here. Is he still here, what happened to him?"

"Oh, he's still here but you see very little of him. The man keeps a very low profile now. And Dr. Van Doren is still his chief resident, but they just seem to keep out of one another's way except over patients."

She bent towards me knowingly. "I hear he's still hitting on the women, however. But your nephew is great to work with and wouldn't be in charge if he wasn't good at what he does."

She jumped up suddenly feeling guilty at the time she spent gossiping with me.

"I could sure use a cigarette. I'm going out back for a while, see you!" She flitted out the door.

Mike came in later than usual, pushing the blood pressure machine.

"You're doing a double shift? You'll be dead tomorrow, Mike."

"Mrs. S, I do double shifts quite often. Don't worry, I'll see to it that you get down and outside with a minimum of discomfort, okay? We'll even put a pillow on the car seat for you if necessary, just don't tell management I'm giving away their pillows."

He was shoving a thermometer in my mouth so I couldn't speak or complain at that moment. Blood pressure done, temperature taken and respiration counted, I was given a clean bill of health.

I closed my eyes and felt peace and rest for the first time in a long time.

I had finally finished with all the procedures. I was going to be healthy…I had a whole bright future in front of me.

I awoke to a pair of smiling green eyes looking down at me.

"I didn't hear you come in, Kurt, sorry."

He took my hand, felt for my pulse, and then held my hand for a minute. "It's my job to come check on you, lady. Your daughter saw Dr. Rainey after surgery, did she tell you? He said you're fine. I think you're doing great, really great. She didn't get to meet me, just the big cheese; the cheese nips like me don't count. Tomorrow's my day off. I won't be here when you leave so I thought I would come in, see you and Holly and leave. Where is she?"

"She left me in your good hands and went home for the rest of afternoon. She needs to rest—she does a lot for me." I continued to hold on to his hand.

"I have to run now, lot to do yet. But I want you to know I think we should keep in touch. You are, after all, my Aunt Maggie?" Looking at me with those green eyes, he smiled, raised my hand to his lips and kissed it so sweetly. Remembering himself, and embarrassed at what he had just done, he dropped my hand, patted my shoulder and left.

I was astonished at the courtly send-off. He disappeared around the corner quickly, but I called out, "Kurt, take care of yourself. Bye, sweet man." The last 3 words were said quietly, almost to myself. I'm sure he didn't hear them as he went down the hall.

Moving away from her room, Kurt smiled at visitors, nodded his head to the nurses, and realized he was blushing. Maggie didn't see that part at least. I hope she doesn't take offense at that silly gesture of mine. You are an old fashioned idiot to go kissing the hands of strange ladies, especially patients. You'd think she really meant something to you. Oh hell, let's face it, she does mean something, she's my "almost" family. I'm going to miss her. Must get her address at the therapy place and visit. He followed the stretcher and concentrated on the swaying IV in front of him. He watched as the fragile old woman was gently lifted into the new bed. He smiled warmly, sat down in the chair, took her tiny birdlike hand in his, and prepared to ask a few questions before beginning his examination.

I was both sad and flattered that Kurt seemed to want to be my friend. But I was fired up with the idea of a decent meal on my way home later in the week. Then the big day tomorrow. Kurt was lovely, sweet and a passing fancy, that's all. He sounded like he had enough trouble in the hospital to keep him amused. I'm sure a man like that—good-looking, unattached—would not have trouble finding company. He didn't need me any more.

Mike came back in and we talked a moment about the surgery and how glad I was to have it all over. "Well, hallelujah, Maggie! It's going to be all uphill after this." He high-fived me.

"Yup, I'm with you," I answered as I saw a tall figure swiftly move out in the hall. He glanced briefly my way, our eyes met. He raised his hand slightly as he flew past. My heart skipped a beat, as I realized the little gesture was for me alone to see and not to share. In his rush, he didn't forget me. I was thrilled. I still had a wonderful crush on that sweet man.

She saw me as I passed her. I'm going to miss you, lady, more than I realized. She's what, two years older than me, I think—nah, none of that crap, been through that enough, not again. Anyway she's got a neat career, things to do, family, doesn't need anything more than a casual friend. I have to get the name of her rehab center. Hope she remembers to eat better. Better get Fred Kelly to check on that supplement. I'm fretting about her already, and she has not even been discharged yet. Oh hell, let's face it, I hope she remembers she's my family now.

Chapter 8

I settled in and turned on the TV. After a while there was a very faint knock on the edge of my door. The loveliest lady I have seen in a long time came into the room. Her hair was totally white but curly. It was cut skillfully and capped her head. Her figure was that of a woman in her 30s, but this lady was obviously closer to my age, if not older. She approached in her well-cut white nurse's uniform, something unusual to see in a hospital these days. I could see the clearest blue eyes set in perfect skin. Her professional smile showed off straight even teeth. I hated her on sight, just for her beauty and figure. She was a classic beauty that had aged gently. I would guess her age at 50 but anything from 40 to 55 would be appropriate. She carried a small notebook in her hand, and placed it in the pocket of her uniform as she approached my bed.

"Mrs. Suit, my name is Nora Feeney and I'm the night supervisor of this surgical wing." She stood next to my bed looking at me intently.

Suddenly there was ice in the pit of my stomach. Those eyes were shrewd and cool. I get to meet Nasty Nora, and she's nothing like I pictured her. I just knew she was skeptical of my relationship to Kurt and even though I was smart enough to pull the wool over Dr. Rainey's eyes, as I looked into these clear baby blues, I did not feel as confident.

The best defense is an offense. In this case, I had to be careful not to burn myself in my anger. "I understand you placed a complaint with Rainey about my nephew, Ms. Feeney. It would have been better had you or one of your spies or minions come to me to get the straight story before running off at the mouth to the surgical chief. I'm sure the entire administration was notified, too." I was quaking inside but the words tumbled out and they were astonishingly good I felt. I lifted my chin slightly and looked her square in the eye.

She seemed to deflate some. Fiddling with my bedclothes, folding my housecoat and placing it carefully on the chair next to my bed, she said, "I came to apologize, Mrs. Suit. I was informed of something irregular going on and felt it my duty to discuss it informally with Dr. Rainey before any formal actions were taken. I only have one question. Dr. Rainey indicated you are the widow of Dr. Van Doren's Uncle Charles. And that Charles was a brother to Dr. Van Doren's father, so how is it your name is Suit and not Van Doren?" She was very formal and stiff and standing there quietly interrogating me. I could have cheerfully strangled her. She really had me this time, she figured.

I became just as determined and gave her what I felt was an evil smile. "Why, Nurse Feeney, Charles was my first husband and not the father of my 3 children. He was a lot older than me and I was widowed young. My second husband, Jeffrey Wyatt Suit, and I are divorced. He's currently married to Amy Paulson Suit, the former CEO of this hospital, didn't anyone tell you? Amy is a nice woman and a good friend. Jeff and Amy were a great help to me this summer when I first became ill."

Boy, was I ever skating on thin ice now. It was true that Jeff was married to Amy. It was also true that she was the former CEO of the Center here. How this popped into my mind and why I blurted it out, I don't know. It was all true, except for the Charles Van Doren part. I figured by the time she reached Amy with the story, my butt would be long gone from the hospital, and the whole situation would die a natural death. Rainey was clearly on Kurt's side in this and what could they prove? I hope that man learns never to start friendships with ladies and spread rumors again. This was costing me emotionally.

"I see, that explains it then, doesn't it? Surprising that you keep such close contact with members of your first husband's family. Especially since you remarried after his death."

"Miss Feeney—"

"Mrs. Feeney," she corrected me.

"Mrs. Feeney, then. When you're working in a new city like I am and you've only one daughter and one nephew here, you keep in contact. They're a great comfort to me at holiday time. Kurt is all I have here and my daughter, Holly. I cherish and love both of them. We do birthday dinners, I enjoy cooking for them."

I looked straight at her with my heart in my throat, and hoping my memory was not failing me, I answered, "Holly's birthday is coming up at Christmas time, she's a twin you know to Ivy, who lives in North Carolina. Of course Kurt's isn't until June, did you know that, Mrs. Feeney? June 30 to be exact."

She smiled and walked out quietly. I got her! Only wish Kurt was here to see it.

Chapter 9

Wednesday arrived at last. I waited all day for the paperwork to come through and for Holly's call, signaling she was on her way. By late afternoon I was annoyed with the hospital, Holly, and everyone who came into my room. By 4:30, the patient coordinator arrived with my release papers, and Holly was right behind her by a few minutes.

"Sorry, Mom, had a meeting at NIH and just drove right over here afterward. Is everything ready? Are we all signed out?"

"No, you have to go down to the office. Go quick to catch the woman. Run if you have to and get the papers back from her. Meanwhile I'll get dressed. I've been gathering stuff up all day and have it all packed up. Hurry!"

She flew out the door. I sat up and started throwing things on the bed that were still in my bed tray. Toothbrush, comb, lipstick, dried Popsicle stick—I picked it up and started to toss it when I realized I put it in there one night after eating a frozen juice bar with Kurt. What the heck, it was a souvenir of my fling with Dr. Gorgeous. I threw it in the suitcase.

An out-of-breath daughter arrived, laughing, "Got her on her way out. You're free, woman, ready to rock and roll as soon as we get Mike or someone, to help us downstairs. This is a great day, no more emergencies. You're good to go!"

She was bubbling, and I was feeling her excitement. I was scared about getting in the car but willing to give it a try. There would be lots of scary things I would have to relearn, and I might as well start now. Mike showed up with a wheelchair. I hopped into it myself with little or no help.

We headed down the hall, me waving, Holly thanking the nurses, dropping off my flowers, and extra candy. Suddenly I was out the door and Holly was pulling the car up. It was show time for me, prove I was ready for

50

this car ride.

Mike took my arm as I moved slowly toward the edge of the sidewalk. Holly parked away from the curb so I could step down. I felt suddenly like a queen stepping into her carriage. I was in a car for the first time in months, not an ambulance—what a great feeling!

Holly started the car. She tried to start the car again. It would not catch. The motor turned over but it was grinding and we were still sitting there. The car was stalled. She was upset and I was frustrated and cross at the car and the whole day. I had waited and planned for this time, and here I was, stuck.

Drivers behind us were getting impatient and a few horns started. Holly got out and gestured she was having car trouble. People moved around us to pick up loved ones and employees finishing their shifts. A bus lumbered around us, still we sat there.

She pulled out her cell phone, fished out her membership card and called the car club. We had about an hour's wait they told her. Slowly and with a little effort, Holly and Mike, my nurse, moved her small car closer to the curb and put on the emergency lights. It was hot, so I had Mike help me out of the car and back into the wheelchair.

"I think I'll hike over to that station just beyond the hospital, Mom. See what they can do for us. Let me put you in the lobby and you can maneuver around and get a soda or magazine while I get this bitch back on the road again. I can call Cooper, too, but first let me see what the station can do for me."

I sat in the lobby feeling frustrated. Poor kid's been busting her butt all summer taking care of me, and now when it's almost over, this has to happen. Damn Damn Damn!

Someone passed me quickly while I sat fuming, ignoring the world. I heard a familiar voice, "Maggie, is that you? What are you doing down here? Didn't they release you? I just came by to pick up some work for my research paper, going home to write like crazy tonight."

"Good for you, Kurt," I replied in an angry tone, "I'm sitting here with a broken down car and a daughter who's at the gas station waiting for the car club to come in an *hour*. You know what that means? A good *two* hours if I remember my car club days."

He towered over me and finally squatted down to my level his hands resting on my chair, those green eyes of his looking concerned and so sexy. I caught a whiff of his shower soap. I recognized that scent whenever he was around; it was distinctive and disturbing. Another memory I would have to put behind me—how nice he always smelled.

"You're disappointed. Damn, what a nightmare. You've sure had enough disappointments this summer, I know. Look, why don't I get my car and take you to the rehab center myself? I can pop you in the little green machine and have you there in no time."

Calming down a bit, I patted his hand. "Thanks, Kurt, but what about poor Holly? She's stuck here with the car, and I feel I should stay with her. To tell you the truth, I've never driven to the place except in an ambulance and don't know the address. It's stupid, but not driving, I just don't know."

"Look, here's my cell phone, call her and tell her you're getting a ride to her house. She or Cooper can take you to the center from there, how's that?" He handed me his cell phone.

"I guess I can try to get her on this." I dialed her number and it rang 3 times. Holly answered. "Who is this? Mom, is that you?"

"Yes, Holly, the nice doctor I told you about is here and has offered to take me to your house to wait while you get the car done. Does that sound okay? That way you don't have to worry about me and can concentrate on the car. Cooper can load me up and get me to the rehab center since I can't give Kurt directions."

"It's not what I wanted to do, but if you could get home, tell Cooper to be ready to come get me if necessary. Never mind, I'll call him and explain. If he's not there or leaves, I'll have him keep the door unlocked for you to get in the house. Go slow and be careful, Mom." I gave her Kurt's cell phone number and hung up.

I turned and handed it back to him. "Okay, my favorite nephew, you're on. You're really nice to do this."

I again went out to a waiting car. Heck, I would have gone with him in a kiddy car. Turned out that's exactly what he had, a little low green sports car. Standing there, I wondered how I would manage. We got Mike, who was on his way home, and the two men practically lifted me into the front seat.

I looked back as we pulled out and waved to my favorite nurse. On the way out of town, I shared my Rainey story with Kurt and my little interrogation and triumph with Nora the Nasty. Beautiful as she was, she scared the hell out of me for some reason. I shuddered thinking about those cold blue eyes of hers. Her and Rainey were a pair in my book, a scary pair.

We inched our way along in rush hour traffic. Kurt was frustrated by the traffic but we were free of the hospital. I was part of the real world for a while and was enjoying it.

We laughed, talked, made plans, and changed the plans. He encouraged me to keep working hard on my strength. I promised to do everything in my power to get on my feet as quickly as I could. He reminded me to eat. It was the third week of September and I told him I had set a goal for myself to be back at work by December first. I had a lot to work on and fast.

"Which way are you going? I'm lost now, Doc. I don't recognize this area at all, I think you have me in Georgetown. Are you zipping up Wisconsin?" I asked.

He looked at me and nodded. "Hey, since I got you crammed into this little car I figured I could lift you out of it. I thought we could stop and have a bit of dinner somewhere. Even if it's a burger joint, I'd love to see you have some solid food and not just ice bars."

"Oh, come on now, it's your night off and here you are chauffeuring me out of town and taking up your research time. I'm sorry you have to do this." The man was certainly making it hard for me to lose my big crush on him.

He laughed and patted my knee. I noticed how nice his laugh sounded, and how good it felt to be out of the hospital and going anywhere with him. I was acutely aware that we were crammed together in this tiny car with the windows open and top down. My hair was blowing all over the place, I felt 16 again and it was fun.

At a red light he glanced over and said, "Maggie, I'm glad I got the chance to see you and say good-bye again. We're friends, practically family, after all that lying we did this past week. Hey, what's family for if not to impose?"

We cruised up and down several quiet streets looking for a good place to eat. He found several but there was either no parking or it was too difficult for me to navigate. Finally I spied a small neighborhood restaurant.

"Look, there's a nice little place to stop. What does the sign say, Raymond's? I can get out with your help and you could park in that lot over there."

He swung the car right up to the door of the tavern. He kept it away from the curb, was no traffic. It was early evening; the sun was starting to go down, cooling it off a little. He unfolded from his side of the car, came over, and with what seemed very little effort, pulled me to my feet. He handed me my cane instead of the walker. "Stay right here if you can, I'll only be a second. If you have to, go sit on that bench over there, can you make it?"

"I'm sure I can, but I'd rather stand. I need the practice and to comb my hair!"

He whipped the little car around and drove into the parking area behind the small shopping center. He appeared on foot a moment later, came over took his hand and helped me brush my wind driven hair back in place. He then gently took my arm. "Let's see what we have in here."

***

We walked into the very dark little restaurant/bar. It looked cozy to me. Actually, after 3 months of only seeing hospitals and rest homes, it looked great. And to be here with Kurt was a special treat.

The place had obviously been here for a long time. Signs of age were unmistakable. Tables and chairs were scarred but clean. Posters, stage props, and autographed pictures were hung high and low on the wall but it was hard to make them out in the dim light. The few posters I could see were advertising great stage shows: *Moulin Rouge, Oklahoma, Guys N' Dolls* were the ones I could just make out. The bar was small, but looked well stocked and men stood or sat on stools around it. Others were seated at tables surrounding a small dance floor. There was the smell of good food, baking bread, and everyone looked friendly. I thought we found a nice snug little place for dinner.

The bartender looked up, surprised, and then smiled as we settled at a table. I sat there looking around, marveling at my freedom. The music was a bit loud and more frantic than I would like, but it was fun and more than I had heard in months.

When my eyes finally adjusted to the dark, I realized the tiny dance floor was filled with men dancing together. I kept looking, thinking I was wrong. I even thought I saw a familiar face in the crowd. But then I realized, no, I was mistaken. We had stumbled into a gay bar. My first night on the town and I find myself in a bar "for the boyz" as my daughter, Holly, referred to these places.

The bartender walked over, handed us menus, and lifted his pad to take our order. I was not at all uncomfortable and hoped that Kurt would look past the obvious, relax, and order. The music stopped briefly, and I looked over at him and said, "Order something good for both of us. I trust your judgment."

He seemed either to be completely unaware of our surroundings, or like me, comfortable with it. He asked the waiter, "What's the specialty tonight?"

The bartender grinned at Kurt and said, "All of our soups are homemade. This evening there's a good prime rib, our salads are divine, and the desserts are all baked right here so take your pick."

Kurt looked over the menu and ordered.

The music started back up and they were playing some old hard rock 80s numbers. Kurt leaned in toward me and practically yelled in my ear, "When the salad comes, I want you to try a little bit of it on a plate. I think something that tastes really good may give you an appetite."

54

"I think my mouth's watering for some of that bread. If it's half as good as it smells, I'll be just fine." Grinning at him, I shook out my napkin and placed it carefully on my jeans. This was exciting, a handsome escort and food not ruined by the District Hospital Center.

I think we were both relaxed and enjoying the music. Kurt was keeping time with a spoon on the table, smiling at me; it was too loud to make small talk. Suddenly a tall dark-haired man came over to our table.

"May I have this dance?"

I looked up, smiled, and said, "Thank you, but I'm just out of the hospital and I don't have my full balance back yet."

"No, I meant the gentleman. He seems to like the beat so I thought he would enjoy getting out on the floor."

Kurt looked startled. His face showed how uncertain he was and unwilling to accept the invitation. He started to say something when I interrupted, "Don't keep the nice man waiting. I'm certainly going to enjoy watching."

He looked at me, his eyes pleading to get him out of this. I shook my head again giving him an evil grin that said, okay, fella, you're going to get out of this one on your own. I could see his discomfort as he replied, "I'm here with my friend and I hate to leave her alone." He again gave me what was now a desperate, silent "help me" look. I continued to smile sweetly, nodding my head.

When he realized no help was coming, he got up and followed the man who, by now, had exchanged names with us. As they walked out to the dance floor, Kurt glanced back at me with sort of a defiant look that said, "Okay, I take your dare." I was astounded. I figured he would continue to backpedal until the man got the message. Rare the straight man who could pull this off, or who would even be comfortable enough to do it. He certainly is one in a million. Steady girl, this is your heart and imagination working overtime.

The song ended. Kurt came back to the table shaking his head laughing and sweating. He put his hands on my shoulders, bent down and kissed me lightly on the cheek. I was surprised and smiled up at him feeling a blush rise as he took his seat. I just knew turning bright pink would betray my feelings. To cover up I tried for lighthearted, "You two made a nice couple. You dance divinely, Doctor."

He leaned toward me and sarcastically replied in a low voice, "Thanks for the help, *pal*. I had no choice after you let me down."

I shot back, "Consider it a payback for all that Aunt Maggie crap you stuck me with back at the Center, *pal*." I emphasized the last word the same way, sat back, and gave him another evil grin.

He leaned forward, looked around and said, "Okay, okay, *Aunt Maggie*, I agree that paybacks are hell! He then leaned back and pulled his shirt away from his chest to cool off. Whew! That takes a lot out of you. Dancing is hard work when you're not used to it." He gulped most of his iced tea. He bent toward me and murmured. I explained that we just picked this place at random. That we had no idea it was sort of a club for men only. Cliff laughed and told me it was okay to say hangout for gays, or fairies, or whatever I cared to call it. But I couldn't call them that, not my style.

"Kurt, you amazed me. I know I wasn't much help. But it was such a funny situation; I just had to see what you would do. I didn't know whether to laugh or take pictures. Believe me, not many straight guys could handle what you just did. Most would have fled the minute they noticed where they were."

"The whole point of this evening is to get some nourishing food into you, that's why we're here. And, hey, I admit I did leave you hanging a few times, so if dancing with some perfectly nice stranger is payback, we're even." With that he finished up his soup, pushed the plate away, took some of his salad and placed it on my plate along with warm bread. It was plain to me I loved both him and the attention.

"Eat, woman, you need some meat on your bones."

"You're bullying me now, but I like it. Been a long time since I've had this much fun, or been fussed over like this. Who knows, I may even eat all my soup and the salad."

"Go for it, Cinderella. We still have to get you home at a decent hour before my green machine turns into a pumpkin."

Nothing more was said about the misplaced kiss. I knew it was a statement to the men in the place that he was having fun but was straight. The memory of that touch and kiss would be with me for a long time to come. We finished our meal laughing and talking about nothing and everything. He paid the bill, and we left. He steered me outside, and I stood waiting on the curb. I think by this time I realized that this extraordinary man was more than a crush. I was going to have a hard time forgetting him.

I stood on the sidewalk struggling to maintain my equilibrium, not just physically but emotionally.

Kurt pulled the little car up. Two men just entering the bar helped me off the curb, and held the car door open for me. Kurt jumped out, came over and took my arm. He stuffed me back in the little open car and I noticed that they eyed him up like choice sirloin. So much for the big night out.

When we pulled away from the place he started to chuckle, then laugh, and

I laughed with him. We were zipping up Wisconsin Avenue by this time, top down, my hair again flying in the breeze. I was still giggling about our adventure in the little bar.

"Mag, from now on when I take you home from any hospital, it will be just a big burger with everything on it, okay? I figure the Golden Dream's our only safe place after this."

As we raced along past storefronts and tiny parks I replied, "Kurt, we had a wonderful time in there. The music was fun and those men were great company."

"You're right, but I have to confess, I've never danced with a guy before. I guess I'll chalk it up to experience." He glanced over at me and then said mischievously, "Of course, if you ever tell anyone about that, I'll have to kill you, you know that."

He looked happy and relaxed as he drove. Then he gave me an impish grin and said, "It was fun though, wasn't it?"

The whole evening was wonderful and as he said this, my heart flipped over in my chest. He was so kind, so funny, and so comfortable in his own skin I doubt anything could disturb him. I realized that this is one of the great perks of middle age, you become so comfortable with who you are that the little things younger people agonize over or consider gauche, don't bother you at all. You are simply not afraid to swim against the tide.

The territory became more familiar and we detoured past my office building. I pointed it out and a few minutes later realized we were very close to my house. I talked about my old life before I got sick. He listened and told me stories about the hospital. I felt on safe ground out away from the place so I thought I would bring up the things I heard from the staff.

I checked out his profile as he drove the little car in and around traffic. "Kurt, I understand I'm not the only point of gossip concerning you. One of the aides told me you had a run-in with a Dr. Packard and got a black eye out of it. But to hear the story he got the wrong end of it with a broken nose. Is that right?"

He looked straight ahead and I could tell there was no humor in his next words.

"Who told you that crap, Maggie? Whoever it is shouldn't be blabbing out of school. I suppose you heard what led up to the boxing match? I hate to say this, but Packard's a bastard and the real truth is he was actually annoying that woman down in the administrative office. He hung around and flirted and wasted her time. Her supervisor was getting hot under the collar about it. She telephoned me and said the problem had to stop. I only did what I was asked to do. I talked to the man."

Kurt took a quick dive for an opening in traffic and continued, "You probably know the type. When you confront a self-important bastard with a huge ego, there's trouble, that's all. I took care of it and we see little of one another, and when we do it's strictly professional. If he still feels like going another round, I told him we could do it properly in the gym with gloves on this time."

He looked over at me, tilted his head. "So far the creep has declined. I hope he keeps it that way. Where do we turn here, Maggie, right or left?"

Between the two of us we got my body out of his little car at Holly's house. No one was home but the porch light was on. He steered me carefully up to the front door, we got it open and I walked into her kitchen. Kurt's cell phone was ringing and he answered it as I went over to phone Holly that I had arrived.

"Maggie, will you be all right? We have an emergency at work and I have to go back down to the Center. Our resident on duty just went into premature labor and she said she's not sure how long she can hold out. I have someone covering with her right now but I have to leave you. I hate to do it, but this is a problem."

I was sitting safely in Holly's wing chair. I smiled and waved him off. "It's the nature of the job, sweet pea, go make sure that lady gets help and the baby gets here safely. I'll be fine. Look how the two dogs are glad to see me. I'll just sit here and wait for Cooper."

Stupid and Puddy were jumping and racing around the company. I would have let them out for a run but decided if one of them knocked me down I would be in trouble. They begged for attention and petting, which I gave them, and then I dialed Holly's cell phone again and got no answer. I dialed Cooper's phone and got him on the second ring.

I sat there waiting for Cooper to arrive, thinking about the evening. I realized I was now totally in love with this man and that this was not a good thing for me. He's attractive, funny, very outgoing, no financial worries. He has too much going for him to be on the market long. Some beautiful babe would catch his eye and reel him in sooner or later. I just had to forget Dr. Gorgeous, I told myself.

Chapter 10

Kurt got into his car and called the hospital. The young woman was doing fine, the nurse assured him, but how long before you can get here was her next question.

"Sorry about being so far away but was taking a friend to dinner, it *was* my night off you know." He thought that was a good way to explain Maggie, his good friend. She certainly looked better in those jeans and shirt than the hospital gowns. Kurt felt a pang of sadness that she was no longer waiting for him back at the Center.

Sitting in Holly's house was great. The place looked good to me after 2 months of the hospital and rehab center. Cooper' reassuring voice came over the phone, "Maggie, I'm on my way to get you and take you to rehab. Holly's car is fine now. It was a vapor lock and after she got back to the hospital it started up on the first try. Talk about frustration. She's on her way home and we've been waiting for your call. Did that guy kidnap you?"

"Nah, he took me out to eat, it's a long story, Coop."

Ten minutes later he helped me out of the house. I laughed and told him about our encounter with the "boyz' bar," as Holly would refer to it.

Cooper and I arrived at the rehab center entrance. We slowly made our way past the big double doors and I settled into a wheelchair to go up to the third floor.

Over the next two weeks I worked hard at gaining strength. The physical therapy room was my second home. I practiced my walking and using weights. I gradually became adept at getting myself to the bathroom alone. I made rapid progress.

Thoughts of Kurt would come late at night and I would try to read and put him out of my mind. This was not an easy thing to do; he was so much a part of my life for that short 10-day period, and I discovered I missed him. I found it hard to believe at my age I was in love. But, like all good things, the brief encounter was over as quick as it started, so lovesick or not, I needed to put it in the past and continue the effort to get back on my feet.

I had friends and family visit but every time I heard footsteps near my door, I secretly hoped it would be Kurt. Disappointed, I got ready for another graduation, another scary set of obstacles to overcome.

Tuesday before I left the therapy center, Holly took me out for an evening at her house. On Thursday afternoon we packed up the trunk of Holly's car with my accumulated possessions: flowers, clothes, books, television. I was off to Mannington Avenue for this final phase.

Ivy and Mike came all the way up from North Carolina for a visit, bringing my geologist son, Tim, whom I had not seen since the day of my heart surgery. I was happy and so busy that I never had time to think about the hospital. I tried not to give Kurt too much thought either, as it was painful. I felt at times I should get in touch with him. He's forgotten about me and gone on to prettier and younger by now, I told myself over and over, but it still hurt deep inside.

I was starting with the new and improved Maggie. Much thinner, overcoming the nausea, gaining strength, enjoying company that came by to see me and to visit with Cooper and Holly. I was getting back into a more normal life. It was good not being confined to hospitals and rehab centers with bad food, boring colors and sad inhabitants.

Over the next weeks I gained strength and even drove a couple of times. I was healing. I needed to go home! Kurt was the past—I was putting him out of my mind and heart slowly.

Kurt sat down and sent an email to Steve.

> *Told you about Maggie. Figured we would stay in touch, we seemed to be on the same wavelength with our matching offbeat sense of humor. We had one fun evening together at that bar I told you about, but not a word since. I've called her house several times but no answer. Guess she may still be in rehab. Shit, don't have time to worry about it but I kind of miss not having her around. On a happier note, how is the house and godson? Life treating you okay? Hey, it's been two days since I heard from you. Kurt*

Chapter 11

Hurrah! After 3 full months, I was home! It was a lovely dry Sunday in October. My cats, Serge and Tulip, were aloof and tried to ignore me at first, but in a couple of hours they were cuddling up on the bed, begging for attention. I was home, the groceries were in, and I was ready for my new life to begin.

I started up the computer and made my announcement to one and all. Lots of congratulations were coming in. My next chore was the voicemails on my phone.

I returned several calls. One especially intrigued me, it was from the hospital. I listened to an impersonal voice ask for Mrs. Suit and ask me to return the call. It was dated late in September.

I ignored it in light of the next call. A familiar voice came on asking for Mrs. Suit, Aunt Maggie, if you will. Could you please return this call? "This is Dr. Van Doren from the hospital, and I'm doing a routine follow-up on you. I can't locate any other number so when you return home, please call."

There were several of these calls over the past month. I felt guilty. There were nights when I remembered him, his touch. Suddenly I was shy but eager to return his call. I wanted to make sure Nasty Nora had not caused more problems since I left. I dialed and got a secretary's recording. I left a message for Dr. Van Doren to call me, his Aunt Maggie, that I was home.

Exhausted after my second day home, I pulled the phone near my bed after a long hot shower. It felt good to have one each day and not be scheduled. The idea that I could shampoo my hair any time I chose to was something I would never take for granted again.

I was drifting off for a nap around 9 at night. The phone rang. I checked the caller ID and did not recognize the number. "Oh hell, must be a solicitor," I said out loud to the cats as I pushed the talk button.

"Is this Mrs. Maggie Suit? The Mrs. Suit who was at the District Hospital Center for an aneurysm repair in September?"

My heart did a flip as I recognized that familiar voice on the other end.

"Cut it out, Kurt, you know who it is. You must know my voice even after all this time. It's Maggie."

"I should have known you'd answer that way. Where the hell have you been all this time, at the PT place? I've looked all over for your daughter's phone number and address and couldn't find it. I was in such a rush that night I got you home that I forgot to get it. How are you doing? Can you walk yet? I have a hundred questions to ask you. This is great. I have this set of survey questions here I have to ask. It's how I finally got your home number. I used this as an excuse to keep calling you. Normally, our clerk does this, but I told her it was a family member, and I would take care of it."

He went through the five questions and I gave him the answers. When it was over he asked, "Are you able to get around by yourself?"

"Yes, fine. It's so good to hear your voice. I've wondered about you often after I left the Center. Has Nora bugged you any more?"

He ignored the question. "It's just great to hear from you. It was dull after you left. I automatically turned into that room the day after I took you home and someone else was there. I just excused myself and left. And, Maggie, I trust you're keeping my dancing career a secret? I'm really glad—"

"Hey, slow down, Doc, I can't get a word in here. I'm fine. Walking, I need all new clothes, getting my house in shape. I get up and down stairs and use the email. My stamina is a bit low yet. Enough about me, how have you been? I mean really, are you getting any rest and eating properly? And those meals we shared were the worst kind of fatty crap you could eat."

I was as happy to hear from him as he obviously was to hear my voice. Information tumbled out from both sides of the phone.

"I'm still tired and still thinning on top and some gray now."

"You were thinning on top when I was there and you were obsessed with it. Relax, you look okay with or without hair, I promise you that, Doc. As for the gray hair you're gaining stature and dignity with those gray hairs; wear them proudly, you earned them with all your hard work."

"Oh, you say that to all the doctors I believe, Maggie, you're a flirt."

"Like hell I do. So when are you coming out to see me?"

"Love to, but I'm tied up here pretty much all the time. I'm working on the final draft of my research paper for the next few weeks. It's almost finished and I add more initials to my name. Right now my life is pretty full and my dance card is topped off. I can hardly find a quiet place to work these days between the job and roommates. But I do want to get out there and talk to you soon. We've had some strange things going on here and I've been in the middle of it. I really need to spend a little time just getting it off my chest."

"Hey, if you need a quiet place to unload and to finish your paper in the next few weeks when I go back to work, you can use the house here. You can use my home office right now as a matter of fact. I also have an ear you can bend. Hope the problems aren't that bad."

"I've been up on some serious charges here, and I'm not so sure Nora's behind it. They called it careless on my part, but, Maggie, I'm not careless. Listen, I really need to talk to someone not involved in this whole thing. I'll get over there soon. I promise."

"Like I said, the house is here any time you want it, remember what's family for if you can't impose."

"I said that, didn't I? That night I took you home. Let me think about it. But for now, tell me about the walking. I have a hundred questions and no time to ask them, let alone listen to your answers. Tell you what: Do you mind if I call in the evenings when I'm slowing down? I usually get a break or so around 9 or 10 pm but if that's too late just tell me."

"That's fine I'm a night owl lately."

"Great. I'm going to go get something to eat. I'm glad you're okay. I figured you were alive and well and hiding somewhere out there. I knew you'd surface eventually, it was a matter of time. Will talk to you later in the week?"

"Any time. And cover your ass, okay?"

"Believe me I am."

He hung up with a promise to call me back later in the week. I was concerned about the developments in his life, but how serious could it be? He was still working at the Center. His comment about being in trouble sort of rattled me. Must be that Nora again. I smiled to myself as I recalled our night on the town, the kiss, and I hugged the covers, falling asleep almost immediately.

He hung up and sighed. "She's doing fine." He then did a little two-step as he left the lab where he had used the phone and continued out loud to no one in particular, "She remembers me and we're getting together." Walking slowly down the dark hall he thought, I need a friend right now, someone who can listen and I know she'll have suggestions. And talk about a fighter, Rainey said she almost bit his head off defending me. My aunt, no, just plain Maggie. See you soon, lady.

***

Indian summer spread itself over Maryland, warm sunny days and crisp, chilly nights. A great time for raking leaves, buying apples and cider at the local orchards, shaking out the woolen blankets and checking winter coats. Most of all, preparations for the start of another holiday season were starting to mix in with Halloween and Thanksgiving decorations. I was busy reading through catalogs and shopping online at my favorite websites: www.overstock.com and www.smartbargains.com. I had yard people out to clear up the piles of gorgeous yellow and red leaves and debris from a summer of neglect. I went out in the mornings and walked up and down the aisles in grocery stores, discount stores, the mall—anywhere, just to gain stamina.

Several days passed before I heard again from Kurt.

"Maggie, it's me, did I wake you up?" the voice on the other end of the phone asked one evening.

"No, I told you to call whenever. How's work?"

"Keeping us all busy."

"At least you're busy, and time flies when you're busy. I almost wish I were going back to work this week instead of in a month. But I'd never be able to do a full day yet. Working my way up to it, however. How's the problem? Anything you can talk about?"

"Is the offer to come over still good, that's what I called about? I really need to fill you in. I have another couple weeks to work on this paper, sort of polish it up. Need to concentrate and life here is hectic. At home it's worse with the guys coming and going on shifts and their music and horseplay. They can't help it but the place is only three bedrooms and I need some quiet. The hospital library is fine, but people can page you if they think you're around. Right now I have a real need to be away from the Center as much as possible, at least until I can get this paper done and figure out what's going on. The university library is just too inaccessible. What I need is a place to plug in my laptop, drag my books out, and just be able to scratch, relax and work. So I'm hoping the offer's still good?"

I answered, "Sure, if you want, let me give you my email address and send you directions and the address, you have the phone number?"

"You're sure about this? I don't want to put you out. Will your roommate object if I'm there? She doesn't know me, and it might make her uncomfortable if I'm around and she's there and you're gone."

"Hey, don't fret. She's a nice woman but almost never home. You'll meet her when you come over. I'll email her to expect you."

"You live in the same house and do that? How come?"

"Her hours and mine don't exactly coincide. She is out from 6:00 a.m. to about midnight a lot of nights. I'm in those hours lately. So, we email one another about stuff like packages, pet problems, and now this pest who will be coming to visit me and study. I'll put you under pest problems, how's that?"

"You sure it's okay?

"Kurt Van Doren, listen to my voice. If I thought you were going to be a problem, I would tell you. I offered you the use of the hall and I meant it. I offered you the use of my ear and shoulder and I meant it. Anyway it will be fun seeing you again and you'll have a whole house to bang around in come December. You'll see my stabs at holiday decorating, which will be few and far between since I'm spending Christmas with Holly."

"There's a chance I'll be working on Christmas if I can't get anyone to cover for me."

"Oh, Kurt, don't do that to yourself. Get on a plane and go to your folks. Make the reservations now so you won't be left out."

"I have a reservation, but it all depends on my work schedule. I'm a lowly cheese nip, not the big cheese. Remember what I told you: I'm not exactly able to pick and choose my hours, you know that."

"I would think with all the covering you've done for others and all the holidays you've worked that someone could cover the Center for a couple of days at least."

"Some of our busiest days occur in the so-called season of peace and good will. Holidays are the worst time. I can't promise anything, but I'll be outside at some point. Don't think I can make Christmas Eve or Christmas Day, but let's talk about it later, closer to the big night."

"Good."

I sat there at the computer, excited to think he was coming to my house. I was going to do my best to get the place up to my standards if it took the rest of the week. Maybe I could get one of those housecleaning services in for one day. I'll call in morning. But now to develop a set of clear directions to my place and to Holly's.

Email to Steve from Kurt: *I found her! Kurt*
Email to Kurt from Steve: *Confused? Just who the hell did you find, Stanley or Livingston? Steve*

Chapter 12

I emailed directions to the house. He remembered me showing him my neighborhood that day he took me to Holly's house so it was easy.

I got off the computer and went downstairs. A few minutes later the phone rang. "Got the email but afraid I won't have much time, I never do. I'm really anxious to see you and get your take on my situation here; someone has it in for me, big time. I've been having one stupid problem after another for the past month." His voice became lighter and he seemed as excited to see me as I was to see him.

"You can sample Christmas cookies. I'll fix lunch or we can send out if you get here sometime in the afternoon."

"Deal. You owe me anyway for all those very, very expensive fruit bars I bought you. Why, I'll bet I must have spent all of three or four bucks on them that week. Throwing my hard-earned money around like that warrants a cookie or two."

It was so good to hear his voice and to listen to him tease with me. We went back and forth for another minute or two, and then he was off.

Later that week, I got the cleaning people to come, and they did it all. I also did a good job cleaning up my computer.

I could hardly wait for Saturday. Looking at my rather shabby house, I suddenly realized this man came from a very upscale background, what was I thinking having him here? I couldn't change much at this point, so I decided what I needed most was not new furniture but a new hairdo.

Friday morning I went around the corner and talked the newest lady in my salon into a wash, color, and cut—something short but stylish. With the new hairdo, I looked and felt years younger and brighter. I studied myself in the salon mirror. Not too bad for a lady who's been ill for a few months. My figure was much slimmer and I needed an outfit that was not falling off. I hauled myself off to the local women's store. This was the first time I had on clothes that really fit and the mirror reflected a smallish blonde with a new body. The clothes looked nice but the salesgirl insisted I needed a smaller size.

She brought me a beautiful soft red sweater in cotton with a high neck. The color looked good. I decided then and there I would come back for more as soon as I felt up to it. She piled up some new underwear and a pair of slacks. I paid for my new clothes feeling like I had accomplished the important stuff at least.

I tossed my purchases in the car and as I was driving up the block to my house, I noticed an annoying little car riding my bumper up the road. Turning off Georgia, the car was still there. I started bitching out loud about bad drivers. "Good grief, why can't some of these idiots learn to drive and keep their distance? If this wasn't a new car I swear I'd slam on the brakes and let him rear-end me." I kept glancing back and could see the image of a man at the steering wheel. I deliberately slowed down. Let this fool get impatient and maybe he'll realize he's annoying me and drop back. I slowed the car some more, practically crawling up to the stop sign on my block. The little car stopped, hesitated and then turned and followed me up my block.

"I'll bet that's the guy that bought the house up on the other corner for that outrageous price," I said out loud to myself as I turned into the driveway. The little green car drifted past my house and then stopped up the block from me. I got out of my car slowly and using my cane got myself to the step on my front porch. Suddenly I remembered another little green car. Oh no, it couldn't be. But it was. I just knew it...a day early!

The familiar figure unfolded himself from behind the wheel and hollered, "Maggie? I thought that was you. I saw you in that shopping center and followed." He came up the side of my lawn asking a million rapid-fire questions, hopped on the porch, and said, "Do I get a hug or what?" He then proceeded to grab me and lift me off my feet.

Kurt hardly recognized the blonde who climbed out of the car and made her way to the front porch. She was small, smaller than he remembered, and her hair was different. No glasses. She moved smoothly as she walked from the car to the porch with a cane over her arm but not using it until she got to the porch. Bet she was working out at that gym when I saw her at the shopping center. Glad I got her the flowers at the store, not much but they are bright and pretty.

***

He handed me a bouquet of flowers. I grinned, hugged him back then said, "Thanks. But, Doc, this is Friday, I thought you were coming on Saturday? I'm not prepared at all." Fumbling for my keys, and juggling the flowers, my hand shook. Seeing this man was a little more emotional that I planned or wanted him to see.

He carried the packages for me as I got us inside. The flowers were put on the table and packages on the steps. He grabbed me again in another hug like a long lost relative, which in his mind, I guess I am.

Lifting me off my feet he exclaimed, "Oh, wow! You've lost more weight, too much from what I can feel, you're light as a feather. Look at that hair and the old eyeglasses are gone; the contacts are really great. You're just wonderful, I can't believe you!" He held on to my shoulders and stepped back giving my sloppy black sweats an appraising eye.

Flushed from the hug I replied, "I never expected company today or I would have dressed better. I'd planned to fix some lunch for us tomorrow and now I've been out all morning trying to find something decent to wear."

My Dalmatian, Stupid, was yapping and rushing around the two of us, sniffing this strange man; looking at me for a treat or for permission to bite him, I didn't know which. My two cats, Serge and Tulip, were peering at this phenomenon from the stair landing. What possessed him to drop by a day early, I thought. I looked a mess and the plans I had were all shot to hell now. Better make the best of it, I suppose. At least my hair was done and the Snappy Maid Service had been there.

Kurt was walking around peeking out the back door, checking out the family room and then the kitchen. "Nice house, Maggie. Somehow I figured it would be like this, homey."

"Oh, that's me, old Aunt Maggie the frumpy old lady with lace curtains and chintz covers on the furniture." I removed my coat and took his rather worn brown suede jacket and put them in the hall closet.

He was gesturing toward the house. "I meant it has the feel and sort of atmosphere of a place that's used and loved—homey, cared about. The Center's kind of impersonal and cold, I guess that's natural, but I spend a lot of time there so it's almost like my home. Lately, there's been such weird stuff going on that suddenly a place I felt comfortable in, doesn't feel safe any more." He stopped by the back door and looked out the glass panels to the backyard.

"It just feels like a real home, something like when I go to Chicago to my Dad and Annie's."

I walked into the kitchen and realized this man really wasn't used to this kind of place. How sad. I opened the fridge, took out hot dogs, rolls, and store bought potato salad I had thought to get Thursday evening. "Have you eaten?" I looked over at him as I said this. He shook his head.

Snooping in the laundry room he went into the small bathroom and shut the door. He hollered out to me as the toilet flushed. "I only had chips and coffee this morning after surgery." Water in the sink running and door opening. "See, I've found my way around here already. Where does that door lead to, Maggie, the garage?"

"Don't go in there, you'll get lost forever. It's not been properly cleaned since Tim was home 2 years ago." I got busy shoving hot dogs in the microwave, laying out plates, potato salad, mustard, and ketchup on the small kitchen table.

"You really don't have to feed me. I can grab something at the dorm, I don't mind."

"It's no trouble, only a little better than what you'd get at the Center, I'm afraid. Would have had better food if I'd known you were coming today."

"Anything will do and taste better than there. What's to drink, can I get stuff? I know, we need glasses, where are they?" With that, he started opening cabinet doors and found the glassware. Putting two on the table he grabbed napkins off the top of the refrigerator, opened the door, grabbed two diet Colas, shut the door with his foot as he turned and put them on the table. "Since you went to the trouble I guess I can shove a few dogs in my face."

I slapped the hot dog rolls on the table and said, "Damn, man! It's not like I expected you. If you'd come tomorrow I could have cooked us a decent meal. You need real food after what you eat at the Center for days on end."

We ate and I nagged him. "Your whole lifestyle is crazy. I don't know how you survive it."

Kurt spread out his long legs and tilted the chair back. "It isn't any worse than it was in college. I could afford to live alone. Nora was right. I have the means but I enjoy the idea of being with the others. It really does work out fine most of the time. Your problem is you want to jump in and rescue people. I really don't need rescuing, I promise, not yet at least."

I turned and looked at him as I rinsed dishes for the dishwasher. "This 'dorm' idea of yours, it may not be what you want, or you may not be able to handle it if these stupid things keep happening. You could sublet the place and get another one of your own."

He looked at me, stood up, and taking my hand led me to the living room, and said, "I'll think about it. Now let me tell you what's been going on since I last saw you. After that, you can show me the rest of this place. I'm anxious to see this office of yours where I can sit around scratching when I study." We both laughed.

He sat down, got comfortable on the sofa and started. "Right after you left, Rainey called me in and explained what had happened with Nora and the complaint. He said he talked to you, and you cleared the air completely, that you explained about the relationship. He said you were quite forceful when you defended me. He's not exactly a fan of yours. I don't know what you said, or did, but he's a fair guy, been in my corner for years so the whole matter was dropped.

"That was, of course, in September. Toward the end of the month, a man came to our service suffering from a rather rare type of heart disease. After reviewing his chart and history, Rainey and I decided he would be an ideal candidate for a clinical trial we were doing for the National Heart Lung and Blood Institute at NIH."

I smiled and nodded having had years of work with NIH and the Blood Institute in Bethesda.

"To make a long story longer, we explained the situation to him. I told him of the risks and benefits, gave him a patient consent form and then left him and his family to decide if he wanted in on the clinical trial. He decided to go ahead with the enrollment and signed the papers. We got his papers filed, gave him a physical and then prepped him for the treatments. Rainey left the whole thing up to me, as I'd been more or less running the show for months now. I had four other people enrolled in the trial and was following them closely. So far everyone was doing fine and there were no complications."

He reached down and started scratching Stupid on her belly. Serge moved downstairs cautiously and sniffed his shoe, then moved away. Tulip did not move from the top step. Stupid was in heaven and his slave from that moment on.

"It was just around the first of October and the staff nurses were putting up autumn and Halloween decorations all around their station on the third floor, I remember. I got the tests finished on the man, ran all this by Rainey, and then went to the pharmacy and personally retrieved the medication from our pharmacist. Our day pharmacist, Bob Thomas, is a good guy and remembers discussing the medicine and dosage with me at length. It's a good thing he did, because it helped to save my butt later on."

I shifted in my chair, looking at him. I could see he was upset. What he had told me so far was building up to something bad, I could tell.

Chapter 13

He continued the story. "October first was a Monday and seemed the perfect day to start this new medication. I had given it to the staff nurse, Ida Phelps, who was the day supervisor on my patient's floor. I figured the dosage and was very clear when I wrote it down. I then mentioned it to Phelps again. I went to great lengths to explain that we were putting him on the clinical trial Rainey was running. I reviewed the protocol and medication with her and asked her to do the same with the nurses at the station as they came on. I don't know why I did that, normally I don't pick about details, but somehow, knowing this drug was powerful and experimental, I wanted to make sure the people on both the day and night shifts knew the dosage and what to look for in case he reacted. Again, I was saved by someone else's memory."

He piled more pillows behind him and leaned back as he talked. "The medicine was started and I went into my guy's room and personally handed him the pill along with his other meds. And yes, I had checked to see there would be no drug interactions with the other stuff he was taking."

He got up and paced around the living room, went to the dining room door and looked out. Facing away from me he said, "I was working late that night, one of those long shifts we all pull, when I got a call from the third floor. My patient was reacting to something and reacting badly. They had a call out for me and then came a call for a crash cart. The full team was there and working frantically by the time I arrived on a gallop. They rushed him out of his room and down the hall to the ICU. I helped, naturally, but afterward all I did was stand around and answer questions about what the medicine was, when it was administered. By the time anyone paid attention to me, the man was stabilized."

He continued in a sarcastic voice. "Nora was there in all her glory. This time I had screwed up big time in her book. She was looking daggers at me and already had pulled his chart, called Rainey and the administrator on duty at night. She was making sure I didn't get away with anything."

He turned around from the glass door, looked at me, and said, "Maggie, the man was a fine candidate, he was in good shape for the medicine. Somehow this whole scene seemed bizarre to me. When Rainey arrived, the man was breathing okay and ready to go to the ICU for the night. The first thing Rainey did was grab the chart from Nora, hustle me into a conference room and shut the door. Together we went over it. Now comes the bizarre part. Someone had upped the dosage."

I stared at him, aghast, at what he just told me. The man was being framed, obviously, and a patient's life was put at risk. "That's just awful. The dose was changed, but how? How did you know it was changed? Did Rainey believe you? Who would do such a thing and why?"

I motioned to him. "This is scary as hell, sit down, finish, finish, give me the rest of it."

He came back, sat down on my shabby old sofa, and explained, "Rainey looked at my notes. We looked very carefully at the medications I had prescribed. And there it was, when you looked close you could see a '1' put right in front of the 5mg. So he got the one 5mg dose I personally handed him and then the nurses did what they do each time, checked the chart, filled the pill cup and put in 15mg of the medicine not 5mg as I prescribed. That poor man got almost three days of medication in one. No wonder he crashed on us."

"He could have died, for what? Someone's idea of a joke? Someone out to get you in trouble? Maybe someone who knew the guy and wanted him out of the way? Is that possible? His wife maybe? She wasn't a nurse by any chance, was she?"

I knew I was asking a million questions and grasping at straws but it was scary to think what would have happened if they had not reached the man in time. "Could they have charged you with anything if he died? I mean this—"

He interrupted me, "Slow down, Maggie, we thought of all those scenarios. Rainey, for all his cold demeanor, is a smart guy and fair. He's been working back to back with me for years now and even he could tell, as small as the mark on the chart was, that it didn't seem to match my usual scrawl. The '1' was too perfect. Like the rest of the doctors in the world, I have lousy handwriting and a tendency to scribble stuff. When you're charting for about 20 or 30 patients and you're tired, your handwriting tends to get sloppy sometimes." He nodded at me. "Okay, most of the time, I guess."

He continued, "Nora was all for reporting my ass to every hospital administrator she could find. She followed us into the conference room, figuring as the night supervisor she had a right, I suppose. We sat and discussed the situation knowing we had to answer to the man's family, our front office—down the line to the Heart Institute, possibly our insurance people if he sued us. Christ, it was a holy mess.

"Nora wanted it put on the front-page of the *Washington Post*, I could tell. A full public whipping then rub salt into it would have been her idea of punishment. She wanted to call the cops about this, saying I tried to deliberately induce this reaction for the 'sake of science' as she put it. That woman made me out to be a regular Dr. Mengele."

I guess the seriousness of what he was saying showed in my reaction. I was appalled at what this woman wanted to do. Any man or woman who worked as long and as hard has Kurt did, deserved at least a fair hearing.

"The worst part of it is that I think Rainey started to think I did make a mistake. He's known me for years. I've made some dumb mistakes but he's there behind all of his residents and damn few get past him, I can tell you.

"I explained to him that I didn't even start this procedure until I ran it past him. 'Remember, I came upstairs and suggested we use the 5mg dose?' He agreed that I did say something to him and remembered we discussed the medication. He didn't remember all the details but he was at least remembering my actively seeking him out and going over the file with him.

"Nora was sitting there with tight lips just waiting to pounce again when Rainey said to her that he thought the chart had been tampered with. He examined it and the change seemed deliberate. He took a magnifying glass and we looked again, this time with Nora there. Under magnification we could definitely see the ink color was slightly different. The handwriting of the number '1' was very different. Even Nora seemed shaken when she realized I was telling the truth. Rainey told her the matter would be taken up with the administration and possibly they would want an investigation into the chart change. I was not to be suspended or reprimanded pending the administration's decision, and she was to remain silent about the whole thing."

He sighed to himself and kept going. "Rainey, as the principal investigator on the project, would speak to the man and his family. He would quietly explain about his reaction to the medicine and then remove him from further participation in the trial. All three of us agreed that was the best course for now. But, that woman scares the hell out of me and I don't think I trust her to keep her mouth shut."

While telling me this, Kurt had gotten up again and started pacing around, looking out windows. "And that's not the worst of it. Word got out among the staff that the dosage was wrong and Van Doren was being hung out to dry. Either from Nora, or those who were on the crash cart team that night, I can't say for sure. A few friends supported me; others started treating me like a pariah.

"When I was writing orders I could tell the nurses were uncomfortable. If any procedure I ordered was even slightly out of the ordinary, they went to their supervisor, Nora, or to Rainey for confirmation." You could hear the hurt and anger again in his voice.

"For a few weeks there was no confidence in me on the staff's part. I felt like a third-year medical student being checked, rechecked, and humiliated by floor nurses and technicians. Maggie, it was a bad month."

He sat there dispirited. I sat in my wing chair feeling sympathy for him, anger at the staff, and admiration for Dr. Rainey. I now wished I had not been so high-handed in my treatment of Kurt's chief. He was in the man's corner and that made him okay in my book.

"That's the most bizarre thing I've ever heard. Who do you think is behind this, and why? It sounds very much like Nora, but you say she was as shocked and upset as you and Jules when you pointed out the discrepancy in the handwriting. Who else has it in for you?"

I bent forward. "Now be brutally honest here with me, have you been fooling around with one of the techs or a nurse who might be jealous or infuriated that you dropped her? I mean that's something that can happen in a place as large as the Center. With the usual single-guy track record, it's almost understandable. I'm not asking out of curiosity, not judging you, I just need facts."

"Maggie, I've gone over this in my mind until I'm groggy. First of all, believe it or not, I'm either at the hospital or at the dorm and not in the sack with any nurse, not for years. No one could be coming at me from that angle. Hell, it's been almost two years since I've had a damn date! I don't lend money. I've never covered for anyone's mistakes. I simply can't figure out why this happened. I only hope it won't happen again but somehow I don't think it's over."

"What about the traffic that night at the nursing desk, anything unusual there—visitor, stranger, family getting in the way?"

"No, we all went through that scenario together. Everyone who should've be there was there and no one else. No one saw anything out of the ordinary." He shook his head.

"That's the scary part. Not knowing what could happen next and who it could happen to. I mean to injure or possibly kill an innocent patient just to get even with you or your surgical service is crazy. But then this person must be a little crazy or desperate about something.

"But *what*?" He shouted the word more in desperation and anger at the situation. "*Why* me for heaven's sake? Or is it the hospital they're trying to discredit and I'm their dupe? What did I do to anyone to piss him or her off that bad? I even reviewed patient charts for this past 6 months, thinking maybe I hurt someone or insulted someone. Or we all screwed up somewhere. The incident with Nora and you and Rainey is all I could think of and that wasn't in the records. I can't see you sneaking around with your cane and that baggy sweat suit and forging meds down at the Center. It has to be someone on staff or who's around there all the time. *But who, dammit, who?*"

By this time he was in the kitchen, sitting at the table and munching on the remaining potato chips in the bag. I went over to him and patted his shoulder and gave him a friendly little backward hug. It felt very good to me to be that close and even his smell was making me forget that he wasn't mine to hold. I resisted a powerful urge to kiss the top of his head and I turned away.

"Why don't you leave it alone for now? You've given me the story, now let me think about it in my left brain way. I may come up with something you didn't think of. Then again, maybe I won't, but for now try to concentrate on work and getting your paper ready, the holidays, and your trip to Chicago. Christmas will be here soon and maybe this nut will forget all about you in the hustle of the season. Let's hope so. I'm going to give this a lot of thought."

I took his hand and pulled him up. "Come on, I'll show you the office and upstairs and get you settled in for any day you want to come. I have an extra key here." I pointed to the top of the refrigerator.

He walked over and found the key with no problem. I forgot how tall he was. We went around the house, and he asked about the computer. We made sure he could use his laptop if necessary by plugging and unplugging mine. He crawled around under my desk and we decided it would be best if he brought some type of device he knew about to use on both computers. He asked if he could download some software to my machine, checked and discovered the computer was fairly clean and clear. We set a time for him to come by on Saturday. He grabbed his shabby brown suede jacket, pulled it on and was off to the hospital. He went out the door, pulling his cell phone out of the holder as he walked to the little green car, his beloved green machine. I shook my head in wonder how a man that large could fold himself up into that little car. I learned later he had the seat specially set back.

***

That evening Kurt emailed his friend in Chicago. Now it was Kurt's turn for advice. He wrote to Steve.

Remember the patient I told you about? Well, buddy, Maggie is who I found!!! She ain't no old lady. I guess you should know, more like my age. Not sure what it is we have but for now we're friends, enjoy one another's company. It's the damndest thing but seeing her after almost 2 months, I'm like a kid! I feel happy and even with all the crap at the hospital, with Maggie listening, making suggestions and volunteering to help, I feel I can get to the bottom of this. She's looking better, downright cute, and she's so light I can toss her up in the air when I hug her. Not that she allowed me that privilege but once. It's not like Elaine, buddy. I remember you staying with me, drunk as hell, but trying to talk me out of it the night before the wedding, remember? We really did do it for the kid and made a mess of it and now I miss little Mellie. Maggie's different, special, sort of, you know what I mean? ... Kurt

Reply from Steve: *Look, guy, I was drunk as hell that night, but I won't apologize. You talked about nothing but what was best for the baby that was coming, the whole time you two planned that marriage. I never once heard you say how much you cared about Elaine, how you two got along in the sack, if she turned you on, nothing but shit like, oh, it will be fine, it will be okay. What the hell did you think I was going to do? I felt it was a mistake, and I interfered, that's what a best man is for. I know you love Mellie, she's your child, your only chick. Speaking of which, we suspect we may be on the way to number two, nothing definite yet. And, hell, you stuck with Elaine a long time after it got bad. Listen, if this is important, take your time. I want to meet her. Got to go now. Baby has ear problem, Ginny's in the bathroom 10 times a day and yelling it's my fault ... Behind at work ... STAY OUT OF TROUBLE!!*

Kurt laughed when he read how he signed it: Steve the Stressed.

Chapter 14

I was gaining strength. The first of December was looming large on my calendar. But first, I had to get through Thanksgiving.

Holly called me one cold drizzling day full of holiday plans. "Mom, you don't have to do a thing you don't want to. Cooper and I are going to fix the turkey and if you could just sit and supervise the dressing as we fix it, that would be great."

It was wonderful to hear interest, joy, and excitement in her voice. Her summer was as bad as mine, if not worse. She had balanced a demanding job with being my advocate with doctors, HMO people and rehab centers.

We agreed on a menu and I put down the phone and went back to writing out checks for bills and looking at HMO statements when it rang again.

It was Kurt. "Maggie, just wanted to let you know I've been working myself to death and haven't had a chance to get over and take advantage of your study offer yet. Gonna get there tomorrow though."

Before I could extend an invitation to Holly's house for dinner he continued, "Sam Pleasance, you know my office mate here, invited me for Thanksgiving but I'll be working most of the day."

When Holly phoned again about Thanksgiving, I told her about Kurt coming to visit me and his plans to come over to study the next morning.

Just as I expected, she started preaching at me. "Mom, that's ridiculous that he would come out there just to spend a few hours studying. I think this guy is after more than a place to study. Be careful, you're too trusting. Suppose he's one of those guys who schmooze old ladies into leaving all their possessions to him and then kills you."

Old ladies? She was on a roll. "Hell, he's a doctor, he could figure out a hundred ways to off you and we'd never suspect. With you being so sick this summer it would be a perfect set up. You sure he *is* a doctor? I mean, did you talk to the nurses about him—to the guy who did your aneurysm, what's his name?"

I defended myself. "Holly, he said the same thing. I'm too trusting. Yes, he's a real doctor. He was with Rainey and the team that worked on me. He was holding my hand in surgery. I even punched him when they turned me over on the operating table. He saw you, and you probably saw him in the hall afterward but you talked to Rainey, not him, that's protocol. As Kurt explained it to me—you get the big cheese, not the cheese nip in a teaching hospital. He's on the up and up, believe me. I trust him, Holly."

"Hell, I just know he's after something. Watch yourself and if he starts to hang around too much or tries to sell you something, Cooper and I will come over and set him straight pronto."

I did not want to get into his rather sobering troubles at the Center; it would only fuel her fire. "He has a lot on his plate right now," I told her. "I guess I'm a shoulder to moan on, that's all. Stop being so darn suspicious, Holly."

Her voice was edgy. "Look out for yourself, okay? Be careful and remember I'm warning you he's up to no good."

I hung up and sighed. Goodness, that girl was a crab at times. I ate a light dinner and fed my dog most of it. I wasn't hungry. I'll bake something good for morning; homemade sweet bread would be good. I pulled out the recipe book and looked for something to toast and eat along with oatmeal.

The next morning, I was roused out of a sound sleep by my roommate, RJ. "Maggie, there's a big guy at the door that says you're expecting him. He kept knocking and I finally got up." She was plainly annoyed at being awakened at the stroke of 7 on a Thursday morning in November.

I nodded to her to let him in. She huffed out of my room. "If I have to keep answering the door, I might as well find another place to move where it's quieter."

"RJ, you've been saying that for 3 years. Get over it." I got up, stretched, and went into the bathroom. Shut the bedroom door, showered in record time, dried off, jumped into new jeans and my famous red sweater and ran a comb through my hair.

I then called downstairs, "Come on up if you want and get comfortable in the office. I overslept so my food schedule is slightly off."

I could hear Kurt taking the stairs two at a time. He popped into view as I started to shut the door and slap on some makeup. It's never a good idea to race out of your room to greet a handsome man without makeup, at least as much makeup as decency allows.

"Hey, sorry to startle the roommate. I know I'm getting you up early. For

78

some amazing reason we had a light night, and I got to sleep and decided to start out early. With my hours, I forget the rest of the world works and lives on a 9 to 5 schedule." He paused at the office door holding a large, battered brown briefcase bulging with who only knows what. He was telling me this through my partially shut door.

I called out to him as I put the finishing touches on my face, "Any new developments on the mystery of the forgery?"

"No, and for now things are quiet there. Nothing I can't handle so far. Some people still stare at me in the hall."

I tugged on the hairbrush, opened the door to hear better. "Kurt, has anything else that would even remotely be connected with this happened to you in the past week or two?"

"You know my car was broken into, or I should say tossed. Others, too. I leave the old girl unlocked and just keep trash and reading material in there. I think it might have been kids. Seems stupid but it has happened before to folks there."

"Was anything taken? I mean, was a lot of stuff disturbed?"

"Hell, yes, Maggie, everything was tossed around and the doors were left wide open. My old notes, a trash bag, and my shaving kit were opened and dumped. Probably kids, like I said, looking for prescription pads to forge. I was over at Children's for the whole day when it happened. Stuff was thrown in my car that belonged to others so I'm sort of under suspicion again. But most folks who know me just think the junk was tossed and landed in my car by accident."

Just then, RJ ran up the stairs with her towel and went into the bathroom across the hall. She shut the door firmly. I could hear the click of the lock. Water sounded in the shower.

"I guess I ticked her off." Kurt's head peeked out of the office and tilted toward the bathroom door.

"Don't worry about it. She had to get up for work. She's amazing. She can shower, dress and be out of here in 20 minutes," I said quietly so she could not hear me over the spray of water. "But a great roommate."

"I'm going to get started and pull my stuff out. Maybe I can just leave some of this for now, that's why there is so much of it."

I finished looking at myself in the mirror, patted the newly brushed, newly lightened blonde hair and walked out of my room. "Make yourself at home. There's a partially cleaned bookcase in there. I'll be getting rid of things in there from time to time so you can just fill up all the empty spots you find. Now I think I'll go down and start coffee and some oatmeal. I'll call you when it's ready."

"Seems like you are always feeding me lately. I really do owe you."

I went downstairs thinking about the car break-in. I started coffee, got a pot out and looked for the familiar blue and red oatmeal box on the shelf. While the oatmeal simmered. Kurt was moving around upstairs unpacking and probably smelling the coffee and food, making him hungry.

He called down, "Is the coffee ready? I'd love some, if it is."

"Everything's ready if you can take a break for a few minutes."

He came into the kitchen, glanced out the window and said, "Look, it's snowing and sleeting again outside. Kind of early for that around here. Now in Chicago we get this crappy weather from Halloween on but unusual here. Hope this isn't a foretaste of a long nasty winter. I hate cold weather, bad for my knee."

With that, he poured himself a cup of coffee, sat down, and drank the orange juice in one gulp. "Snow, sleet, and warm oatmeal—good meal for a nasty morning. You just instinctively know how to fix the right thing."

"You suggested it, sweet pea," I said as I dished out the sticky mess. "It was your idea to have oatmeal, don't give me credit. I just cooked it up."

We turned on the TV and watched the early morning show on the only channel that came in on my tiny thirty-dollar TV. We finished eating and I piled the dishes in the sink as he went upstairs to work.

I didn't disturb him, the rest of the morning all was quiet. I could hear him up there working on his computer and occasionally pacing up and down in the room. I went to the store. Later I hauled a box of cookie cutters off my shelf, and looked up cookie recipes.

Chapter 15

We established a pattern after that morning. The days Kurt was there we talked and ate together, either lunch or breakfast. He stuck carefully to his pattern of working from early morning until 1 or 2 each day. I almost never bothered him so the house was quiet. He managed two more visits that week and three the next.

Thanksgiving week rolled around. That Wednesday was a lovely warm fall day, almost hot by some standards. The cold, wet, snowy weather of the week before was a memory. We were in the midst of a golden autumn morning when Kurt showed up as I was struggling with a large Christmas wreath to hang on my front door. I was concentrating and didn't hear his car pull up.

"Here, let me help you with that." He grabbed the large wreath and carefully took the back string and placed it up high on the door hanger. "It looks nice. Did you make it yourself?"

"As a matter of fact, I did. Went up to the craft store, got some gilded fruit and that gold bow and put it together, then took a can of gold spray paint and just lightly put a touch on the green leaves. It's really pretty, I think."

"You've been planning Christmas for weeks I'll bet, I have taken in 3 packages left on the front porch for you and you must be getting more every day. Aren't you going out to the mall at all? It would help the stamina thing, you know."

I opened the front door and let us both in. "First of all, you have not been coming here for weeks, just two weeks. And, yes, I've been walking around Aspen Hill but not the really big malls. I prefer online shipping costs to the crowds. I love Christmas—the preparations, the baking, the wrapping, and all the mess that comes with it. It's sort of my time of year."

He looked at me and smiled. "I have a surprise for you. Today we celebrate. I've turned in the final paper; it's my last project. I've been examined, poked, prodded and defended my research magnificently and brilliantly, if I say so myself. I can now officially say that soon I'll be awarded my degree from your old alma mater, Maggie! How does that grab you, lady?"

He was excited, proud, and expansive. He hugged me and danced me around my living room. "You've been feeding me meal and after meal, and today, it's your day. I'm taking you out wherever you want to go and feeding you whatever your heart desires. Kurt Van Doren, M.D., Ph.D., sounds pretty good, doesn't it? And I'm spending it all this afternoon. My treat, so don't say no. I'm just too happy to have anyone say no to me today."

I looked at him and grinned as he put me down but held on to me. Having our bodies pressed so close felt wonderful and I wondered if he was enjoying it, too. I moved away, embarrassed at what I was feeling. His hands lingered around my waist.

I said in a soft voice, "I could never say no to you about anything. You can take that to the bank. Now, let me go so I can get gussied up a bit and I know just the place to take you in Olney."

He grinned and turned me loose. "Slap on the war paint, lady, put on your jazziest dress, and off we go. You helped me get over the hump here. I owe you big time—your food, the computer, and your office programs for my final graphics. Now git, gal, I'm going to feed your face today."

I started up the stairs, trying to figure out what to wear. I had expanded my better fitting wardrobe more so I had a choice of things. I called over my shoulder to him, "I'll be down in about 10 minutes, or you can come up and wait with me while I pick something out and slap on makeup. I don't mind if you do, I can get dressed in the bathroom and you can help me pick something to wear."

He hesitated then said, "I don't know about women's clothes, Maggie. Put on what you think would look good and be quick about it. As for war paint, just put on a little, you look fine as it is."

Chapter 16

What fun, a handsome guy taking me to lunch! I whipped out my one good black dress, pantyhose, shoes—washed my face and applied makeup lightly, but I took a little time to get it right.

A voice called up the stairwell, "Why didn't I just kidnap you the way you were? I'll bet you're up there fiddling with makeup and other crap. Come on, Maggie, times a' wasting and we need to celebrate!"

I dabbed some cologne on my wrists, grabbed my shoes, and started downstairs. "That didn't take long and I wanted to make sure I looked halfway decent for you. After all, you have a reputation to uphold as a swinging bachelor, a handsome man about town. We can't have you appear in public with a woman who looks like something the cat dragged in, now can we?"

"Swinging bachelor, my ass, ain't had a date in years, all the women I know are married or over 80 except you." He bent towards me and sniffed my neck. "You look great, and you smell wonderful. That's a very sexy smell. Best be careful or I'll have you back upstairs and lunch forgotten."

His sniffing tickled and I flinched a bit and giggled. Then I grinned and said playfully, "In your dreams, Doc, let's go." I got my coat and started for the front door. My heart pounded as I remembered our closeness a short while ago. I knew he was teasing me. Like I just said to him, I now repeated to myself—in your dreams, lady.

We went outside to find the warm, golden day had retreated and we faced a cool overcast sky. Fall weather does that—one minute sun, next fog or rain. I stepped off the front porch and realized I would have to ride in that little green car of his again. The thought of the way he tore out of my street each time he left told me he drove like the wind normally, and I'd be terrified. We'd been in heavy traffic the only other time I rode with him.

"No you don't, Kurt, I'll drive my boring car. Yours is too small for both of us. It's so low, I'd have a hell of a time getting in and out. Hope you don't mind." I took out my keys and started toward the driveway.

He gently took the keys out of my hand, grabbed my elbow, and escorted me around to the passenger side of his little car. "Nope, I've been planning this all morning. I have my heart set on you riding up the road in my green machine. I got you in and out in September for dinner and to Holly's so I can certainly do it now. Even if we can't put the top down I want to chauffeur you again, or do you want to drive?" He extended his hand with the keys, and I was flattered. He really was very possessive of this old wreck.

The car business was firmly settled. Not the way I wanted, but I had to admit I enjoyed the ragtop last summer. At least the damn thing had seatbelts. How bad could it be? After all, we were only going about five miles up the road.

Getting me in was not as difficult as the September drive. I buckled up as he started the motor and pulled the car out of the driveway. I must say he drove carefully out to the main road. So far so good, no rushing, no weaving. Hell, I may survive his driving yet. I reached over and put my favorite golden oldies station on. The Supremes came blaring out at us. Kurt looked over at me, grinned and started to sing the words along with Diana and the girls.

We flew up Georgia Avenue, warmth seeping in the windows as the sun started to peek out from the clouds again. The traffic was not heavy as we passed woods, a smart new housing development and the new shopping mall they just completed. I could see kids from the local high school were swarming the McDonald's. Kurt was quietly singing along as Diana and the ladies poured their hearts out at top volume. His voice was soft and sexy and I had to concentrate hard on the scenery. It was affecting me in ways I didn't want or need. Still, I was happier than I had been in months. This was the way I remembered that drive in September. Oh, let it last just a little longer, I prayed.

I looked at his profile as he drove. I was tempted to reach out and touch his cheek. Nothing sexy, just to touch him, that's all I wanted to do. Instead, I remarked, "So you know the words to some of these oldies, eh? I think the one they just played was a hit 30 years ago. Guess I'm getting old, Kurt, the new stuff doesn't do it for me. I sound ancient when I complain about the kids not being the same as when I was young. Holly thinks of me as practically prehistoric." I thought of her advice on the phone and cringed inside for a moment. Old lady, never!

He looked mischievously at me, winked and said, "You're too cute to be an old lady, Maggie. But you're right about the music. I love the old stuff. It had style, rhythm, and most of the songs told a little story of some kind. You could relate to it. This new shit is just that, shit."

I indicated for him to take a right turn. "And you know," he glanced at me, "leaving some of it hidden for our imagination is what makes the old songs so sexy and wonderful."

"Make a left up here, old fart," I said.

He started to make a left into the shopping center. I was going to direct him to the top part of the lot. Just as we made the turn something cracked and we suddenly tilted. Kurt hit the brakes and that started us to spin out.

I yelled, "What's wrong?" We were swerving and then spinning. I could hear cars slamming on their breaks over my beating heart.

He was fighting the wheel and holding on. His good reflexes were strained to the limit. I was frightened and started, in my panic, to grab him, when I realized he needed all the room he could get to just control the little car.

The road, the stores, everything was tilted at a crazy angle and moving in a circle around us. In a way, it was like being on a crooked merry-go-round. We were sliding now, and smoke was coming from the front wheels. It smelled terrible. I was terrified we were going to catch on fire. You could hear cars slam on their brakes as we continued to coast in a circle. The new fear that flashed into my head was one of them hitting us. I could see oncoming traffic pulling over into parking lots to avoid us and the screech of their brakes, too.

My head hit something and I was thrown forward. I felt my chest tighten as it strained against the seatbelt. Kurt had not bothered with his belt and the force of the car's motion was causing him to fight the wheel even harder. His body pushed against the door as the front of the car swerved to the left. That door flew open but somehow he managed to hold on to the steering wheel. I made a grab for him but my seatbelt held me tight. He righted himself and by the time I got a grip on him, the car had lurched to a stop and was crumpled up against a large sign at the shopping center entrance. The huge sign was tilted ominously over the car.

"Get out quick, Maggie, get your belt off, move, move, and move!" He straightened himself up and tried to find the buckle on my belt. I grabbed for it, too, and with both of us fumbling we only made it worse. Finally, I found the damn thing on the right side and pulled frantically. The belt moved away from me. I opened the door and literally rolled onto the pavement to get away from the car. My jacket took a good hit but at least it kept my elbows intact.

The car, now huddled up against the tilted sign, continued smoking. Traffic had come to a complete halt. Drivers were getting out of their cars to help, I guess. Kurt climbed out of what once was a door but seemed like a mangled piece of metal sprung and bent upward. He ran around, grabbed both of my arms, and pulled me up and away from it.

"Get back, get back, I don't know if it's hot enough to catch fire!" He gestured to the helpful drivers coming forward but kept an arm around me and helped me away from the smoke.

We made it to the sidewalk and he looked at me with such tenderness as he held me out and checked me over. "Are you okay, Maggie, are you hurt anywhere?"

Kurt checked her over feeling nothing but fright and fear for her and for himself. She's shaking, what a scare. She has to be okay—if she's hurt, I'll never forgive myself. I just need to hold her, make her feel safe, secure. That's all I want to do, just hold her. But not like this, because of a car wreck. Good God, what's happening here? Just a coincidence, nothing more. Oh shit, not more trouble. Please let it be an accident, nothing more.

His arms tightened around me, calming me, checking me for pain. He kissed the top of my head. Then without waiting for a response, he flew back to the car and turned off the ignition. He again put his arms around me. I leaned in, dazed and frightened. My dress was filthy and torn. My jacket was ruined. My shoes and purse were missing. My head and chest incision hurt, and I was crying from tension. But his arms around me felt reassuring and good.

I raised my head and glanced over at the little green car. It looked rather forlorn sitting huddled up against the bent sign, half on the sidewalk, smoking and leaking.

A nice older man dressed in sweats and a baseball cap came running over to us. "Someone called the cops and the fire department, mister, help's on the way."

The nice man took my arm and led me away from the sidewalk and toward his old silver car parked in the lot. Opening the doors on the passenger side, he steered me into the seat. My knees were weak and I sat gratefully. "Why don't you and the little lady rest until they get here?" He said to Kurt, "Are you okay, fella? You look like you need something for the cut over your eye."

It was then that I realized that Kurt was bleeding from a gash over his eyebrow. It looked like the rearview mirror caught him as he wrestled the car to keep it on the road. Another Good Samaritan handed him some Kleenex. He gingerly patted the cut and then the blood from his eye.

A crowd was gathering. People came out of the grocery store and drug store. Others were standing and speculating about what happened. I could hear isolated words.

Another man appeared wearing a Fried Chicken jacket and paper hat. He came out with a plastic bag containing ice for the cut and cold drinks. It was a thoughtful gesture.

Seeing all that blood, I was concerned with Kurt's damaged forehead. The nice older gentleman, whose name I never got, thanked the man for us, then took the drinks and put them on his car's floor near us. Out in the distance we could hear sirens.

Traffic had started to carefully move around the little wrecked car. It had left a trail of various fluids all over the street, making driving hazardous.

I was holding on to him and trying to brush away imaginary dirt from his cut face. I wanted to scream at people to get the ambulance there faster. He looked pale and shaken but was, as usual, taking charge of the situation. He let me fuss for about one minute then he strode out to the edge of the road to meet the fire trucks.

More onlookers gathered, pointing and speculating. Two big fire trucks pulled up. Men jumped down from the cab and pulled large extinguishers out. The truck engines were loud as they dwarfed the little car. The ambulance, with lights flashing, quietly slid into the parking lot right behind the trucks. It pulled to a stop, and Kurt walked up to the driver and spoke briefly. He practically dragged the EMT over to look at me. He quickly switched from victim to physician, and took charge. The EMTs seemed confused as to whether to treat him as a patient or doctor. I was ready to strangle them.

Still shaking with fright and fear, I answered the techs as they asked me stupid questions about what day it was and who was president.

Finally, I could stand it no longer and almost yelled, "For heaven's sake take care of that man, he's bleeding all over the place and needs help. I'm fine. Please help him!"

They looked at me and turned to Kurt. The wound in his head was still bleeding. He was using cold, wet paper napkins from the Chicken Man's donation to stem the flow.

The tall heavyset tech went over and directed him to please sit down while they checked him over. Kurt reluctantly leaned on the bumper of the ambulance while he checked the cut. A pressure bandage and some tape was applied and he was handed a couple of wet wipes to get the blood out of his eyes and off his face. They started to ask him the same stupid questions but he ignored them and walked towards to the now quiet, crippled little car.

"Ma'am, we want to get both of you inside now. We're going to take you over to the hospital emergency room. As soon as the police ask a few questions we're leaving."

I was still shaking, but taking a sip of the ice water seemed to soothe me. I was handed a couple of damp wipes and I started to shake the dirt off my ruined black dress and torn jacket.

A tall county policeman approached me carrying my black purse and shoes. I took them and thanked him. I leaned on the ambulance as I put the shoes on. The purse seemed closed and in order. I knew I'd need my hospital card for this trip. I was well versed in hospital protocol by now.

Everyone who was standing and watching realized nothing more exciting was going to happen so they started to leave. The firemen took a tank and sprayed the front of the now ruined little green car for the second time. Kurt, ever in charge, was trying to wedge his way between them to inspect the damage.

The EMT followed him, took him by his arm and steered him back to me. He was firm but polite as he requested, "Sir, Doctor, please keep still, will you? The police will be here in a second. After they take some information we're going to transport you over. You can sit in the back but you'll have to go with us, okay?"

Kurt was pissed. "Man, that's my car in the middle of the street. I can't let the thing just sit there!" He was exaggerating. The car was safely up on the sidewalk; it was no threat to traffic. Unfortunately, the big crooked sign looked like a threat to traffic and pedestrians at this point.

Since the EMT wouldn't let him move around much, he came over to my side and was holding me in one arm and gesturing with the other. I could feel him still trembling with fright and anger.

The same tall policeman came over with a clipboard. He talked to the EMTs. Suddenly it was decided that we would go immediately to the ER, and he would talk to us there. He assured Kurt they would take care of the car. He handed him a card with an address on it where he could find what was left of his precious green machine later in the day.

The firemen had stopped traffic and were busy hosing down the street and removing a bit of broken glass from the driver's side window. One big truck rolled out of the parking lot, noisily shifting about ten gears and pulled away.

The policeman took Kurt's driver's license information. I heard him give the District Hospital Center as his work address and my address and information.

With the crowd gone and one truck left to mop up, I felt relieved at not being the center of attention. Kurt was plainly annoyed and frustrated but cooperative.

The EMTs were getting us ready for transporting. He refused the gurney and took himself up in one long step. I gazed at the huge high ambulance entrance and shook my head. "I can't get up there, guys, it's too high."

Randy, the heavyset blond attendant, according to his badge, looked at me and said, "We're going to have to put you on a stretcher to get you in. It's not too bad and you only have a couple of blocks to go."

I grinned at him and replied, "Randy, I've ridden in more ambulances this past summer and fall than you I bet."

They pulled out the stretcher, and I promptly lay down and was buckled in. Kurt got back out to help as they pulled me up and into the back door. They told him to get back in and remain quiet. It rankled, I could tell. We then sped off with Randy filling out forms and asking us questions.

Chapter 17

Two minutes later, we arrived at the ER entrance of our local hospital. We sat there while he finished his paperwork. Neither of us was a critical case. By this time I had calmed down. Kurt had managed his temper and his frustrations. He smiled at me and held my hand in the ambulance. I explained to the EMT that Kurt was the doctor who operated on me this past September.

He glanced up from his clipboard and said, "She's your patient, Doc? Wow, my surgeon sure never took me out joyriding in a sports car after my appendix came out."

He grinned and patted my shoulder as Kurt and the other tech pulled the stretcher out of the ambulance. The wheels jarred to the surface of the cement and I was pushed inside.

"Well, well, well, look who's here," Jonesie, the tall good-looking ER nurse remarked to his staff members. "What'd you do this time, Maggie? Is it your heart or too much holiday cheer, baby doll?" He greeted me like an old friend and walked me down the aisle of the now familiar hospital.

I had been there three times this past summer and he had an almost elephantine memory for faces and names. Green curtained cubicles lined two sides of the large room. The central office area was busy with nurses moving in and out, and what looked like physicians on different phones. Everything was quiet. A typical suburban emergency room, none of the big city drama in here.

Kurt followed behind my stretcher with the two technicians guiding me.

Jonsie said, "My goodness, Dr. Silver will be sorry he missed you this time. But he's on nights for the next month."

I struggled to sit up and said to Jonesie, "Get the damn buckles off this thing, will you? I'm fine, I just couldn't do the step in the ambulance. Their solution was to strap me on this roller-skate and load my big butt into the ambulance. And guess what, Jonesie? I brought my own personal physician with me this time. Meet Kurt Van Doren of the bloodied Van Dorens. We were in an auto accident around the corner."

Jonesie stopped at the end of one aisle, turned and shook Kurt's hand. "Glad to meet ya, Doc, sorry about your head. If you step this way, I can see that you get stitched up pretty quick. Won't hurt you a bit but we'll have to charge you." He turned and winked at me as he pulled the man into the cubicle next to mine. He had checked the good doc out thoroughly and realized he was a hunk.

I managed to get the buckles off the stretcher with help from the EMTs and I pulled myself to a sitting position. Still gritty from the road, I was starting to feel cold and knew both of us were going to be stiff after this little escapade.

I got off their stretcher and stood. I yanked the curtain between the two cots back and watched as Jonesie looked at the nasty cut on Kurt's forehead. He gave him a clean pad to hold and disappeared around the corner. After a few minutes, a young doctor I did not recognize appeared. He walked into Kurt's cubicle, the two men shook hands. Then the male pissing contest started. Get two men of the same profession together, introduce them, and it happens. Kurt, appearing macho, hopped off the cot as they talked, comparing school, hospitals, and specialties, until I thought I would scream at them.

His badge read Rogers and as the testosterone flew around, I called out to him, "Dr. Rogers, would you please look at that bloody cut? I don't care if you went to school with Adolph Hitler, I want his cut fixed. It's deep and ragged and I was wondering if by chance there's a plastic surgeon around today who could do this work?"

Kurt was by now almost completely composed. He grinned at Rogers. "Don't pay any attention to her, she's just a fuss pot where I'm concerned. I'm sure you'll do fine." He then joked, "And with a good mirror I can supervise. I am, after all, a surgeon and used to trauma surgery. Got any of this new…."

They walked off together to find a suture kit, I expect. Kurt was asking something I didn't catch. I jumped up as they came back laughing about some story he was telling the staff. The tall good-looking doctor who had turned up as a patient on this slow afternoon in December mesmerized them all.

I was a little put out by all the camaraderie. I "flounced" off my ER cot and announced, "If no one's going to pay attention to what I say, I'm going to the bathroom and try to regain some dignity."

Kurt stared at me and snorted, "Going to be hard to be dignified, Maggie, with the whole back of your dress muddy and half torn off." Rogers was working on his cut and he was sitting on a chair next to his bed and waved his hand at me. He sat there composed, legs crossed in front of him, laughing at me. "You caught the back skirt part there in the door handle as you rolled out of the car and off it went. That's why I was sort of standing with my arm around you out on the street, my dear."

So much for dignity. I was down to picking grit out of my hair and shoes.

They took Kurt's insurance information. I think mine is encased in plastic next to all the computers in this ER. They finished up his head and Rogers figured he knew about aftercare. His tetanus shot was up to date, he assured them. I was given a clean bill of health after an EKG and a thorough going over by Dr. Rogers with his newest colleague, Kurt Van Doren, watching every move the man made. After much laughing and promises to keep in touch, Kurt walked us out to a waiting cab in front of the hospital.

The taxi took us to my house, where he called his insurance man and then the local car rental place the insurance man recommended. We both got cleaned up. I changed into jeans. We brushed his pants and jacket as best we could. We drove back up to Olney to the rental place to pick up his car. They promised to deliver one to my house before 5:30. We stopped and bought him a clean shirt. He lost his tie somewhere between the accident or at the hospital. He put it on in the store and we dropped his suit coat in the backseat of my car.

"It's now 3:45, we've been screwing around with this for 3 hours, and I for one am starved. The place I was taking you for lunch is right here. Do you feel like eating early dinner now?"

He looked at me with his puffy eye, a big white bandage and grinned, "You know me, I'm always up for food. Let's do it. But no booze for you or me, okay?"

"Fine." I grabbed his arm and we finally went off for the promised lunch.

Chapter 18

The parking lot at that time of day was almost deserted. The big crooked sign was now pulled down, and there was no trace of Kurt's little car. I drove, and he looked wistfully at the spot where his beloved green machine had been sitting. All you could see was a large grease or oil spot. We pulled up in front of Mama Lucy's.

The sign inside said: "seat yourself" so we did. While waiting to order our lunch, we both started to unwind. Kurt looked around and took in a deep breath. "I love the smell of a good Italian place, the garlic and Parmesan, the yeast dough, it's great, and all the cheeses, great, just great!"

The dining room was almost empty. A couple of late lunch folks at window seats only. The large room held round tables with yellow tablecloths and silverware that awaited dinner patrons. The Mama's staff obviously had started decorating for the holidays, with twinkling little white lights woven in the greenery over the bar/deli. Little bunches of dried flowers in red, gold, and brown were arranged in small glass vases set primly on each table next to tiny turkeys. I had forgotten that Thanksgiving was the next day. The walls were adorned with hand-painted murals of Italy. Behind the long bar and attached delicatessen, the cooks were busy preparing homemade pasta, pizza, and desserts. The long, glassed-in deli case held platters of pastries and salads, ready for the early evening takeout crowd and diners with a sweet tooth. The yeast smell of the different dough being prepared was drifting over to make us aware that our stomachs were empty and waiting.

We watched the cooks move around getting ready for dinner. The bartender had only one customer and both were leaning against the bar watching some basketball reruns. Kurt kept glancing the customer.

"Looks like my buddy Packard there is waiting for someone," he commented.

"Here? Packard? This is a little out of the way for him isn't it?" I turned to stare.

"Well, you know what they say, 'Of all the gin joints in all the world...'" He let the quote go as we both noticed two rather seedy looking men meet Packard at the bar.

"He can see us from there, Kurt, do you think we should leave?" I asked.

"Hell, no. We have every right to be here and we both need to eat now after that scare. It does seem a coincidence that he would show up here at the site of the accident a few hours later, doesn't it?"

The two men stood and laughed at something Vince said and then moved off toward a table full of women and children at the back of the place. Packard turned his back and resumed his conversation with the bartender. A few minutes later, a young woman walked in, gave the handsome doctor a light kiss on the cheek, and they left together.

"I wonder what that whole thing was about, Maggie? If I thought he put you and me through this I think I would—"

I quickly said, "Looks like a nice out-of-the-way place to meet a lady—not your wife, if you ask me. Probably just a coincidence and if not, I'll help you break his nose again." We both relaxed and laughed.

Packard forgotten, Kurt leaned back and said, "We'll have to come back some night when I get an evening off—if I can get over the fright of making a left turn here, Mags. If the food is as good as it smells, I think this could be a favorite of mine, too."

He leaned across the table and said, "I'll have to take you down to O'Malley's near Connecticut Avenue. It's just a bar and they do very simple food, sandwiches, and steaks. But the fries, that's what they're famous for. They're so crisp and good, big hunky ones, too, not the presliced frozen suckers you see at Mickey D's."

Our waitress approached and it was obvious that she thought that Kurt was as tasty as a great O'Malley French fry, the big hunky ones— not prepackaged. I thought he looked a bit seedy after his early afternoon experiences but the girl gave him a wide smile and all of her attention while we ordered. She was dressed in a black skirt and white shirt, which had two buttons undone. It barely showed off a rather good cleavage.

We made small talk and watched as other diners appeared and were seated near our table. This was the early-bird special crowd of seniors mostly. When our salads arrived, the waitress managed to bend over and give us a shot of her attributes. I noticed there were now three buttons undone on her white shirt. A short time later, when the linguini with clam sauce for me and cream sauce for Kurt arrived, we were given another shot of the chest as she cleared away the salad plates and placed the steaming dishes on the pale yellow tablecloths.

My hero, not immune to a good view, looked at her, smiled up, and thanked her in his most charming way. I thought the girl would start squealing with delight any moment and was prepared to catch her if she fainted. He tapped the back of her hand and thanked her for the service.

She looked into his eyes then checked his bandage and puffy eye. She then glanced over at me briefly.

Just to be smart, I looked at her and said, "I beat him regularly."

She looked surprised. I don't think she believed me. I got the impression she was assessing my relationship to this man: wife, mother, sister, coworker? She sort of shifted her shoulders as if to say whatever you are, sister, you ain't got my body.

I felt uncomfortable at being appraised by a kid and at the same time jealous as hell of her shape and youth. Straightening up and filling her well-endowed chest with air for emphasis, she looked toward the handsome injured man and murmured, "I sure hope you and your friend here enjoy the meal. Just let me know if you need more bread or anything else. I'll be over behind the counter. Just wave or nod and I'll come back. Okay?"

Adjusting his napkin on his lap Kurt smiled sweetly up at her, touched the back of her hand again, and said, "My wife and I want to thank you for the lovely service. I'll surely let you know if we need anything."

I kicked him under the table as she walked away. Her demeanor seemed just a little more professional and less blatant. I gave him another kick, practically leaned my breasts into the linguine in front of me, and said in a quiet voice, "You rat bastard, flirting with that kid in front of me. Then you go pumping her up with the hand thing, and telling her I'm your wife. What next? You going to boink the hostess on the way out? I may give you another black eye and matching gash if you keep this up."

Kurt took Maggie's hand in his, and covertly glancing over at the deflated young lady behind the counter he turned it upward and tenderly kissed the palm. It was not only a ploy for the benefit of the flirtatious waitress but a sexy move he saw on a TV movie one night.

He glanced over at Maggie as his lips touched the soft warm curve of her hand. She feels so good. Even scraped and bruised she looks good. You know you've wanted to do this for a long time but for now she thinks this hand thing is a joke. I need to keep up the romancing. She'll catch on sooner or later, I'm sure. Maybe she'll make a move and show me how she feels, too.

***

That kiss was so sexy and felt so good that my heart skipped a beat and like the smitten waitress, I was almost ready to faint. Only I knew this tender act was just that, an act. His eyes holding mine gave me a conspiratorial look. I'm sure to the uninitiated it looked like a tender moment between husband and wife. He murmured more to my palm than my face, "You sound like a real wife bitching at me about the flirtation, my dear. I'm only having a bit of fun. We did something similar at the hospital in September, so why not here and now?"

I laughed at him, I couldn't help it. This man was a bedraggled, bandaged rat bastard, and I loved every minute of it, and him. I was remembering the last time we were out at a restaurant; the strange little bar in Georgetown.

He was just plain enjoying himself. Getting into character, I reached over and tenderly touched his face. I loved touching that sweet face but it was more in the spirit of the game at that moment. I was so grateful to the powers that be that we were not injured when his damn car fell apart. Accident? Was someone deliberately doing this to him? The next time it could be fatal. I shivered and my hands went cold with fear thinking about that.

Kurt smiled, straightened up, and started eating his linguini. Our sweet domestic scene was over and the patrons and our fluffy waitress were looking embarrassed and anywhere but at the battered couple in the throes of marital bliss. It was mean, it was fantasy, and it was fun.

Chapter 19

I wasn't prepared at all for the Thanksgiving feast the next day. Kurt had left me full of linguini and laughing over our little scenario at the restaurant. We both realized we had a close brush with something serious and tried to put a good face on the whole incident. I wished him a happy "turkey day." He pushed off for a late shift at the Center in the rental car. I watched as he disappeared around the corner, and the thought occurred to me that he might not be safe…what if the accident wasn't really an accident? I rushed off to the grocery store and ended up baking a pie and some rolls late that night, downing aspirin and moving slowly as I got stiff.

Getting to Holly's was easy, but I knew helping with dinner and cleanup was going to be tough as sore as I felt. She kept asking about Kurt and about our accident and she finally accepted by explanation that he was not an old lady schmoozer but a casual friend.

She sat down and lectured me as we prepared the dressing. "Mom, look, you're lonely and with Ivy in North Carolina and with my job, Cooper and his kids, I know I haven't always been as attentive as I should. But, Mom, I care about you. I want you to know that. Now let's have the truth about this Kurt guy. Don't be embarrassed to tell me anything, I won't judge you. You've just made a few hospital visits and a lift home into something more than it is. I don't want you to be hurt or make a fool of yourself."

"Holly, if I was imagining things, making it into something it's not, I would tell you right here and now and be done with it. But Kurt's a nice person and a real friend. I don't know how to convince you. We really did wreck his car yesterday, and I feel 100 years old today. If you care to see my bruises I can pull off—"

She interrupted, "I believe you, you did him a favor and he was trying to pay you back, that's all. If the guy's your friend, as you say, I just don't understand how I could have missed him at the hospital, or how I managed to miss him when I come over to the house with Puddy."

"Holly, when was the last time you were at my house?"

"Let me think, oh, I dropped Puddy off just last Friday. I remember that clearly, and then I picked her up around 5:30. There was no handsome doctor drooling at your door at that time, Mom."

I turned and looked at her. "Yes, you dropped her off. For the past month you've been there exactly twice and that was to drop off the dog, in and out quick. Face it, Holly, you've not been there enough to run into the milkman, the postman, or any other *man* in my house. He's a friend I keep telling you, your inheritance is safe with me!" I was beginning to lose my sense of humor about Holly's suspicions.

She sensed I was getting steamed. She took my meaning and without a word she got up from the table and started clearing it of old mail, magazines, slamming some half-dead flowers in the trash. She removed the old tablecloth and pulled out a new one from a package and fluffed it out to place on the table.

"Don't get fussy, Mom. I don't want or need your money. I just said I hadn't met him, and you've talked about him a lot. If this guy is real, you've built up something in your mind about him that may not be healthy. I just don't want you to make a fool of yourself. There's nothing more pathetic than a woman your age chasing a man down, trying to get him to care about her. It's disgusting in a way. Look, I only mean for you to be happy, but not thought of as a fool by your friends, the neighbors and even us."

I put the silverware down on the table with a thump and glared at her. "Trust me, the man is real, the friendship is fine, nothing more, nothing less. Now drop it!"

The rest of the day was splendid. We laughed, and overate. Cooper and the kids watched parades and football. Holly and I put an old movie on the DVD and enjoyed it, and then it was clean up time.

That evening we emailed Ivy, Mike, and Tim in North Carolina and sent pictures of our day. Suddenly I was home and it was over. Monday was December 1, and I was excited.

I started back to work after the holiday. Greeting old friends and making the acquaintance of folks hired since I left 5 months ago was exciting. I was working from 7:30 a.m. to 1:30 p.m. each day. It would be a lot to handle, but I felt strong and up to it. I came home each day and napped. It had been days since I had heard from Kurt. I guess my self-fulfilling prophecy was right. He was busy with work and finishing up his studies and was too busy for me.

I missed his voice, the smell of his old suede jacket when I was near him, his silly jokes. Each time the phone rang I was disappointed. I began to wonder if I was the fool Holly thought, but I was determined not to let her win that one.

At the end of that week, I pulled around the corner and passed a strange car in front of my house. Was that the stupid rental I couldn't remember? My heart thumped in my chest, and my new valve sounded absurdly loud as I parked. I deliberately checked the mailbox and slowly walked up the driveway to the house. In my mind, I was racing for the door and throwing myself into waiting arms inside. Instead, when I opened it there was no sound but Stupid padding down the steps to greet me.

Where was Kurt calling out a hello? Maybe the strange car belonged to a visitor next door. I listened, no sound at all. I went up to the office we had shared for the past few weeks. His notes and notebooks were scattered over the desk and the trashcan was amazingly full. I had emptied it yesterday. Someone had been here…where was the man?

I went downstairs and called out calmly, "Kurt Van Doren, where the hell are you hiding out?" No answer. The house really was empty. Suddenly, a movement, then a shadow moved across the back door. I crossed the living room and looked out. There, outside in his old suede jacket, jeans, and sneakers, was Kurt doing battle with a lawn rake. He was gathering up leftover debris from the two shedding gum trees in the backyard. The yard cleaning crew did a wonderful job that November but he was getting up the hundreds of sticky ball seeds that fell from my neighbor's trees each December.

I opened the door, which was now full of nose prints from my animal herd, as Kurt called them. Stupid flew out and stood next to him. "Hey, what are you doing, working off the pounds from Thanksgiving?"

He looked up, leaned on the rake, a dazzling smile spreading across that face that inevitably turned my knees to jelly and had my heart pounding. "Maggie, there you are. I thought since I was off today and fully recovered from the stiffness and bruises, I would come over and clear out my stuff from your office and clean up this backyard for you. Good exercise and I love being outdoors this time of year. I even got my stitches out, see." He pointed. "How's the job coming? Getting used to the grind yet?"

I wanted to hug him but even I knew that would not be dignified, so instead I opted for a light tone. "Hey, I'm useful, and they said I was missed, what more can a girl ask for? I'll make some coffee and fix us something for lunch, how does that sound?"

***

Kurt looked up as he worked on the yard. She looks a little tired but you can tell she's happy to be back to work. I missed seeing her all week, should have stayed away. Probably best if I do to protect her. I don't know if that crash was an accident or deliberate. But shit, man, here you are doing yard work. Face it, you have no willpower where she's concerned.

"If it's my pay for this work, good deal." The weeds and seeds from the gum tree were piled in one corner of the deck, the rake leaned against the tree. He called Stupid and started for the house.

"Gotcha," I said to him as I went to the kitchen to make his favorite, tuna fish. I made it in a happy daze, humming to myself all the while.

The office did not get cleaned out that day. We sat and ate and he told he how he felt about his divorce and about seeing his little girl. He told me how he had never been close to Mellie as his ex took the child's time up exclusively. "I think she poured all her feelings into the baby, Maggie. I was completely left out from the day she was born. No wonder we didn't make it as a couple."

He sat back in his kitchen chair as I started mixing up a big batch of chocolate chip cookies for work. I flipped on the oven to bake and set the temperature and proceeded to stir. He took the heavy mixture from my hands and with sure capable strokes and more muscle than I could muster, moved the big spoon around in the dough, making it creamy and smooth as he talked.

He got up, opened the refrigerator and got out the milk. I could tell he was preparing himself for that first batch out of the oven. A big glass of cold milk to accompany those warm chocolate chip cookies would hit the spot. There goes the cookies, I figured.

He settled down again at the table to wait for his treat. Time flew as he related memories, both happy and sad.

The first of the cookies were out of the oven. I removed them from the pan and put them directly onto a plate. "Be careful, the hot chocolate in these cookies can burn your mouth." I then slid another tray into the oven.

"Sure, I'll have some later." Cookies almost forgotten, he continued reminiscing about his childhood, schools, friends, funny things and sad things that happened in his Army life, med school pranks—just wonderful stories.

We went over the problems at his work again. I even got out a pad and paper and we made a timeline and list of things and suspects but nothing inspired us. Conversation drifted to other things. I began to throw some back to him and we began talking about old movies, favorite songs, and TV shows. We laughed and dug up great old memories, argued about who was the best cowboy or comedian. A set of cookies burned in the oven during one hilarious debate. He got up and taking a set of hot pads grabbed the ruined cookies and just dumped them right into the sink. He flipped off the oven, covered the bowl of dough and put it in the fridge for me. I just sat there completely happy with this whole afternoon. When he picked up the cookie sheet to clean it, I finally got up, put my arms around him and gave him a hug.

He turned his back to me and ran water on the cookie sheet. I could sense he was enjoying this time together as much as I was.

Finally, he said, "You know, life was not so bad in those days. Anyway, that's all in the past now. I have a whole new life ahead and I intend to throw myself into a new job soon and live the good life from now on. Make more good memories for my retirement years."

It was late afternoon by now. The cookies were either burned or baked. We spent the best part of it talking and now Kurt was due to leave.

He turned, and in a surprise move, kissed the top of my head. "Hey, thanks for listening, it was really fun just hanging out. It's been great not talking too much about the stuff at work, too. There's been nothing new for a while and I hope it stays that way. I'm watching my butt and Nora was so rattled with the patient being hurt she's been a little more friendly."

"I don't trust her, Doc. She could be hiding a very dark sick mind underneath all that starch. Don't rely on old Nora...she could be the one. I have her top on our list and Packard and Sewell right behind."

"I feel the same way, Maggie, and wonder if there is some hidden motive she would have to do all this to me. I'm asking quiet questions about her husband, Phil Feeney, too. Between the two of them it could have been carefully worked out with her on the inside problems and him on the outside stuff. She still thinks my appointment as Rainey's chief resident was a put-up job but I find it hard to believe she would be that careless with an innocent man, a patient she never saw before that night when he was in ICU. Anyway, thanks for the afternoon, it's been fun but I have to get back to work."

The magical afternoon was ending. I could tell he hated to break the sweet rapport and fun time we shared. He said softly, "Hate to go."

I smiled as he pulled on his jacket and softly replied, "I hate to see you go."

He hesitated and glanced at me. I could have sworn it was the same soft loving look I got the day of the accident. Oh hell, Holly's right. I guess I'm reading into situations again.

"Got to run but will see ya soon. And, hey, I'm taking those cookies with me for a souvenir, hope you don't mind." He was all business again and waved the bag at me as he went out the door.

In the emotion of the moment I never noticed he had packed them up. He left and I went back to a kitchen with the smell of burned chocolate chip cookies.

Kurt pulled his cell phone out and called the hospital. He spoke to Dr. Rainey and got a brief update on the day. He explained he would be there shortly. Oh hell! She had me baking cookies today. What next, dusting, embroidery? It was so relaxing just to sit and remember things from the past, trade stories, laugh together. But face it, guy, you're not exactly Lance Romance sweeping her off her feet. Look what happened when you took her out? You wrecked your car and she was a good sport about the whole thing. I guess I need to go slow. Get her to think of me as more than a friend. Maybe court her a little, take her someplace a little more glamorous than a gay bar, an auto accident and the emergency room. Oh shit, let's face it, the way I feel now I could no more walk away from her than I can walk out of my own skin.

> Email to Steve from Kurt: *I'm sort of in love with the woman. I guess I am. But she doesn't seem inclined.*
> Steve's delighted reply to Kurt's email: *It's about time you noticed. Even I could tell from up here, you dufus! What's stopping you from telling her? Get on with it, man, get her in the sack, that's the final test, old buddy!!!! Of course, you could end up like me, house, mortgage, kids, carpool, not exactly the happy bachelor life, but then again... Steve*

Kurt shut down the computer grinning and hummed to himself as he got a page to go down to administration.

Chapter 20

After Kurt left to go back to work with our cookies, I cleaned up the kitchen, did some chores, and started heating some dinner. I glanced up at the clock and was amazed to see how late it was. I was putting the baking sheets away when Stupid went crazy—barking, pacing, and growling at the front door. It was dark, and through the glass panels I could only tell there were two people standing on the porch. I flipped on the light. A large man wearing a suit was holding a badge up to the front window of my door. I opened the big door but kept my storm door closed.

"Yes, may I help you? Is that a police badge?" I asked brightly with ice in my stomach. With a son who had been in and out of trouble for years, I never knew when something could happen to him. I suppose they would notify me this way. I was suddenly weak-kneed and shaking inside.

"Ma'am, I'm Detective Walters from the D.C. Metropolitan Police Department. This is my partner Tanya Jackson. We're here to talk to you and ask you a few questions, that's all. You've done nothing wrong but you may be able to help out a friend. If my partner and I could come in, I'd appreciate it or you could put on a coat and sit out here with us on the porch."

Now I was very confused. Why would they send a D.C. cop to talk to me? The man and the woman were dignified, well dressed and did have the appropriate badges, I guess. I was impressed. I opened the storm door and invited them in.

The detective was a man of my own age or a bit older and rather heavy-set, with salt and pepper hair and a face that reminded me of my daughter Ivy's bloodhound. How appropriate, I thought that he would look like that breed. His partner was a lovely young woman, very slim and pretty, with dark eyes and smooth dark skin, her hair pulled back severely. She did not look old enough to be a police officer. She was dressed in a dark pantsuit and white blouse that made her seem even younger, like a little girl playing at grownup.

"Come in, sit down, and tell me what this is all about please, Officer. I can offer you a soda or I can make some coffee if this is going to take a while, I even baked some cookies today. Oops! They're all gone, I forgot."

I realized I was babbling. They waited patiently. I wound down, and they both indicated they were fine and did not need refreshments. I realized, of course, this was not a social call. I was nervous...not guilty, just nervous.

"Mrs. Suit, do you know a gentleman named Kurt Van Doren? He says you two are good friends, is that true?"

"Oh, no! Something's happened to Kurt. Is he all right? Did someone finally get around to hitting or hurting him? Of course I know him, he's a good friend and often uses my office and my computer here to study when he wants to hide out from the world. He just finished up his research work and we celebrated last week before Thanksgiving. He was here today, as a matter of fact. Can you please tell me if he is all right?" I was babbling again.

The gentleman looked at me in a kind but detached way. Questioning people 20 times a day they don't tend to get too involved, I could see.

"Mrs. Suit, your friend Van Doren is fine. Now can you tell me about today? What time did he get here, what did you do, what time did he leave?"

"Wait, why do you need to know that? Is he in trouble? Listen, I have a son who's had problems with the law, and I know how you guys work. I want to make very sure he's safe and has an attorney before I talk to you. What's this all about anyway?" I thought I was being forceful but I guess I sounded more hysterical.

The detective, Walters, looked at me, made a decision as his face relaxed a bit. "Mrs. Suit, did you turn on the news tonight at all?"

"Yes, I turned on the 5 o'clock news a while after Dr. Van Doren left here, why?"

"Did you hear about the attack on a nurse at the Center this afternoon? She was beaten and left for dead in the little area behind the cafeteria where some of the nurses sneak out to smoke. This happened a little before noon today. We're just asking routine questions of people who may know something about the assault. Dr. Van Doren is one of those people we're checking on, that's all."

I looked at him and said, "Bullshit, Detective, you've arrested him and taken the poor guy and are holding him on some evidence. Look, I've been through the court system with my son, Tim, since year one. I know how all you bastards work." I glanced down and apologized. "Sorry. I'm upset, that's all."

I was very near to tears and frightened for Kurt. I knew if the cops thought they had their man, innocent or guilty, they would try to make a case. It's scary as hell. He needed an attorney. I'm sure his father would certainly help out. I was trying to think of who would be able to help him. All this raced through my mind as I struggled to keep from crying.

"You know I was cleaning up the kitchen and I do remember something about an assault. They said a suspect was in custody. But it was later on the news, not at 5, I'm sure it was the one later—the 6 o'clock news. Now, dammit, man, that suspect is my friend, isn't it? Does he have an attorney? Has he called his father?" I was babbling again, I knew it.

"If you would just calm down, Mrs. Suit, and help us out here we may be able to clear this all up this evening. But if you continue to question us and waste our time, your friend may spend the night in jail downtown. Now can we continue?" He was firm and in charge. I realized immediately he was making more sense than I was.

"Now, Mrs. Suit, you say he was here. What time was that, do you know?"

I took a deep breath, forced myself to calm down and realized I could only help Kurt if I did. So I started. "I've been ill. I started back to work Monday after being on disability for several months. I work from 7:30 a.m. till noon or 1:00 each day this month. When I got home about 1:30, he was out in the backyard here doing me a favor. He thought the weather was nice, he was off work, so on the spur of the moment decided to help me out by raking up the sticky balls in my backyard."

For the first time his partner said something in a soft voice. "You don't look like you've been that ill to me, Mrs. Suit, and sticky balls? What are those?"

"I have these big gum trees that belong to my neighbors and if you look outside you can see them. I have no idea what the trees are really called, just gum trees to me, but in late fall and early winter they shed these horrible seeds that I call sticky balls. They're small and sharp and annoying so you have to really rake them up a few times before Christmas."

"Oh, being a city girl, I don't know about such things." She smiled sweetly at me, and I realized she was trying to put me at ease. It did help some.

"Anyway, I got home around 1:30, and he was in the backyard working on the sticky balls. He had them all raked up and piled near the patio. If you go out, you can see where they are."

Detective Walters made a note and then looked up and asked, "You're sure he did them today? I mean, was he doing work around here regularly, or was it just a spur of the moment thing like you said? You didn't get home until 1:30, so no one saw him before that then, say, around noon today?"

I thought of Loren Lee next door. Maybe she talked to Kurt. She knew him from the Center and they often talked when he was going in and out.

"I think it was spur of the moment for him. He's never even been in my backyard before that I know. And as for anyone seeing him, the only person I know who could vouch for Kurt may be Loren next door. She used to work with him at the Center, and they often speak when he's here. You may ask her if she noticed someone in the backyard and recognized Kurt, or he may have heard her out with the baby and talked to her."

"Yes, we'll do that, but for now you can only vouch for 1:30 or so. What time did he leave here, Mrs. Suit?"

"We baked cookies and he ate most of them while we talked. He packed some up in a little white bag and went off before dark sometime, saying he was going back to work. I don't know. It was almost dark but it got so cloudy this afternoon late. Let me think, I don't know the exact time. I was still baking, I do know some time after he left I turned on the news and it was channel 7. Oh, I guess he left before 5 p.m. closer to 4, I would say. But it was not until the 6 o'clock news as I was fixing dinner that I heard about the arrest."

Detective Walters, turned to Tanya and just nodded his head. Without a word the woman got up and went to my backyard and looked closely at the pile of sticky balls and the rake. She came back in and went out the front door. I figured she was going to talk to Loren or even Peter if he was home. I prayed for them to be able to help Kurt at this point.

Detective Walters and I sat there in silence. I guess he felt he shouldn't ask any questions until Tanya got back. But suddenly he broken the silence, "What's your relationship to Dr. Van Doren, may I ask? Are you related, lovers, friends or what, Mrs. Suit? I understand you met him earlier this year at the hospital, is that right?"

"Oh, when I was a patient we got to be friends somehow. Just found out we had the same sense of humor and similar ideas on things and he visited me often when he was not busy. We told folks I was his Aunt Maggie…it was easy to explain it that way."

"So you technically aren't his Aunt, I take it? Just an adopted relationship, right? Sort of like when you bring your best friend home to meet your kids. I understand, I have an old Uncle Pete like that, too."

Tanya was gone for a while and I was getting nervous. However, the longer she was gone the more I felt Loren may have had something to say to her about Kurt's time at the house. Oh, let her help, I prayed.

106

"Mrs. Suit, if it was Dr. Van Doren's day off, why didn't he go home?"

He was interrupted by a soft knock as Tanya reentered the house. "Can I see you outside, Walters?" she said.

He got up and they went outside and walked down to my mailbox where they could not be heard. She took out a notebook and they compared notes on something. Let it be helpful please, I thought.

Detective Walters walked back up the lawn and stopped below my steps. "That's all we need to know for now, Mrs. Suit. You've been a help to the doctor, I believe."

I looked at his retreating back and called out to him, "Detective Walters, before you go, please keep in mind that when you came out here from the District you should have traced the exact route he took to my house. Comparing his sign out time with here and the mileage should help also. He's a man dedicated to saving lives, not damaging lives. Maybe you should know that this is only one incident. There was another rather nasty problem in October that involved Dr. Van Doren and it was traced to a forged…. Oh, never mind, that may be damaging…but talk to Dr. Rainey about the October problem with the medicine and the forged change on the patient's chart. If I know Rainey, he's copied the chart but kept the original one in his office just in case. It may shed some light on this whole thing. It's a little more than this incident today, I can tell you."

Walters turned and came back up the lawn. He looked up at me and said, "You're saying there's been other problems with Dr. Van Doren at the hospital?"

"No, you idiot, I'm saying someone's been playing around, trying to hurt or discredit Van Doren. This isn't the first incident. I'll bet your ass or mine that there was plenty of evidence connecting Van Doren to this assault, right? Just how dumb do you think a man of his caliber would have to be to assault a nurse then leave so much crap around you would arrest him almost on the spot? Sorry, you're not an idiot—I'm upset. And this campaign against him is escalating. Oh, hell, forget I said anything, okay?"

"No need to call names, Mrs. Suit, I'm only doing some background work on this. I'm sure someone has checked his times. I've made a note of it here. Also, I've noted that something happened to discredit the man earlier. I'm writing this up on the pad and I want you to initial it, please?"

A voice behind me spoke up. "Peter Lee," it said, and then my neighbor extended his hand to the officer. "Attorney. Now, I'll tell you what, after you write it up, I'll take it inside and copy it and then *you* can initial it, Officer. Mrs. Suit can initial it afterward, if she sees it's in order."

Peter Lee—savior—was standing right behind me. His voice was calm, reasonable, and sensible. I could have hugged him right on the spot.

He said, "Make sure you write that correctly…something was done to discredit Dr. Van Doren. He did nothing to discredit himself."

Walters looked at us both. "I'm not stupid, Mr. Lee, and Tanya is writing it up now. You certainly are free to initial it and so will we—after you agree that what we wrote is correct."

Calmer somehow with Peter's strength there and Loren smiling from the front porch, I felt much better and not so alone. "Why don't we all go in the house where it's warmer and get this done?"

Tanya walked up, tearing the note from her pad as she said, "No need, I have it written down. If you can read it inside, we'll wait in the car."

Peter took the paper from Tanya and walked over to his house as I followed him in. He read it carefully, handed it to me. "I think they have it right, Maggie, don't you?"

I read her rather rounded handwriting, agreed and initialed it. He took it and went outside and talked to Walters.

I turned to Loren. "Please say you heard or saw Kurt this afternoon, did you?"

She described her morning. "I was heating food getting ready to feed the baby early, way before noon closer to 11:30 or so. We had a doctor's appointment later around 1:00 and it takes about half an hour to get there. I heard Kurt outside with Stupid. She was barking and carrying on and he was scraping or raking, I could tell. He had the back window open and was singing along with the golden oldies station. You know anyone who knows him would recognize that nice voice. He used to sing at the hospital, too. I called out and asked what he was doing over there. He said manual labor, kind of jokingly, just the thing on a warm fall afternoon. He was nowhere near the hospital when that girl was attacked, I can swear to it."

I felt such a sense of relief my knees got weak and I sat on their steps. Loren got me a glass of water and when Peter finished copying the little page for us we left their house. Loren and Peter and the cop escorted me back to the front porch. I hugged her and she told me not to worry. I hugged Peter and thanked him for his strength at being there for me. I shut the door after they left and burst into tears.

What an awful ending to a lovely day. First our lovely afternoon trading stories and just enjoying ourselves, then he was arrested, humiliated, and probably handcuffed. Oh, this is awful. Let's hope they realize they've made a mistake. I had work the next day and I didn't know how I would manage it. Maybe I could work at home, I brought my stuff with me tonight to work on.

Looking at the clock it was only a little past 9 p.m. Their visit seemed as if it took forever, only an hour passed but it seemed like a year in my mind.

Chapter 21

I dozed off on the sofa and slept for several hours. I was thinking about getting up but still trying to get comfortable on the sofa when I heard a soft tap and key in the lock and the door opened. I figured it was RJ so I did not stir.

Suddenly a tall shape stood over the sofa. I could feel the cold on his clothes from outside as he said quietly, "Maggie, you asleep?"

"No, not really. Are you okay?"

"Christ, what a night!"

"I'm just glad you're here. Was it awful?"

"Frightening."

He sat on the floor next to me with his back against the sofa and leaned his head back to rest it. He was very close. I was so relieved and happy to see him. I wanted to put my arms around and him and say it would be all right. Instead I sat up and switched on the lamp.

He looked tired and pale, his hair mussed as usual, his clothes were wrinkled and sweat stained. "They let me go about an hour ago. I got a ride to my car at the Center. I swear I started for the dorm but found myself pointing in this direction. I wanted to be here instead of answering questions at my place. It feels safer here. Hope you don't mind."

He moved away from me slightly. "I think a few days from the Center wouldn't be frowned on at this point. I need to get a hold of Rainey in the morning to talk to him about it."

"What the hell time is it?" I asked.

"It's 2:15 in the morning. I'm sorry."

"Don't be."

I reached over and brushed his hair tenderly with my hand. Not daring to do more, I sat up straighter. "I'm working at home tomorrow so don't worry about it. Are you out on bail, or did they just let you go? Do you want something to eat? I have sleeping pills that may help. Take Tim's bed, we can talk in the morning."

He sighed and stayed on the floor with his back propped up against the sofa and then leaned on my knees. I think we both felt reassured by the closeness. He shook his head. "No, I don't want anything but a shower and a bed, if you don't mind. This has been a damn nightmare. They took me out the back door of the cafeteria where they have the garbage cans, like I was garbage. I was in handcuffs. There were reporters around but no one saw us behind the dumpsters. They didn't get a good shot of me being arrested."

He sat there with his head down, looking defeated, and humiliated about what had happened. "Goddammit, I feel like shit! I look like shit! I smell like shit! Oh, Maggie this was awful. The worst part of it is the kid that got hurt, Millie Prentice, she's in bad shape. They don't know if she'll make it or not. Someone sure has it in for me to do something this rotten."

Millie was the surgical nurse who came to check on me after the surgery in September. We talked for a bit and she seemed very nice. "I get the shakes thinking about what she went through. Did they tell you why they picked you up for questioning? They probably had others there, too." I did not tell him Millie had explained the Packard fiasco to me in lurid detail.

"If they did, I didn't see them. They had enough evidence pointing to me to haul my ass in and question me for 6 or 8 hours. I think you're being optimistic, it was a frame-up, aimed at me alone for damn sure."

He stood up, and taking my hands helped me off the low sofa. We went upstairs and I got him a huge bath sheet and cleared cat toys and clothes out of my bathroom so he could shower. I gathered his things and put them in the washer so they would be ready in the morning. I was keeping busy which kept my feelings in check.

After a shower, he dressed in some of Tim's sweatpants and certainly looked and smelled a lot better. He took 2 pills, curled up in Tim's cold bedroom with the covers piled on, and was asleep in no time. I straightened up a bit then peeked in to reassure myself he was here and safe. I wanted to crawl in with him.

Back in my room, I was now wide-awake, thinking about this whole mess. Kurt always appeared to me to be so gentle but there was the nagging fear in my mind that I really did not know him that long. We have only had phone calls, a few hospital and home visits. I started listing what I knew about him. He was certainly stressed at the accident but kept his cool and cooperated with the fire department and police. Loren next door was positive about him in her conversations to me. I remembered nurses who talked about his kindness and consideration. They knew him a long time and under very stressful circumstances and had nothing but good things to say. I was sure Kurt was doing my yard work. Loren vouched for him so the police must have believed her. On the other side, I knew he punched the Packard man, and brought on Patricia Sewell's anger just because he was appointed to a position she coveted.

There was something mysterious going on with Nasty Nora, too. Was it a secret he did not want to share? Was it something in her twisted brain causing her to act out? She certainly has the means and opportunity but I was not sure at the motive. Is anyone else out there enraged enough to injure an innocent person? It may be that he unknowingly crossed someone. It could be any one of hundreds of people who work there. I fell asleep counting reasons.

Both of us slept very late the next morning. We were both exhausted from the ordeal. I awoke to sunshine streaming in my window and a dog making humming noises.

I looked over and there was Kurt sitting in the chair next to my bed, absently scratching Stupid's belly. She was on her back, legs in the air and squirmed with pleasure at his touch. I decided I would do that, too, if ever given the opportunity.

"Hey, do you know it's almost 9 o'clock, sleepy head? I've been up for a few minutes and talked to Rainey on the phone. He agrees with me that I need to take at least the next couple days off to get myself reoriented and the staff to forget the awful shock of seeing or hearing about me in handcuffs. We're hoping Millie will be awake by then and able to identify her attacker or at least clear me completely."

He got up and moved toward the doorway. "Listen, I managed your strange coffee pot downstairs and have it ready. Get yourself together and come down. My turn to fix you something to eat, even if it's your own food."

I called work. Then I took a quick shower, and plastered on makeup to hide the circles under my eyes.

"Come on, let's get out of here and get some coffee and breakfast somewhere nice. We can talk about this later after we enjoy the morning a little."

Kurt looked up from the paper he was reading and nodded.

We headed out for the local Starbucks in Leisure World. I figured a ride in the sun and some coffee and Danish would do wonders for us both. Starbucks was full of retirees on that weekday morning so we ended up at Pansy's deli and bakery instead. It wasn't crowded, we found a nice quiet booth in the back. We got our coffee and several pastries, then settled in to gorge on goodies.

I hated to break the silence, but I finally looked over and said quietly, "Did they put you in a cell or were you just interrogated? I mean, how awful was it? I know how it was for my son, Tim. And he was usually guilty of doing some stupid thing and brought on his own trouble. But for you to sit there knowing you were here being helpful to me. And that poor girl, Millie, I wonder how she is today?"

I was not making any sense. My mind was going faster than my mouth. I had the victim all mixed up with his jail cell. I needed to slow down, I could see.

He pulled his coffee cup over, leaned toward me and quietly answered my questions. "Maggie, I took the cookies and munched them on the way to work. I guess I got back sometime after dark. It was almost evening when I left your place, but with the cloud cover it seemed later. They were waiting for me at the main administration office in the hospital. I had no idea what had gone on. I was not paying attention to my radio. I had no inkling why I was being paged down to administration. I just walked in and bam! I was cuffed with my hands behind my back and my rights read to me. I was hustled out the back door behind the cafeteria to a squad car. I kept asking what it was about. I just knew it was another frame-up but somehow a hundred times worse."

He took a sip of coffee and winced. It was hot. "They refused to talk to me at all. Silence, total and complete, all the way to the main police station. I was angry, humiliated, and those damn things hurt my wrist. Hard to sit with them behind my back." He demonstrated where and how his hands were cuffed.

"For some damn reason I kept thinking about Dr. Richard Kimball, the fugitive, how he had gotten away in the movie. Now I know why guys run. I was so scared, and had no idea what the hell it was about. It took me the whole time I was there to piece it together."

"Did you call an attorney or your father?" I was eating, but he was just sitting there with the pastries. Letting food go to waste was not his style. A couple came in and sat in the opposite booth, their annoying kid kept racing around hollering. I ignored the brat and listened to his story.

He finished his coffee and got up for another cup. He came back with his refill and continued, "I didn't want my family to help, I figured I could handle it. I told them only where I was and what I was doing, but kept my mouth shut about anything else even when they started their little games. They try to get your sympathy, tell you it will be easy if you confess, it's really lousy the tricks they tried to pull, but I just kept my big mouth shut for once. After a while, when I got the story pieced together, I was really having second thoughts about a lawyer at least, and if it kept up I was going to call my father. I'm sorry I had to drag you and Loren into it, but I was cornered and had nothing else to give them. I was here. I was doing a friend a good turn. It's a good thing that thing I was."

"It kept your ass out of the slammer. Loren and I were more than glad to help. Whoever did this must have known when you left work. He or she figured you might be alone. They don't know about this place yet, or they didn't think you would be here for some reason. Another close call, Doc, this is getting scary."

The brat got to us, so we capped our coffee, piled in the car and started for home. As he drove, I continued my thoughts out loud. "Kurt, I'm afraid I blabbed about the other incidents to that guy Walters, the detective, last night. I think you may be pissed at me for it, but I was trying to help. He wrote the stuff I told him down and then, God bless him, Peter Lee appeared out of nowhere in my yard right after they talked to Loren. He insisted the cop initial and hand over what I said. He had me read it, verify and initial, then took it to his house and made copies for me, you, the cops, and Rainey."

He gave a huge sigh, and slapped the steering wheel. "Jesus, Maggie, can't you keep things to yourself? I don't think telling that cop will do anything but make me look worse in their eyes. Let me see what you had the cop write down, will you?"

We got back and I handed a copy of the notes Detective Walters had Tanya write down. He started pacing while he read and I could tell he was angry with me. He kept glancing up from the note toward me as his body language said "fury." He handed the note back, then looked out the kitchen window.

"Damn it, you told them about the other stuff that happened. That's going to look bad for sure. No matter how much you and I, and everyone who matters at the Center know I wasn't at fault in those incidents, they were not as clear-cut as this. This time I have Loren and can prove this was not me. What you told them only makes me come under suspicion of forging the chart and endangering the man's life. Dammit, with this," he snatched it up and waved it at me in anger, "you've probably made all of it a police matter now."

He turned and shouted, "Didn't you think? Didn't you realize that stuff never went out of the department? Oh, for Christ's sake, that was a dumb thing to do! And I was stupid to tell you about it."

114

Suddenly, he grabbed his jacket and slammed out the front door. I had never seen him in a temper before, and it scared me. The old familiar fear I felt last night about him being a relative stranger came back. I watched carefully as he strode down the street past his car.

Fuming, Kurt walked around thinking to himself that women are just not logical. Christ, what kind of a mess am I in now? Defending me, yes, I guess in her way she was. She's always defended me but this arrest surely has killed my chances with her and possibly my whole career will go down the toilet. After all the years I spent in school, I'll still end up back in my father's construction office, pushing a frigging pencil for the rest of my life. Jesus, what was she thinking!

He slammed out but I was now angry, too. Pacing around I started talking to Stupid who sat there by her water dish. I guess I was justifying my actions with the cop to the dog, as if she would understand. "I was wrong but I was trying to help him any way I could. He doesn't see it that way."

He showed up in about 10 minutes, cold, and in a slightly better frame of mind. While he was out stomping about the neighborhood freezing his butt off, I had discussed it with the dog and was now upset with him, too. I was convinced I was right to tell Walters about what had been going on. When he came through the door, I shot him a look and said, "Now slow down, Van Doren, you've been the victim of an obvious frame-up attempt twice. I'm not even sure that car thing was an accident and neither are you. Have you talked to the mechanic yet? This cop, Walters, is experienced and no dummy. If he looks at what Rainey has kept and thinks clearly about what's going on here with the attack, he's going to see you're the victim, not the aggressor."

I moved closer and said, "And maybe I shouldn't have spoken about the problem, but I was frightened for you. I was also backed up against a wall. I was fighting for you, mister. I was using everything I felt I had in my arsenal to get you free last night. The thought of you in that station just made me wild."

The anger and frustration of last night and the exhaustion and tension were too much. As I spoke I started to cry. He moved toward me, but his body language still said anger. He was working on controlling it, I could tell. Instead of saying anything, or touching me, he paced. I cried. We both were at the end of a long emotional rope. Our reactions were different, but they were both powerful and frustrating. The worst part was I think we both felt helpless and frightened about what had occurred.

I wondered where this would all end. If he went off to prison for something he didn't do, it would kill him. I cared so much for this man, I know it would have been hell for me, too. I'd move heaven and earth to prove him innocent, if I only knew how—had a plan—had a clue as to who was causing all this and why.

He pulled me to his chest finally in a big bear hug. The kind of hug you give your aunt or sister, but I clung to him and we sort of gained strength in being close. It was over in a couple of seconds. He pushed me back holding my shoulders. "Maggie, the bastard, whoever he or she is, has me grasping at straws and yelling at you now. You did what you felt was right. It may or may not become a police matter, hell, I don't know. I guess we're both still in shock. It's been a terrible strain. I should never have pulled you into this mess, and I'm so sorry."

I turned to face him and suddenly I knew I wanted this man desperately. He had to know, too. I wanted him with me every day for the rest of my life. I reached out to take his hand but he moved quickly away. I felt as if I had been stabbed. I watched in silence as he crossed to the stairwell and grabbed his coat off the newel post.

Kurt thought she was signaling to him that she wanted more. It was all he could do to keep his body from responding. He felt vulnerable and foolish as he moved across the room grabbing his coat. He knew he had to break it off for both of them.

But he could not say the words. She's doesn't know what she's doing and you almost got her killed once, don't get her involved any more. Let her have a life without you and your problems. This is your chance to protect her. Not have her humiliated or dragged into any more of this shit. If they arrest me again and I have to go through a trial, I'll be ruined—no medicine, no life at all. She deserves better than that. But…but… He knew this was something that had gone too far to stop.

He paused at the door and looked back at her. There were tears in her eyes but she was tight-lipped. Dear Lord, I think she's pissed off. "Listen, we need some space here. I have to go, get home, I think. Hey, I'll call you." She laughed at him then, a sharp bitter sarcastic laugh that stopped him in his tracks.

Chapter 22

I knew I made a terrible fool of myself. Holly had been right, I'd overstepped the bounds. He had been my friend. I made it more because of my selfish needs. He did not need me making a pass at him. He had enough problems without a desperate, love struck woman hanging on him.

I looked at my feet, embarrassed. My chest was hammering, my face was hot, and I felt alone and stupid. What I had done was so obvious, a cheap move on my part. It was too late now to back down. I might as well say what I wanted. Get it all off my chest and let him flee for good.

"So go…get out of here. But before you do, I want you to know that everything I did was in friendship. And please, please, don't feel obliged to call."

He stuttered, "Maggie, for now I just think it's—"

I interrupted him and poured out my feelings. "Are you trying to embarrass me? Okay, I love you. Happy now? I'm sorry if I offend you by saying it, but I just have to get it out. I guess I've loved you since that first day we met. Stupid, huh?"

To my horror, I was crying, blubbering in fact. I turned my back to him in my humiliation and practically hollered at him, "Go back to your damn dorm. And please don't call."

Except for my crying, all was silent for a moment. I stood facing the wall, tears running down my face. I was too humiliated to face him at this point, the pain of losing him was almost physical. I turned my head slightly and literally hissed at him through my shame and pain. "Just get the hell out of here and leave me alone. I'll get over it. You can bet on that."

Suddenly he was across the room, his hands on my shoulders. He turned me and took me in his arms. "Oh, Maggie, I'm sorry." He pushed me away gently, taking my lowered chin and tilted it up. Our eyes met.

"This has been hard on me and I know you've been with me all the way. I had no clue how you felt until now. Maggie, honey, it's just not a good time for us, I need you to be safe." He held me and was now kissing my hair, my forehead and the tears from my face.

He looked down and smiled. "Until now, I thought I was just another one of your pets, another needy adopted whatever. I don't want to be a pet, Maggie. I'm not Serge, or Stupid, not just one of your special projects."

I looked at him as I shook my head. "Oh, Kurt, you're not a pet and I don't need protection. I don't want anyone else, I only want you, even with the problems. I want us together. Hell, I'm in it already and it's probably better if we can share, find out who's causing this. Face it together."

He kissed my ear, holding me tighter. His voice was soft and husky, he murmured, "I've loved you for a long time and needed you. I wanted you so badly. Oh, Mags, you're home, you're love, and you're safety—just everything to me. I didn't know how to tell you, to show you. And I could never tell past the joking how you felt."

"What a jackass I am," I whispered.

"What?"

"A jackass, a fool."

He had his arms around me in an instant and pulled me up to him, pressing his lips against mine, and I was kissing him back, throwing my arms around his neck, standing on tiptoes to meet his mouth. After a few moments he moved to the base of my neck. It was like an electric shock. My breath caught in my throat. He was breathing hard too, and his hands were firmly in control.

"Uh, Kurt?"

"Hmmmm?" He found my mouth again, kissed me more deeply, his tongue running along the edge of my teeth. Then in one swift movement he pulled the sweater over my head and dropped it on the floor.

"Is this such a great idea?" I managed to ask in a great gulp of air when he broke away and took a step back.

"Why? Don't you like it?"

"I like it a lot."

"Then what's the problem? I thought—"

"I did! I do! I just mean I don't want to mess everything up."

"Maggie," he said as he stepped closer again, traced just one shoulder blade with his index finger, "shut up."

I was shivering. "But…" I gasped and braced my hands against the wall to keep from falling over as his mouth explored me, his hands firmly on my hips.

118

He raised himself to face me again, smiling. "Rendered you speechless, haven't I? Must be love."

"It *is* love," I said quietly.

"For me, too," he whispered in my ear. And he picked up my sweater and led me by my hand to the bedroom.

Later that afternoon as Maggie lay sleeping, the covers tangled, her arm thrown out toward him, Kurt slipped out of the bed, booted up his laptop and wrote to Steve.

> *Mission accomplished, Stevie boy!!! Better than I ever could have imagined. She loves me. Imagine, all this time she loved me, too. And talk about fireworks, it was great! Guess you don't have to worry on that count! We're compatible.... Oh yes, very, very compatible!! Kurt*

He signed off and returned to the bed. In spite of the problems, he knew they would get past it—they had to now. Maggie turned in her sleep and made a tiny sound of pleasure as he gathered her in his arms. A feeling of peace came to him, something he could not remember ever feeling before.

Chapter 23

Kurt called the Center the next day and found out that the nurse, Millie, had awakened but recalled little of what happened except someone grabbed her. He was a white male with reddish hair on his arms, she claimed. She was in critical condition and later that day she died in spite of all efforts. The police now had a homicide investigation on their hands.

Kurt knew it was linked to his problems. He moped around my house for another day but went back to work. In fact, Dr. Rainey called and demanded his return, claiming no one understood him like his chief resident and everything was going to hell without his careful attention to detail and scheduling.

I went through the next week in a haze of both apprehension and happiness. By now the police were convinced that the girl was the victim of a junkie or mugger and the situation had just gotten out of hand.

Several days after Millie's funeral, I picked up the ringing phone at my desk.

"Maggie, hey, I think I have hit on someone who may not be my biggest fan. I should say Sam here reminded me about a nurse who used to work here, Sheila Cowan. The more I think about her the more I'm convinced this is something I need to look into. It's a long shot, she's a nice person, and I can't imagine doing anything like this but at least it's worth discussing."

"I'm grateful that someone remembers something," I said. "You only have me left as a suspect at this point."

"Listen, babe, meet me at that pizza place this afternoon, the one around the corner from you. It's half-price night and we can grab a bite and I'll explain this to you."

"Why can't you explain it to me now on the phone? You've got me curious. How do you expect me to function with this on my mind all day?"

"Calm down, it's probably nothing, but at this point I'm grasping at straws. See you what time, 3:00 or 4:00? And someone else is meeting us at 4:30."

"Make it 4; I can't get there sooner. This better be good and worth waiting for."

"It's good but what's worth waiting for comes later after the pizza."

"No garlic, I take it?"

"No garlic. See you at 4."

I arrived to see my man walking into the bar and order area. I followed him in. He ordered, paid, and we sat with Cokes while they produced our pizza. I was trying to act cool and collected.

As soon as we were seated, Kurt blurted out his news. "Maggie, I may have hit on it. At least I hope to get a lead on what's causing all this. The someone who's meeting us is named Sheila Cowen. Remember when I told you I didn't have a date in two years—well, it was this lady I was thinking about. Sam, my roommate, reminded me of her when we discussed this whole ugly scenario. She was in and out of my life so quickly I just dismissed it. Sam thinks it's a long shot, too, but convinced me we should at least talk to her. After all she is a nurse, and she worked with me. She may remember something that we did or said, or somewhere we went that could shed some light here. And I know she has a guy, and he could be a link." Our number was called and Kurt got our food and sat back down.

I picked up a slice of hot pizza and asked, "Who is she, hon, and what did you do, poke her in the nose, too?"

"Don't be a smart ass, listen." He leaned over the table and said softly, "After the big bust-up 4 years ago, I ignored women—I was gun shy. But being a man, things needed taking care of after a time."

I smiled at him, pretending to be naive I asked, "Like what things? Can you explain in more detail?"

He got a bit flustered—after all, we were in a crowded pizza joint. People were going past our table collecting carry out. Guys and gals were drinking beer, and eating at tables crowded all around us. The counter people were busy taking orders, pulling pitchers, and calling out the pizza orders.

"Maggie, honey, it was a long time ago. It has nothing to do with you and me." Playing with the paper placemat he said, "I did it, okay? I'm not proud of it, but I'm not ashamed either, it is what it is."

"I suppose we're made of wood—just around to take care of men's needs," I said in a sarcastic tone.

"Oh hell, I did not mean it that way. It's not like what you and I have, but just—you know what I mean, you are acting cute on me now, I wish you would stop."

I grinned. "Cute? Me? Why, Kurt, I can't imagine what you mean? I just asked you to give me all the facts as clearly as you can: times, dates, and graphic descriptions of unusual positions—just anything to see if I can help." I took a bite of my pizza, chewed thoughtfully, then gave him an evil grin.

"Stop trying to be smart, this is important. To make a long story short, her name is Sheila Cowan. We were two lonely people who got together. We had a few laughs, a couple of dates, and things happened. She left the Center a few months after we stopped seeing one another. I got her phone number from one of the nurses who uses her daycare and called.

"Luckily, she's taking the baby to the doctor up in Olney today, so I invited her to come along, eat pizza for old time's sake and to meet you. We could get an idea of how she feels about me. See what she remembers. We also have the bonus of seeing her baby, Anthony. That should tell us something, too."

"You bet, hon, it could mean more child support for you if he has green eyes and that cute dimple in one cheek like you do."

"I don't know. I'm pretty sure I'm not responsible. I remember we were very careful about that, but I guess you never know."

"Holly and Ivy arrived after 'very careful.' I know about that stuff, hon." I remarked grabbing another slice.

He stood up and said, "Here she is." He walked toward the woman I always visualized myself to be—tall, very slender, and who walked with a natural grace even hauling a baby on her hip. She wore her dark hair clipped back, and a there was a sprinkle of freckles across her nose. If she talked in a perky voice, I was going to toss my cookies. She smiled as Kurt gave her a quick kiss on the cheek. I was not thrilled at his enthusiastic greeting. After introductions, we got a baby seat for the little one who she introduced as Anthony. This adorable boy with his baby curls, light brown skin and large dark eyes was definitely not Kurt's.

She shrugged out of her coat as I helped the baby off with his little blue jacket and matching hat.

"My, it's cold out there and so raw. I hope we get an early spring," she remarked.

"Me too. I look forward to all my bulbs coming up, at least the ones the squirrels don't get over this winter," I replied.

She slid into the seat next to Kurt, and I was stuck with baby, Anthony, patting and playing with the tray on his high chair. I gave him a cracker.

"We got a large pizza with everything, hope that's okay with you, Sheila?

I also got a hot dog for the little guy here. Figured one wouldn't hurt him." Kurt said.

"That's fine." She put her hand out across the table, "I'm Sheila, you must be Maggie. Kurt said you have three of your own, so you've had plenty of practice with babies."

I shook her hand and replied, "Not lately, Sheila, but it's like riding a bike. It comes back quickly."

All this time Kurt was watching me, the baby, and glancing sideways at Sheila. He slid a paper napkin and plate towards our guest and pulled a slice of the pizza off for her. He was being so solicitous I wanted to slap him.

"You look great. I got your name from Pat Jordan. She says the Wishing Well Day Care is a great place for kids."

She smiled, showing teeth an orthodontist got big money for. "Ever since I finished my nursing degree it's what I've wanted to do. Now I have my dream."

"Sheila, did Pat ever mention Kurt's problems at the Center?" I asked, hoping my jealousy was not too apparent.

"Oh, goodness yes. She seems to have a new piece of gossip about you almost weekly, Kurt. This problem of yours is really serious, isn't it?"

The kid continued to play and yell. She bit into her pizza. I wanted to bite her, right on her perfect little ankle, I thought as Kurt explained.

"Too serious, I'm afraid. That's why I wanted to see you. I'm at the point where all I can do is check out old friends to see if they can remember anything or anywhere that I might have given someone a reason for all this."

She shook her head as she ate. "I certainly feel bad for you. But, no, you and I didn't spend all that much time together, but I've thought about it a lot. I knew Millie Prentice, she was a nice girl and actually wanted to go on to medical school, did you know that?"

Kurt shook his head. "No, but she was about the best surgical tech we had—except for you, of course." He smiled at her and she punched his shoulder playfully.

That's it, now I was ready to punch him if they played any more touchy feely.

She took another slice of pizza and dodged stray pieces of a paper napkin and cracker crumbs from the baby. "Lem, that's Anthony's father, and I talked about this when your car was totaled. I told him we were friends and I don't remember that we went anywhere except to a movie, O'Malley's a couple of times for beer, and my place. Pat said a few people are concerned that this accident's part of this whole thing—this situation."

"We don't know for sure about that, but who is this Lem you're talking about? Do I know him?" Kurt asked.

"He's a staff man at Hopkins in Baltimore where I trained years ago. We kept up and over the years decided it was for real. Then a while back, broke up, then Anthony arrived and now look!"

She smiled and put her hand out for me to study the ring better. "Yes, I got it for Christmas. We're planning a small spring wedding because it's the second time for both of us. I'd like you and Kurt to come if you would. I'm sending out handwritten invitations, so give me your address and expect it in the mail in the next month."

I looked at her left hand and remarked, "He has good taste if he picked that out."

I cut up the baby's hot dog and he was managing to eat, yell, and spill all at the same time. Things never change, I realized as I watched him. Sheila was giving him tiny drinks of her Cola.

Kurt smiled at her and grabbed her hand. "I'm glad for you. I sort of knew about him, that he was somewhere out there. Glad you two got together again. I know we'd be happy to come to the wedding. If I'm not in jail or worse."

After grabbing her hand, I was thinking I'd get jail after plastering pizza all over both of them being so cutesy.

"Oh, don't say that, Kurt. After all this is past with you, and the wedding's over you both must come out and spend time. The weather by then will be warm, and we have almost an acre of ground with a nice fenced pool in the back."

"Sounds good, Sheila. I think I'd like that," I lied and then jumped up as the baby tipped Sheila's large Coke. Most of it spilled on the floor. She also jumped, and Kurt slid out and went to get towels to mop it up.

"Listen, I have to go. I can't let my assistant spend too much time alone, it's not fair. It was nice to met you, Maggie."

We got Anthony dried and cleaned up and I helped her with her coat. Kurt was packing up the uneaten pizza for later and doing the cleanup honors as I walked out with her.

I got ready to step outside when she smiled at me and said, "You're perfect for him, you know. He's lucky to have you."

"What do you mean?"

"Just that he's a good man. Almost as good as my Lem, Anthony's dad." Her eyes twinkled with mischief as she nodded at Anthony. "Word gets around, Maggie Suit, especially about Rainey's chief resident. I keep in touch through Pat, you see."

I realized she was being kind. We went outside together.

124

She continued, "You're on his side, right or wrong, you really care about him, don't you?"

I looked down and felt a slight flush spread over my face. She was a nice person and I felt bad about being so jealous.

Sheila shifted the baby on her hip and walked slowly towards her car. "He's a good man and if I didn't have a great guy who finally realized we should be together, I'd fight you for him, Maggie."

I smiled at the both of them, turned and got into my car. Kurt had cleaned up the mess and was walking across the lot waving at us. Sheila was busy putting the baby in his car seat. I pulled out of the parking lot, waived, and Anthony waived back at me. I gave a relieved groan. I was very glad she had the baby's father. I didn't think I would stand a chance next to her.

After we got home, I asked, "Kurt, how come it didn't work between you and Sheila?"

"It just didn't. Hell, if I know. I think we were both on the rebound, me from the marriage and her from the kid's father. I decided after I got free that I wasn't cut out for marriage and family, that's the simple truth of it. She knew that. She had this daycare idea and she told me she was burned out of the nursing thing. Nice how it turned out for her, isn't it?"

That remark about marriage and family stung. I thought we were working towards a relationship, and here he was telling me in plain English that I was just another romp in the hay for him. I got the impression he was warning me off, sort of declaring his independence.

I walked into the kitchen and stood at the sink. The subtle or not so subtle remark about marriage and domestication was a slap. I tried to keep the hurt out of my voice and replied, "How nice for you. Your mind's all made up, I see."

His lips tightened in a narrow line, he started to get a little annoyed. "Hey, it's my decision—no wife, no babies ever again."

I got the impression he was warning me off with that remark, sort of declaring his independence. "No family, no more children, Kurt? You may change your mind in time." It came out a little stronger than I had anticipated but I was annoyed.

"My decision. Anyway, what the hell are you so fired up about? It's not like I'm taking your ability to marry and have babies away. Those babies, by the way, left with your last hot flash, kiddo."

That did it. I was pissed. I know my face was getting red as he threw the nasty crack about my age back at me.

I turned and practically spit at him. "Yes, make a stupid remark and get called on it and what do you do? You start throwing darts back. I'm not even menopausal, you jerk! But you, you're just making a generalization without thinking. Not domesticated, not inclined to be, is that something you're putting out to me to make sure I don't start getting starry-eyed ideas?" I was on a roll, snapping out my words. "Look, Dr. No-wife-no-family, I'm not Sheila. And I'm not walking slowly past jewelry store windows, if that's what you're warning me away from. Ain't my style, mister."

The subtle—or not so subtle—remarks about marriage and domestication was a slap. But the age crack really hurt and I was close to tears.

I sat in my living room and curled up in my chair by the window. I was too pissed to speak.

He followed me back into the living room, plunked himself down on the sofa, looked at me, and then shook his head. "I admit it was a dumb statement. I made my mind up about this after I split with Elaine. It's me, not you. I guess it's something I have to work out."

In a softer tone of voice he said, "And now I've met you. I know you're special to me. I just need time, I guess."

I fumed and he slunk upstairs to check his email. I set about straightening the room. He was busy putting some of the notes and background materials in a box to store in the office. Since he finished most of his written work, his need for the office had dwindled to checking email occasionally and doing hospital paperwork he brought in his battered old brown briefcase.

He sat at the computer and banged out an email to Steve in Chicago.

> *Hey buddy, you know how you always warned me about putting my foot in it. I blew it. I've got both feet in now. She's angry as hell and has every right to be. If looks could kill I'd be gone by now. I'm gun shy about marriage, I admit, but I had to advertise it to her like a warning. She never and I mean NEVER has hinted or said anything about permanence but old doc here had to state his position anyway. If I bend over, will you give me the proverbial kick in the ass? Kurt*

After hitting SEND, his beloved laptop stayed quiet. Later that night a message popped up.

> Reply from Steve: *Consider your ass kicked. She sounds like a keeper to me.*

126

Chapter 24

Still fuming at Kurt, Stupid suddenly started barking and racing around the room. She went to the door, yelped, and jumped up as a figure stood outside and rang the bell. I turned on the porch light and there was Holly with Puddy.

No, this is too much, after bickering with Kurt, now Holly shows up. She was finally going to meet the man.

She came in out of the cold with the dog pushing in ahead of her. Puddy and Stupid started racing around biting one another and having a high time. Holly quickly went to the back door and let them both out to the yard. Arctic air blew in as she shut the door.

"Holly, what a surprise. Glad you're here," I said, knowing Kurt was listening upstairs. His footsteps and creaking in the office stopped as Holly came in. Now I knew he was just waiting for the right moment to make a grand entrance.

The stage was set. After her lectures and put-downs, I figure she deserves whatever this turns out to be.

"Mom, when you told me you got new slipcovers I figured I'd come over and see. Cooper's working today and then off doing some Christmas shopping this evening. I wasn't invited, so I guess he's picking something out for me."

She looked at the sofa and chair and felt the material. "Hey, this is great. Chenille, isn't it?"

"Yes, it is nice." Figuring I would get an immediate rise out of her, I remarked, "Kurt helped me pick it out online about a week ago. I was surprised it came so quickly." I could hear faint squeaks over my head. I was beginning to wonder what he was up to. Whatever it was, I had to be prepared. The noise was very faint and could be explained as the cats playing up there.

"How about a drink, Holly? A glass of wine?" I went into the kitchen, and she followed me.

"Mom, it's December 19th. You have been at this Kurt crap now for months and I have yet to see this man. When are you going to give up this fantasy? So he showed up a time or two but it's not that real, so I don't want to hear any more about it, okay?" She slammed her glass of wine down on the kitchen table firmly. Just a little too firmly, it flew out and on her sweatshirt.

"Fine, Holly, no more about Kurt," I said as I moved back into the living room and sat in my wing chair. Holly flopped down on the sofa, still feeling the material. The dogs were barking to be let in so she got up to open the back door.

At the precise moment she opened the back door, a booming voice singing some kind of school fight song came from the stairwell. Kurt appeared in all his glory in his almost altogether. Wearing only a towel around his middle, otherwise completely naked from top to bottom with his face slathered in shaving cream, he bounded down the top flight of stairs and stopped suddenly on the landing. He bent over and peered at my daughter, feigning embarrassment.

"Oh my, babe, I didn't know you had company. Sorry, I'll just go upstairs and get dressed."

I looked up at him and my glance told him the whole story line from then on. "Oh, don't be such a prude. Holly's seen a naked man before, haven't you, my dear? Come on down for a moment and meet my long lost daughter, Holly, and her dog, Puddy."

Holly stared at Kurt as if she had seen a ghost. Her expression was the old "deer caught in the headlights" cliché you hear so much about but never see. It was priceless. The dog, sensing Holly's discomfort, sat in front of her protectively. She was interested in the stranger, but was ready to defend, it was obvious, never taking her eyes off him. Holly reached down and patted Puddy, reassuring her everything was fine.

Now truly embarrassed, Kurt tightly held the small towel that was keeping him modest. He peeked at us, then stepped down to greet my rather astonished and embarrassed daughter. "How do you do, Holly? Please excuse me, as I'm just a figment of your mother's imagination."

I simply could not hold it in another second. I burst out laughing. Holly looked at me then back up at this almost naked man in front of her. She didn't know whether to laugh or scream or run like hell—her confusion was apparent. Finally, she simply bolted for the door.

I stood in front of it and said, "Holly, you wanted to meet him and now you have. As you can see he's shown you all you ever need to see of him, figment that he is. Calm down. It was a joke. I'm sure you'll see the humor in it someday."

With that, Kurt bounded back up the stairs two at a time. Holly started to look at me, then smile, and then she started to laugh. "You've always been crazy, Mom. I suspect he is every bit as crazy as you."

She laughed out loud and Puddy stood in front of her, head cocked sideways and watched as Holly continued to laugh and sit down.

Kurt returned neatly dressed in jeans, a dress shirt and tie, holding shoes in his hand. He placed them on the floor and went into the kitchen. He came back out with wineglasses, handed one to her, and one for us to share.

"You surely don't think we planned this, do you, Holly? Your mother has a crazy streak in her and so do I. All she had to do was raise her voice. I was completely at fault here. So if you're mad, be mad at me, not her."

Holly shook her head and laughed some more. "I'm not angry at anyone, but do you know what a jolt that was to see a half-naked man wearing a towel and shaving cream come singing down my mom's stairs? This is definitely a first for her."

She looked at both of us. "I was almost convinced she's been making you up. I discussed the problem with Ivy who kept saying, 'No, Mom is okay, she's just having a friend over you don't know.' But, me, I was ready to call the funny farm for her."

The rest of the visit was amiable. Kurt left early to get to work on time.

He took me out on the porch and kissed my nose lightly. "Mags, I know I was wrong to say what I said. I'm sorry if I hurt you. I love you and I'm sorry, is all I can say. Am I forgiven?"

He looked at me with remorse in those soft green eyes and my heart stood still. I hugged him back and assured him he was "mostly forgiven."

Holly got ready to leave, too. "I'll have to email Ivy and tell Coop about my meeting the naked stranger with shaving cream on. See you." With that, she grabbed Puddy's leash and the two of them hurried out to her car.

I was astounded at the whole evening. It went from sniveling, angry, and crying to hilarious in no time at all.

I smiled as I thought that Holly would be telling Ivy and Cooper and Mike this story for hours on end tonight. With Serge and Tulip snuggled up to me, I went to bed and slept like a baby through the night.

Chapter 25

The holidays arrived. Kurt managed to get Christmas evening off and spent it with me at Holly and Cooper's. Christmas morning came complete with freezing temperatures and bright sunshine. I opened my eyes and winced it was so bright.

We got our coffee and the next two hours were a flurry of gifts, phone calls to our family and Kurt's in Chicago. We drank coffee and ate breakfast muffins. We hardly noticed the time. Kurt had to leave and we got him out by 10 a.m., which was later than he planned.

He hugged and kissed me good-bye and Holly winced at the gesture. He raced out the door, late as usual, and called back to us, "Thanks for everything, we have to do this again next year."

Driving back to the dorm, Kurt was smiling to himself, listening to carols on the radio, and feeling happy. Oh hell, I'm sunk. I can't imagine any life without her now. Wonder if my folks will love her as much as I do. And I'll take Rick's I told you so, and his damn knowing grins—he was right, smug little bastard! I'm just going to get through this hospital problem somehow and convince her to stay with me. I think Maggie's right; we can cross Sheila Cowen off the list of suspects. And who knows? Maybe it's over and the killer is too frightened to try anything else. We just have to catch him now.

Christmas dinner was a huge success and cleanup went quickly. We all three collapsed in the family room after Cooper came home from dropping off his kids. It was over, we got through it without any frightening incidents in Kurt's life. I was grateful to the powers that it was uneventful.

Kurt enjoyed his 3 days in Chicago, came home to me full of stories about his daughter. With Christmas over, we both went back to work. On New

Year's Eve, he telephoned. "Babe, I'm at work but I hope to be off this evening. A whole group of folks from the Center are meeting at O'Malley's bar tonight for a few beers and conversation. You get to meet the gang I've talked about so much. Not a formal New Year's thing, but something to do and cheap. I told you about O'Malley's, didn't I? They have the best burgers and those big chunky fries that are so good, I can taste them now."

"You and that stomach of yours. Yes, you mentioned them to me the day of the accident, remember? Where is this place exactly? Do you want me to meet you there?"

"No, you drive on down here to the Center. I'll take over and get us to O'Malley's. Make it after rush hour, around 8:30 or 9. Be hungry—you're going to love this artery hardening food."

"I'll see you out front of the main building at around 9. Don't make me circle the block ten times, now."

"I wouldn't do that to you. I'll be the bum in the suede jacket, tan work shoes and day-old beard; tired but eager."

"Ah, but *my* bum, that's what counts. See you then." I hung up and left work early enough to do animal chores and get ready to meet some of the colorful folks I heard stories about for months. I was looking forward to a fun evening.

It was a cold, clear night as I drove downtown through light traffic. The streets were nearly deserted. Joggers and people strolling toward downtown on foot were bundled up against the cold. It was obvious most people were celebrating New Year's later than we were.

The tall main building of old stone hospital complex announced itself several blocks before my turn. I arrived at 9 sharp. I found Kurt—scruffy looking indeed—lounging against a planter box containing drooping evergreens and a few dead fall flowers. He was talking to a short round man and laughing.

He looked up and smiled in recognition, ran around to the driver's side and opened the door for me. I got a quick hello kiss as I switched seats. He pulled away from the curb like a posse was after him.

We drove downtown and turned right on Connecticut Avenue. After a few blocks, we turned left and pulled into an old pitted blacktop parking lot. O'Malley's turned out to be a neighborhood bar tucked into the middle of that side street. It served a rather mixed neighborhood of colors, backgrounds, and incomes.

***

Damn, what an idiot! Kurt thought, I get a free night and what do I do? I take her to a downtown bar on the most glamorous night of the year. She's too nice to complain, but one of these days I'm going to take her to the best restaurant in the city—or better yet, that cruise ship down the Potomac. I really need to show her a better time than a burger at this hangout of mine.

Entering from the cold parking lot, Kurt tugged at an age-darkened door. The first thing I noticed was that the city's smoking ban was not too strictly upheld here. It was hazy and dark, and in addition to the smell of stale beer and cigarettes, Patsy Cline was singing about walking after midnight on the jukebox.

It took a moment for my eyes to adjust, as we hesitated at the doorway. The whole place was long and narrow, with an old-fashioned dark wood bar spanning almost the entire length of the room. A huge classic mirror sported liquor, cigarette, and beer signs on the mirror and wall. Bottles of imported beer and various liquors, their colors shimmering in the dim reflected light, were displayed on shelves surrounding it. An older, heavyset man in a white apron was working at pulling beers and pouring drinks.

At the end of the bar near the takeout area and cash register was a set of swinging doors that flew open and shut as employees rushed in and out. The help consisted of two middle-aged waitresses in white uniforms and comfortable, worn shoes threading their way among the close-set tables. They held large trays up high over the heads of the seated crowd, serving the house burgers and fries in baskets lined with paper napkins.

Working men lined the bar dressed in denims, suits, and hospital attire. They looked up as we entered, some recognizing Kurt, others turned back to their drinks.

I leaned close and asked, "Why here? It's not that close to the hospital, but I see several familiar faces from last summer."

"It's close to the lowest decent housing values in the city. Since most of residents are supporting families on small salaries, or their wives are working, this is where we all sort of landed."

"But you're not supporting a family?"

"No, but I'm paying child support and that puts me in the same bracket as most of the folks here. A lot of the nurses and technicians have settled in the neighborhoods, too. Remember, my dear, most of the folks who do the heavy lifting in medicine are not that well paid."

The Patsy Cline record stopped and the noise of different conversations drifted past. Several patrons looked up and waved to Kurt, a few offering him room at their table. He smiled, greeted folks but held my hand as he moved us toward the back across the rather small sticky dance floor. All this place really needed was peanut shells, and sawdust, I thought. One good-looking man sitting with two others gave me an appraising look—I recognized Vince Packard from our Italian restaurant. Knowing how he felt about Kurt he was on the top of my suspect list. I would love to talk to that guy, but figured now was not a good time.

In the far corner several people were involved in a hotly debated discussion at a large table. It already was loaded with several empty food baskets, discarded napkins, some bottles and glasses. Loud catcalls and hoots erupted when they spied Kurt. He was rudely invited to "sit his ass down and settle this argument once and for all." Introductions were made and several names flew past me.

The debate centered around speculation on new surgical suites. The discussion then rapidly moved on some surgical technique or method of treating a condition I could not pronounce, let alone fathom. Terms were thrown around I didn't even try to understand. After some questioning, Kurt smiled and then took a pen out, grabbed a napkin and started to draw on it, outlining his points as he went along. I sat quietly watching the man I loved explain, answer questions patiently, and share his experience and knowledge with the people at our table and several curious onlookers. He is such a great, patient teacher, I realized. I keep forgetting it's part of his job.

I recognized Patricia Sewell immediately by her size and her gorgeous red hair. She was seated exactly opposite me on the old faded red leatherette banquette. She had the traditional milky white skin with pale freckles showing underneath and a lovely face, rather round because of her weight. She wore a full set of rumpled Army fatigues that did nothing to flatter her frame. The coloring was bad for her skin and hair. Her eyes were large, an unusual amber brown with full lush lashes. This was a very attractive woman who simply did not have the time to take care of herself.

She looked at me in a distracted way when I was introduced.

"Hi, I'm Pat," she said. I registered somewhere in her mind and I got a rather distrusting look. I saw that very same attitude and look when she was part of the original surgical team that accompanied Rainey to my room in September. For some reason she took an immediate dislike to me back then and now.

She looked me over and commented, "My, you've lost more weight and certainly fixed yourself up nice. Glad everything turned out so good for you." She glanced at Kurt as she said this. The implication was clear.

I offered my hand over the table. "I remember you from back in September, Patricia. You have the most stunning red hair I've ever seen."

Her grip was weak and disinterested. She dropped my hand quickly and immediately turned to Kurt and joined the debate. Except for the distracted exchange she had no interest in me or my presence at the table.

I sat there and thought about her as the person who was behind his problems. She certainly disliked Kurt. She was a large woman, and, if angry enough, she would have the strength to beat and stomp little Millie. She was wearing heavy boots, I noticed.

During a break in the debate, Sam, his good friend, and Kurt managed to get up and start toward the bar. Kurt looked at all of us, made a circle with his hand to indicate he was getting a round for the group. We all nodded. I had no idea what he would bring me back but assumed it would be beer. I hate beer!

I tried conversation again. "I understand from Kurt that this place does a great burger but that its fries are what they are famous for."

The four faces, whose names I had forgotten already, smiled at me as they all tried to make polite conversation with the stranger Kurt had dragged into their evening. It was obvious they were eager to get back to the question at hand, but needed their chief resident to continue when he returned with the drinks.

The beer arrived and the debate raged on. Pat seemed usually strident and forceful in her defense of one of her more controversial points. Kurt and the others all shook their heads in disagreement as she continued to drive home her arguments.

Finally, he turned to Patricia as she continued to argue. "Pat, I think we're being rude to our guest here. Why don't we leave the shoptalk for the conference room? It's a rare time when the bunch of us are all together with a few beers, and tonight's a holiday. Hey, I really prefer to enjoy myself and not be quote on duty unquote." He gestured the quotes.

He was trying to move Patricia off her soapbox. It was obvious to all he was being tactful. I, on the other hand, would have told her plainly to shut up.

Red faced, and charged up on the argument, she shot back at him, "Yes, let's just kick it under the table. It's hard to face up to the fact that I was right and you and Rainey were wrong. That the great doctor himself may have overlooked the patient's medical history in this instance. I was the one who took—"

Kurt again interrupted her. In a firm but quiet voice, he leaned past me and looked directly at Pat. "Not now, understand. This is neither the time nor the place to bring all this up. We were discussing the entire field in general, not Paulson's death. We've gone over and over this with you. What happened couldn't be helped—it was simply his time, *Doctor*. We're not miracle workers. He was very ill and at the end of his rope medically. I talked to the man and listened to him, Pat, really listened. Not just to the answers to his history, like you. I knew how he felt, his fears, his years of illness, his concerns for his family. I could feel it; I knew deep down he was ready to give it up. Now, enough of this!"

The men at the table were plainly uncomfortable with the interchange between Pat and Kurt. They started a quiet conversation between themselves. Kurt turned to me and started to say something when Pat stood up, maneuvered her large body around our table and leaned over the two of us.

"Yes, let's turn the conversation to something more pleasant, like your game playing with old Aunt Maggie here last summer. We all heard about that little diversion. I recall that no one called you on it either. Wonder how Old Ironsides managed to miss all that coming and going in your room, Maggie?" She was referring to Nora Feeney, I'm sure.

She nodded her head in Kurt's direction. "Better yet, let's talk about your high-handed, supposedly philanthropic dorm up the street. Who gets to shack up there, Kurt? Only the right size ladies, the right color gentlemen? No one ugly allowed, no one fat allowed?" she said this quietly, but in a nasty tone, bitterness dripping from every word as she stood there.

Kurt was controlling his anger and struggling to do so. Pat had touched on a sore subject with the Aunt Maggie story and then she lobbed another nasty grenade about his living arrangements.

He turned and looked directly at her. "Pat, I told you there are no openings right now. I don't care about looks. I told you then, and I'm telling you now that with the way we constantly butt heads, I think you wouldn't be a good fit in the place. Now let's drop it. Sit down and I'll buy you a beer."

She looked over at me and then back at Kurt and raised her voice. "No, I guess you're right, you must not care much about appearance, or you wouldn't be hanging around with this blousy old cow!"

Dead silence greeted this comment. Pat abruptly turned, and pushed her way past the folks on the dance floor, and left. Packard got up and casually followed her out the door. Those two could be trouble, I wonder if they could be working together. Right now, I would put money on it. At the same time, I could feel my face flush as her words stung.

I sat there embarrassed. I did not know where the ladies' room was and felt it would only make it worse if I tried to flee to that female safety zone. When Kurt looked at me, I could see cold fury in his eyes. He grabbed my hand, pulled me up, and we started to leave. The whole table exploded in protests. Other tables of people that heard Pat's vicious little diatribe joined in the protests.

The bartender, in his stained apron, appeared and asked for our burger orders, insisting to Kurt that we stay. Apologies to me were called out. A few people came by to assure us Pat was out of line. Sam jumped up, pushed Kurt back in his seat. Another young guy, Roy, pulled my chair out and gently insisted I sit down.

Kurt was so furious he was shaking. I wanted to get him out of there to cool down. I didn't know whether I was more hurt or worried about his fury. But if Pat was just outside it would be bad news. I figured the guys were smart to get him defused in here before we tried to leave.

Roy, the baby-faced guy in the tee shirt and jeans, looked over at me, then to Kurt. "It's her way, man, you know how that woman can be. She's probably PMSing or had a bad run of luck at work. We all get crappy at times." He turned to me. "No one listens to her complaints. She's so big she's the 8th and 9th dwarfs…crabby and flabby!"

"The board listened to her and her supporters last summer when I got the chief's job, Roy. You just came on the first of July so you were clueless to the politics. She yelled discrimination so loud that Rainey and the others were up before them justifying themselves blue in the face over their choice in the matter. She's had it in for me since she was turned down. She seems to think something I said or did influenced their decision."

Someone was telling a story about Kurt's early days at the Center and his owning the condo known affectionately as "the dorm." He was still livid and uncomfortable, so ignoring the story, he grabbed my hand and said, "Come on, Maggie, we have to go. Hey, guys, it's not been great all round, but thanks for your support. Long drive out to the 'burbs for Maggie, and it's New Year's Eve, so all the drunks will be on the road. And most of all, I'm bushed, so I'll see you all tomorrow." He was talking too fast. He again grabbed my hand, pulled me up, and we threaded our way out to the parking lot.

"So much for the famous O'Malley's French fries," I said as we climbed into my little red car and he tore out of the parking lot and headed to my house. He was pissed, I could tell. I decided to keep quiet.

I rubbed the back of his neck as I continued, "No wonder Nora had you checked out and found you were a little better off than the average bear after that condo story first got around. But it doesn't explain why she's so against you. You never punched her out or had to report her for infractions. Must be something more there. Maybe something you're not telling me?"

He sighed. "I never made a secret of the dorm scheme. I really can say only that when I first arrived 5 years ago, Nora was younger and I was

136

younger and she always seemed to be *available* whenever I needed guidance or help with something. You've met the lady; she's really a beauty. She's older than you, babe, I know that for a fact."

He glanced at me and said, "I didn't give it a second thought for years until all this started at the Center, and I looked back and thought about it hard. I could be wrong. I can't be sure, but it's the only thing I've been able to come up with about Nora. Just a sort of crush on me that's long vanished, but the hostility remains. Nothing more that I can think of."

"You could represent something to her. Someone or something else she hated and it pushed her over to do this sort of thing. That lady does have ice in her veins, Kurt."

With that, we pulled in the driveway and he helped me out of the car and into the house. I walked in the kitchen while he let Stupid out to do her duty for the night. I poured kibble out for her.

"You hungry, hon? We never ate tonight. We could have leftovers or Christmas cookies and milk or I could scramble some eggs for you."

"No, Maggie, I've had quite enough for this evening. A huge dose of aggravation is about all I need to chew on for now. Let's go to bed, okay?" He pulled me by the hand and we followed Stupid upstairs.

I sat down in my old wing chair and faced him. Whether I liked it or not, we had to talk about tonight. Pat may have been cruel and bitter, but her words had a ring of truth in them. I started slowly to undress, kicking the shoes over in the sitting room and pulling my panty hose off.

"Look," I said quietly, "you were so furious tonight that I was afraid to say anything until we were safe here at home. I think you shouldn't chew on what Pat said tonight. It was in a bar and probably some alcohol fueled it, so don't let it affect her work or yours. She'll probably regret it tomorrow."

"Maggie, you don't know Pat. She never has regrets. And what she did was cruel and mean, I don't know how I can't hold it against her. She's vindictive and a nasty bitch! On the other hand, she's the best the Center has. A fifth-year woman with hands of gold. Rainey and I both agree she's going to make a remarkable surgeon. She's bright, willing to take risks, absolutely ruthless when she feels she is right, as you heard tonight. As much as I hate to admit it, she's head and shoulders above me in talent and approaching Rainey's level at light speed."

I put out my theory. "But she's kind of twisted and so bitter. Maybe, just maybe, she could be the one. She has access to the records like you, she could have changed the number. She's obviously talented but feels she is being shafted. The job would be hers if she could get you out of there. And her size and those boots she had on could cause any woman a problem if she went after someone Millie's size. Kurt, are you a little jealous of her? Why didn't she get the chief's job? Were Rainey and the others really favoring you?"

"No, they didn't favor me. Rainey had a lot of input and he's a cold analytical man and a great teacher. He looked at her and me and our temperaments and talents, and decided that what Pat needed was more time to be a student, or take direction, to learn a little humility. And remember, Maggie, each section and subsection in a teaching hospital usually has a chief in charge of the educational aspects of the area. I had more teaching experience, so his vote went to me and the others followed, I guess."

He walked into the bathroom. "She knows she's good. She's got the same inflated ego all surgeons have; even yours truly. But she can't handle it too well, as you plainly saw from tonight's outburst. She needs to be able to control her temper and shake some of that bitterness off, or it will color her career. He's trying to help her do that in his own way. Of course, she's not aware of it and after not getting the job, I've been the target of her venom more than once."

He came out and switched on the radio to his favorite golden oldies station—they were doing some New Year's Eve special.

"Packard followed her outside tonight? When she left he got up and sort of just wandered coolly out, but I get the feeling he was following her. If those two ganged up on you, it could be the problem."

Tossing his sweatshirt and undershirt into the hamper, he sat down on the bed to pull off his socks.

"Yes, it was Packard, I noticed him, too. But to tell you the truth, I don't think they are sabotaging me. Why now? I'll finish my residency in less than half a year and so will they. Of course, we could be competing for staff positions, but I find it hard to believe they would kill for a damn job. Even their egos can't be so big they would kill because of a punch or a job slight."

"I was talking this over with Detective Walters and Rainey, and we think the attack on Millie was not meant to hurt her or kill her. Our guess is it was a miscalculation on the murderer's part. But we could be wrong."

One sock flew towards the hamper and missed. "I think what was going on there with Packard leaving O'Malley's was he looking for a freebie from Pat. She's known to be kind of free with her favors and when you get a woman pissed like that," another sock hit behind the hamper, "and you give her some sympathy, you can get almost anything out of her you want. Packard is eternally horny and always looking." Off went his jeans.

"She's right about me being older than you, but it's not just that. It's only a couple of years. But I've been ill, I've lost weight, my hair has thinned out.

Sometimes I feel like I'm never going to get back in shape again."

He came over, pulled me up, took my hands, and started dancing slowly with me as Elvis singing "Can't help falling in love with you." The music was sweet, his arms were sweeter. I rested my head on his chest as we moved together in our underwear to the soft sweet love song. Stupid looked on, shrugged, and moved over to her bed and flopped down.

"You've been sick, but you'll get stronger, and your skin will fit again and glow. Now as for your hair, I never noticed it was thin. I guess guys don't take that sort of thing in too much. It will come back, too. The hair loss is almost universal with anesthesia. You had about 4 doses of it this past summer, what do you expect?"

He kissed the top of my head and I raised my face as we moved slowly to the soft words Elvis crooned. Our lips touched lightly and softly.

"Maggie, I love you."

"Do you think people at the Center gossip about us?" I asked.

He kept dancing with me around the bedroom. "Yup, they gossip about everything there, you should know that."

He started kissing my ear, nipping it softly, holding me closer. "Look how much fun we had with the rumor mill this summer. The story probably goes like this now: Kurt Van Doren is sleeping with his aunt."

I punched him playfully. "Ah, my sweet babe." He held me away from him and looked down at me. "Finish getting undressed, go on."

"After what I just talked about how I feel? Guys are supposed to be interested in legs or big firm boobs. I would think you would notice the extra skin and hair."

"Hell no, Mags, a girl undresses and we're just grateful and leer!"

I whirled out of his arms laughing, ran over to the bed and grabbed a pillow. I bounced it off his head and back.

I yelled at him, "Hey, you want to leer, here!" He ducked as the pillow connected again. He then put both arms up in defense as I chased him around the room, both of us in our underwear, pounding him with the pillow and laughing.

I cornered him between the bed and the nightstand and threw it down.

I held out my arms to him. "Okay, darling, Happy New Year. I've seen the leer, now show me just how grateful you can be."

And he did, it was wonderful.

Email to friend Steve from Kurt, New Year's Day: *Happy New Year. Arrived back in one piece. Mellie has grown and she loved the presents you gave her. We wrote a thank you note, did you get it yet? Folks were glad to see me. Told them about Maggie. Not about the other however, don't want to scare them. They could find this nut and things settle down. Glad you got over the snickering and teasing about how right you were. I know I went on and on about her, but I just can't help it, and oh, Steve, she is a keeper. But stop the crowing now because if you do much more I'll come back to Chicago and kick your smug ass in front of God, your wife and our kids. Kurt*

Chapter 26

By January I had settled into a full routine with surprising ease. My mind was occupied and I was rapidly gaining strength and stamina.

My only personal concerns were for Kurt, not myself. We spent all our free time together. But I worried constantly that something would happen again. He was blamed for things before, but now, since that suspicious car accident, and the girl's death, I was afraid for his safety.

Most of the problems that plagued him this fall seemed past. If Millie's killer is caught, it would be a good year, I hoped.

The end of January brought cold, nasty, wet rain to the area and the prediction on this bleak Monday was for it to freeze overnight. The phone rang in my office. I put it on hands free and heard Kurt's voice as soon as I picked up. "Mags, it's me, you won't believe. Just when I thought it was over, another stupid thing today; a break-in and it was a very clumsy job."

"Don't tell me, the cops are after you about it, right? Are you hiding? Do you want me to come get you?"

"Nah, I'm okay. Not to blame this time."

"Who or what did they leave this time to point to you? Hair samples, a pair of your shorts? Really, this just too much."

"Someone broke into all the lockers down in the staff area, mine included. Lots of stuff was taken—money, keys, clothing. Lot of it was just thrown around. It looks like a vandal got in and tore up the place. Not sure how it's going to be blamed on me, but you can be sure they will find a Kurt connection somewhere."

"Did they call the police? I know petty crimes isn't Walters' thing but you should notify him, since it sounds like another connection."

"Hell, Walters was here when it happened. He was reinterviewing the nurses who found Millie. He rechecked the whereabouts of the two red-

141

haired guys on staff. He told me one was at home with a pile of company to vouch for him, and the other guy was in our surgical offices working on the thermostat with Rainey and his secretary to vouch for him. Everyone was reinterviewed today. Chet says he's just going over everything he can to pick up something, anything about the murder. I told him about Sheila Cowan, too."

"What did he say about the vandalism?"

"He laughed. Said the perpetrator was either a fool or deliberately making me look like an innocent patsy. From the timeframe they put together, I was running some tests on a patient and then talking to Walters himself. Maggie, this is getting stranger and stranger. Chet's right here."

"I think Walters may have something there. Someone's linking you, but in such an offhanded manner you almost always have time to clear yourself. How strange. Another twist in this whole mess."

"Hey, meet us for lunch. We'll drive over now and catch you early. Is that good for you?"

"Always fine when I get to see my main man. We'll go to the Hunan place down the street." I hung up and went back to work.

I was concentrating on a list of terms for a glossary I was creating when the phone rang in my office. I picked up and Angie said to me in her soft southern drawl, "Maggie, there are two gentlemen here to see you. Can you come up to get them, please?"

"Sure, Angie, is one of them very tall?"

"Why yes, Maggie, that would be correct," she answered.

"I think that's the famous Kurt. You've finally gotten to meet the sexy voice on the phone and the mystery man in my life. The other guy is a cop so be nice."

Imagine my shock when the elevator doors opened and I came face to face with Jules Rainey standing right in front of them, hands behind his back, admiring our beautiful reception clock that never worked. Where the hell was Chet Walters?

Behind Rainey stood Kurt, looking pleased with himself. I figured he was coming with us to lunch.

I put out my hand and pasted on my most professional smile. "Why, Doctor Rainey, how nice to see you again. What brings you here to our office?"

He took my hand for the briefest second. You could tell that the man really did not like touching ordinary folks. His demeanor was warmer than usual, however, and I smiled at both of them.

"Angie, we're going downstairs to my office and possibly out to lunch, right, gentlemen?"

Rainey nodded. "We figured since you were indirectly involved we should include you. This is a rare day when we are both off and able to work you in."

I felt I was a kid with a toothache the way he talked about "working me in." But knowing a little about Rainey, I dismissed the formal tone as business as usual with the man.

"We're meeting Walters at the Hunan place up the street in about 15 minutes, so we don't have a lot of time to fool around here," Rainey remarked to me as we headed downstairs.

Kurt had done no more than nod at me, smile and say hello. Rainey was clearly in charge. Then it occurred to me, that Rainey's the boss. He has an opening Kurt hoped to fill later this year. It was just plain schmoozing on his part.

We headed out to the Hunan Forest up the street. Since it was only 11:30 and a short walk, I knew there would be plenty of room.

Kurt was friendly and formal all the way to the restaurant, holding my hand, and making small talk with Rainey. He seated himself next to me. Detective Walters showed up as we sat; indicating to the staff that he was with us. Dr. Rainey sat across from me in the dimly lit restaurant, and Walters seated himself next to Rainy.

Then, to my surprise, Nora Feeney came through the front door and headed to our table. Now I was thoroughly confused. Nasty Nora was eating lunch with us? No way. She approached the table, and Walters motioned for her to sit down.

She removed her coat to reveal a well-cut black silk suit. The combination of the dark suit, lovely turquoise scarf with her white hair and good looks was perfect. She put her expensive leather purse down on the empty chair at the next table, sat down as gracefully as a princess, and looked over at me.

"Why, Mrs. Suit, you're looking healthy these days. I guess rest and better food pays off—along with our medical care, of course." Her tone was light and pleasant. She liked being in control and I had bested her once. She was not going to let me do that to her again.

I glanced over at her, nodded, smiled, and said yes. Anything more would have signaled something, and I certainly didn't want to do that. Silence and smiles were sufficient. Kurt just sipped water and gave me a puzzled glance over his glass. I winked at him.

The smell of Chinese food, and sounds of pots banging and sizzling along with men shouting orders in Chinese was coming from the red swinging doors behind us.

The detective, Walters, took charge of the conversation immediately. "What you need to know is today's my day off, so none of this is official, okay? What I'm doing now is on my own. Let me explain. Even though the case of assault and now murder against Millie Prentice is still open, we have officially stuck it the pending file. This means, for all intents and purposes, that it will go unsolved for now. I'm not giving up on it, however. I'm entitled to keep working on what we call 'cold cases' on my own, or when I'm not busy. I'm intrigued that so many little things have happened around the time of that assault that all point to you, Dr. Van Doren. I saw it firsthand today with the lockers. So now I'm taking my own time to look into this."

He leaned back as the waitress approached our table, pad out and pencil ready for orders. After we finished, I looked over at the detective. "Walters, what other little incidents have happened since November that have pointed to Kurt?" Turning to Kurt I said, "Why didn't you tell me other things have popped up? You kept assuring me all was quiet at the hospital. If you want me to help you, or at least come up with a different perspective, I need to know what's going on?"

He looked at me after glancing briefly at Nora. "I've been busy, Maggie. With moving our department into the new wing and the holidays, it just went out of my mind. When I did remember to talk to you, I was at work or you were at work or it was the middle of the night. I'm not calling you up then to discuss stuff that may or may not be part of some conspiracy to get rid of me." He touched my hand gently. "Look, it wasn't intentional, I've been busy, and so have you."

Walters took up the conversation. "Look, Doc, for what it's worth the forging prescriptions and the break-in down at the pharmacy are both serious situations. They were aimed at implicating you, but we were on to the game. Don't downplay it for Mrs. Suit, she's no fool. Now with the Prentice girl dead we're looking for a murderer, one who's also tried to kill you and Mrs. Suit in your car, too. We got that report back and the tie rod on your side was definitely tampered with."

"Not to mention the stupid vandalism trick this morning," I said. "He told me about that when he arranged for us to have lunch."

"That goes without saying. He was with me when this happened from what we can tell by checking with the staff who used the locker area."

He cleared his throat and continued, "Before the Prentice girl died, she gave us a very vague description of a tall man with red hair on his arms. That lets you out, Doc. But we need to comb through your life to see who you

144

know who would fit that description. Somehow, you're a threat to him. We have to know *how* you're a threat. What you saw, where you observed this person or situation, what causes them to discredit you, kill that girl, and now may do you harm."

Walters shifted position, fiddling with his silverware as he spoke. "Whatever it is up there in your head is making this someone nervous as hell. Since he or she killed Prentice and stuck your name on it, he or she must have sabotaged your tie rod, too. Chances are they'll try something that serious again. You better watch yourself, Doc, 'cause the next time you may be the victim in the true sense of the word."

I spoke up. "Detective, we talked to Sheila Cowan, the woman that Kurt told you about. Her little boy, Anthony, is about a year old and could not possibly be Kurt's child."

"I know, we checked her out as soon as we got word. Seems she's about to marry a Dr. Richardson, Lemuel Richardson. She has all the right qualifications for doing this, but I just can't see her as a suspect. But you never know in cases like this."

Rainey looked over at Kurt and remarked, "Richardson's a Hopkins guy, I know him. I think you met him a couple of times at meetings, remember?"

Kurt shook his head no.

Chet Walters felt around in his coat and took out a little notebook, flipped it open and continued his monologue. "For your information, I got a call on the way over here. A search of your rental car showed all the missing stuff was in your backseat. It may be a rental, but you do keep it locked up, don't you, Doc?"

Kurt nodded to the detective.

"Marks show the person used a rather sophisticated system to get the car unlocked, something the better car thieves are using on these new models now. I'm sure we won't get fingerprints, but they're going over it. You may not be able to use the car for another couple of hours."

I ignored the stuff Detective Walters was telling us and, peeved, looked over at Kurt, who could tell he was in trouble. "So the tie rod actually was tampered with? That's scary. I remember asking you about it. And those other things, the prescription, and a pharmacy break-in. That's pretty serious, Kurt, wish you had told me." In my head I was already yelling at the man that I knew that stupid accident was deliberate. I glanced at Nora who gave me a smug look. She knew, why didn't I?

I was upset and my body posture told him that as I moved slightly away from him.

Rainey reset his silverware and looked over at us. "Some of what's happened has been common gossip around the Center now for weeks. Whether or not you're at fault, the fingers and talk are pointing at you. If this doesn't clear itself up soon, Kurt, as your chief of staff, in order to protect the Center and to protect you, I may have to ask you to resign and finish your residency in Chicago or Dallas, somewhere clear of this situation. Of course, you would have to possibly spend more time there than here."

He sat back, and for the first time in my short acquaintance with Rainey, I saw a genuine emotion pass over his face. He was sad, or hurt, I couldn't tell which, since emotions were so rare with the man. It was obvious that he liked his chief resident, respected his abilities, and would hate to lose a good man.

Ignoring my anger, Kurt looked over at Rainey and then to Nora. "I think you both have been great about keeping me covered and watching over me. Nora, we haven't always seen eye to eye, but you've been very good about this whole mess."

He shook his head slightly as he looked at his boss and said, "I think you've gone out of your way, Jules, to be fair. I can't let you continue to take the heat for me. I'll give it a couple more days and then resign effective the first of the month, if that's okay with you."

Nora reached over, and grabbed a packet of sweetener, twisting it in her hand. I got the feeling she was reaching for Kurt or Rainey's hand but decided against it at the last second, so the blue packet sufficed. "Taking that attitude is not good," she said to Kurt, quite firmly. "Jules didn't say he was firing you or that you have to resign right now. I get the feeling that he's willing to give it a little more time, am I right, Jules?" She looked at the chief of surgery, and I could hear the pleading tone in what she said.

Jules Rainey leaned forward over the table, his pale eyes glancing from Nora to Kurt. "She's right. We're going to try to give this a little more time. Detective Walters is involved now, so maybe we can get to the bottom of it before you have to do anything drastic. We may even be able, with careful monitoring, to keep this whole thing under wraps until you finish up in June. You're too close now for a change. It would not be a good career move for you at this point."

"Good, that's settled then. You stick it out as long as Rainey and you think you can handle it. And the rest of us will watch closely and hope this all may just stop. In a way, you're being stalked." Walters leaned back with this last remark and shook out his napkin, obviously enjoying the prospect of a good meal.

The petite waitress approached our table carrying a huge tray of food. "Yup, we're going to keep a close eye on you, Doc, all three of us. And we

146

need you to keep thinking about what it is that you saw, or thought you saw, that's making this individual so crazy. My feeling is that something will turn up and crack this whole thing open. We just have to keep our eyes open."

I decided to put out a rather wild idea. "It's a shame we couldn't do something to draw this person's fire. Somehow set up a situation where if we were careful and watched, Walters, Nora, or you, Jules, could actually see something being set up."

I turned toward Kurt. "What we need is to put Kurt or someone close to him, like you, Dr. Rainey, or me, in a situation where it's just too handy an opportunity to pass up. By now the person knows Kurt's not being blamed for the incidents. If he or she really wants to get rid of him, they need one good solid act, possibly serious enough, that will put the blame squarely on you and cause your dismissal or force you to resign."

Walters was working his way through the broccoli and beef he ordered. He chewed and finished then looked over at me like I was crazy. "Hey, Mrs. Suit."

"Call me Maggie, Detective, I'm not your granny."

"Maggie, this isn't a game here. This person has caused serious damage and now murdered someone. Tried to murder you two, in fact. We can't playfully decide to hang Doc Rainey here or Doc Van Doren with a big target painted on their backside that says: *Come and Get Me*."

Walters was loading duck sauce on his egg roll as he continued, "It would take a whole army of cops or PIs to keep a watch on the situation you describe—stakeouts in the OR, other areas, following the two docs through those dark tunnels and corridors at night. We'd have to put phony patients and nurses in the place. Can you see cops running up and down the halls with guns or cell phones strapped to their little gowns and uniforms? Nah, sorry but it'll never work."

He shook his head, and took a bite of the sauce-covered egg roll. After chewing carefully, he continued, "We have no one but ourselves, folks. My department's way too busy to play nursemaid to a possible victim, or watch the pharmacy or medicine lockers on the third, fourth, or fifth floors."

I looked up over my food and said to everyone, "I could get in there and nose around some, ask questions of the staff. I could hang out and look like an accident waiting to happen. If I was careful and you all watched over me, I think it might be useful. Maybe we can find this person."

"Nah, Mrs. Suit, that sounds like something you see on *Murder, She Wrote,* not real life, and it could be dangerous."

I answered with confidence I didn't really feel, "Come on, Detective, I'm Kurt's good old Aunt Maggie. I could do it, and I'll bet it would help."

Now everyone stopped eating and started protesting. They all had good reasons not to let me pull such a stunt. Walters protested through his broccoli. "Dumb idea and dangerous as hell given this person's record."

Placing his hand on mine, Kurt said firmly, "Too dangerous and scary. I'd never allow it, Mags."

Nora chimed in, "The hospital would never go along with it either. The danger of a lawsuit or worse would make the administration forbid it on several levels."

Rainey just looked at me. Putting down his fork, he looked over with that lizard-like grin of his. "Bet I could get your old aneurysm to flare up, Maggie. Have you admitted for tests. An aneurysm is a dangerous thing, and as chief of vascular surgery, I did the original work on you. It would be natural that you'd come back to me or be referred back to me for further work."

He was on my side! The only one. Good old Rainey saw my point in this. Knowing him, he could talk the others into it.

"Jules," I said, "I think we have the beginnings of a plan here, but we need to talk the others into it. That's going to be your department. You're the big cheese here and used to giving the orders."

I had finished my meal and took my napkin off my knees, wiped my mouth, and placed it next to the plate. I looked at Jules, took a sip of my cold tea, and over the top of my little cup, winked at the man brazenly. He smiled back, and for the first time I could see some real humanity reflected in that smile. We were comrades—coconspirators you might say. I was beginning to like Rainey more and more.

Chapter 27

The luncheon broke up with Rainey and Walters taking Nora back to the Center. It was Kurt's day off and he walked with me back to the office.

"Look, babe, I'm sorry about not telling you the accident was no accident. But I only found out for sure the week after I came back from Chicago. As for the other stuff, it was so minor I really didn't want to bother you with it. You get very defensive about me, and I appreciate it, but you've had a bad year and this whole situation hasn't helped any. I guess in a way I was shielding you. It was out of love and concern, please understand that."

I turned my head and said, "Oh, yes, I'm such a baby you were shielding me. You came over and spent nights and shared my bed and cooked meals with me, but I'm too fragile to hear the truth? You mean in all this time since December you could not find *one minute* to tell me about the pharmacy break-in? What about the prescription forging? And the car? I was in that car and almost got killed. I think I have a right to know who's playing God with my life!" I emphasized it rather loudly.

I kept walking rapidly, getting mad as I strode back to the office complex. "You could have shared the bit of news about the car at least. I think you're just being typically male, and as for trying to shield the poor little woman from reality, please don't! I'm a big girl now, not some—some—sweet tippy-toed idiot who faints at the sight of blood.

"Let me tell you, Van Doren," I said as I jammed my key fob at the elevator door, "I suspected all along that accident was no accident. Almost everyone who knows about this situation feels the same way. I told you that back when it happened, remember? But no, I can't handle it."

The elevator doors opened and we entered. I stabbed at the button and got us up to the fourth floor. "I even mentioned it to you at the ER that day. That whole afternoon was a blur, but I had a hunch, Kurt, so I'm not surprised."

We were walking down the hall now to my office. He was following, not saying a word. I was talking quietly to him. "I'm disappointed you didn't share this with me. I thought after that afternoon at my house, that wonderful afternoon, we both promised no more holding back, no more secrets, we'd share everything with one another. What happened to that promise?"

I was fuming and realized I had simply trusted this man too much. Trusting any man is bad news, my head was telling me. I should have learned that by now.

He pushed my door shut with a backward motion of his foot, came over and tried to put his arms around me. I turned and moved away, but he persisted and held on. "Look, Mags, when I come home to you, I just want to be with you and love you and not go over this shit all the time. Can you understand that?"

I said, "Don't try to schmooze me, you were playing big hero Rhett to poor little Scarlet here, and I don't appreciate it."

He sat in my visitor's chair, picked up an article I was reviewing, and started flipping through it to keep his hands busy, I guess.

I grabbed it, trying to soften my words, I said, "Kurt, go home. I don't care if home is my house or down to the dorm. I have work to do and I have to get over this stupid mood of mine now. Okay, what you did was not that terrible, and in your heart you were protecting me. I understand that. But don't you see that I felt silly in that restaurant knowing that even Nasty Nora knew about all the other incidents and the tie rod and I was kept in the dark?"

He stood up and looked at me in a distant way I was beginning to recognize. He turned to open the door, and then briefly closed it again. "Look, I apologized. I know you must have felt like an outsider there today. I didn't tell you, Mag, because I care about you." He yanked the door open as Sally walked by; he nodded to her and turned back to me. "I'm going downtown and get some stuff done at the apartment. I'll call a cab and talk to you later this week."

He walked away with a stiff back and shoulders, a look I had seen before. He was mad at me. Probably leaving before he said something more hurtful or that I would misconstrue.

At 2 in the morning he sat down at his computer and emailed Steve.

Damn women. She just doesn't get it!!! I thought once we got together everything would be fine, smooth sailing. Now she's pissed and I'm not quite sure why. Amazing how I had all the answers for you and now none for myself. Ignore all the

150

bullshit advice I ever gave you. She's been understanding and helpful and now after some of the stuff with the nurse dying and the accident, I'm scared for her. Hell, I'm scared for my own ass, too. She doesn't get it. She's pissed because she was not first to hear about a few minor things that happened. I didn't tell her, I forgot! Now she has this wild hair about coming into the hospital and snooping around. And my cool, distant chief, Rainey, is totally charmed by her. Furthermore, he agrees to her dumb scheme. He should know better, he's being an ass. I can't talk the two of them out of this and I'm really worried they'll do it. Shit, what a day! Kurt

Steve's reply a few hours later read: *Man, never even try to figure women out...brain will go into meltdown if you do. Let her snoop, you know the staff are not going to talk to her—keep an eye out for trouble, let her get in and out in a day and forget it. Keep me posted. Seriously, if you need help I'm here and have contacts down in D.C. if you need legal counsel. Keep your butt safe and hers, too, buddy. Sounds like you're both upset and wrong. Anyone would be with what you two are up against. The making up part will be good. I'm sure you both need to do some apologizing. Keep telling yourself she's a keeper. Buy her flowers, roses—big pink ones. If they work as good for you as they do for me—well you get the idea!!! Steve*

Chapter 28

I was upset at being treated like I was an invalid. I had been ill, but I was whole and healthy now. I wish Kurt had waited and not reacted so quickly, I think we could have worked it out. He has to realize I've been on my own for years and used to news—good, bad, whatever came along—I had to take. Someone shielding me brought out anger and my independent streak, when I guess I should have been grateful for his caring so much. This being a couple is hard for me to get used to.

The script I was working on was a blur. I couldn't concentrate. I had mail to answer and calls to make, but the frustration kept coming back. I really hoped he would call or come back. But the afternoon wore on, and the phone and hallway remained silent. I picked at my script, made a few notes. Then I started making more notes to myself on what I knew had happened so far at the Center.

Nothing, absolutely nothing was coming to me and I crumpled the second and third sheets of paper into the recycle bin. There was no connection, no clues, except for the dying comments from the nurse about a man with red hair on his arms. Holly's beloved Cooper has red hair on his arms and he's almost as tall as Kurt. There must be about a thousand other tall guys in this area who match that description. You can't investigate all of them.

Impatient to be doing something, I put in a call to Rainey at his office. He was not in; I didn't expect he would be. I left a message for him to call me at work or at home. Just before I left for day the phone rang.

"Maggie, Jules Rainey here, can I help you with something?" His carefully groomed monotone came over my speakerphone. "Or are you just looking for your long lost love? Let me see, according to my schedule he's off all day today." He was actually trying to be light and pleasant—amazing for this colorless man who the staff had nicknamed "the reptile" because of his unemotional approach to everything.

"No, Jules, he's at home doing whatever he does. I wanted to talk to you about lunch today. You saw some sense in what I said." I smiled at the thought that I had at least one person on my side and a pretty powerful one at that. "Why did you agree with me? If you can come up with some good reasons, maybe you can help me convince Kurt and the detective to let me pull this off."

"Maggie, let me say first of all, that on thinking it over at length after our lunch, I feel they may have a point. It would be too dangerous for you to come in here knowing that you would be putting yourself at risk and possibly Kurt, too. If anything happened to you, he would be the first person they would blame. He would never forgive himself if you were injured or worse. No, I think we're better off leaving it the way it is. The police will come up with something or we can hope that this madman will give up."

Oh no, I had lost my coconspirator. Now what? "Jules, listen to me, I don't think anything will happen to me if I get in there. All I want is a day, or perhaps two, just to talk to the nurses who knew her, look at the layout. I just may come up with some hint or suggestion for the police, for you, for Kurt. I'm looking at it as an outsider, maybe you all are too close to notice some things."

I was desperately trying to think of an argument that would convince this passionless, rational man. "Jules, you're going to lose a good surgeon if you don't help me. I know about the opening at the Center. I have a feeling you were seriously considering Kurt. I know the field is very narrow and to spend 5 years training the guy just to lose him to some two-bit country hospital in the boondocks because of this cloud hanging over him wouldn't make sense.

"Please, Jules, for your sake, his sake, and the good of the Center, just give me a day or two there to look around."

He didn't say anything for a long time. I was afraid he'd hung up on me while I was trying to convince him. Finally a deep sigh. I had hit pay dirt.

"Maggie, how would you be protected? I mean, we don't know anything about who's doing this. I really hate to take the chance just for you to talk to a few staff and snoop around a little."

"Jules, you don't want to lose him, do you?" I was almost jumping out of my seat. I knew he was weakening. If only he would stay on the phone a little longer I'd have him, I thought.

"Hmmmmm, Maggie, what type of procedure did we do on you in September, it was a aneurysm repair, right?"

I almost jumped out of my seat. I had him! I almost yelled into the phone, "Yes, Jules, you remembered, it was about mid-September. They did the angiogram the month before the heart valve surgery. Why? Can you think of a reason to readmit me?"

He was hesitant, but I could hear the wheels turning. "If you had an angiogram we could always say that we were admitting to check for a recurrence. It's not common, but enough to get you in here for a checkup."

"I don't care what it's for if it works. You and Kurt are not going to be doing anything to me, just looking me over. After a couple of days, you send me home with a clean bill of health."

"You need your heart guy, Kelly is it, or your HMO person to see you first. We do have to do it by the book, you know."

"Better yet, Jules, you telephone Fred Kelly. Say I was at lunch with you and some friends and complained. You feel I need a quick checkup and you want me to come there because you did the original procedures. He'll write a referral."

I was on a roll and barely able to sit still at my desk. The night cleaner in my office must have thought I was crazy.

The cold rational voice on the other end of the phone calmed me down. "Look, Maggie, you better talk to Kurt about this first. I'll call Fred and get this set up for you. But I'm warning you that if Kurt doesn't approve, I won't move a finger to do this. Do I make myself clear?"

"Oh, Jules, you're a doll. I know we can do this. Get started setting it up, and I'll get to Kelly and Kurt. You can tell him, too. Maybe coming from you, he'll listen. We can work out how I'll be protected later. Between you, Nora, Kurt, and the friends he has on staff keeping an eye out for me I think we'll be okay. I'll be very careful and keep my cell phone with me at all times. I know it's off limits at the Center, but I'd use it only for an emergency. Anyway, it's only for a day and a night. It may not help, but there's the outside chance it could."

"I think Kurt's lucky to have a woman who loves him enough to put herself in possible danger to protect him. He sounded distant, almost distracted. Then he repeated, "Very lucky, indeed." He hung up on that comment.

Poor Jules, he sounded sort of lonely. I think that cold, unemotional side of his was an act, and underneath he needed a Maggie, too. I was only going in to look around. Kurt knew when he first told me about the incidents that I helped and offered a slant he didn't think about. A fresh eye, that's what is needed here.

I left two messages for Kurt that evening. No return calls. I was hurt and deflated about the whole process by the early morning. But knowing his schedule and that he would be at work tonight late and tomorrow, I figured

Rainey would start working on him, and then I would follow up. Either way, we would convince him I could try for less than two days.

There was no call the next day from Kurt and this disturbed me. I had wanted to hear his voice and be reassured that he was not still angry. I knew he was brooding about my blowup after that lunch. I wanted him to know I was willing to forget the whole thing. I hoped we could work out our differences. I was even ready to drop the plan if he insisted.

I drooped home that night. I threw a Lean dinner into the microwave for five minutes. I was gingerly taking it out with hot pads as Kurt walked in the front door.

I called to him as if nothing were wrong. "Busy day, hon, you must be exhausted. Did you get any rest at all last night or did they have you hopping? I can fix something for you."

He appeared in the kitchen. This was not a happy man. In fact, this was a very angry and unhappy man by the look of his scowling face and cold, hard eyes. He was loud and as each word came it was like an emphatic ice bullet. "Talk about not discussing something with a loved one, Maggie? How about you? Was that little tête à tête with Rainey fun? Did you get him all hot and bothered to agree to this stupid little scheme of yours—this—this," he was sputtering he was so pissed, "grandstanding, that's what this is—hey, look at me, Nancy Drew. Guess you batted those baby blues at him and he just melted, right? He makes a hell of a lot more money than I do—I saw him looking at you at lunch the other day; little slimy looks he gave you while you were eating. That bastard is supposed to be my friend."

He stood over me, his face near mine, almost mocking me. "And just tell me, what do I do if something happens to you? How do I keep that off my conscience? I have one dead friend. She was a nice kid, and poof she's gone!" He gestured broadly with one snap of his fingers.

He turned and walked into the living room, strode toward the door then turned and mimicked sarcastically, "Oh, move over, Millie. Here's Maggie to share your grave!"

He looked back as he yanked the front door open. "Do what the hell you want, but I refuse to be a part of it. *Do you hear me, Margaret?*" he yelled, then walked out, and slammed the door so hard the glass rattled.

Kurt, upset and hurt, stomped across the lawn to his car, yanked open the door, got in, and sped away from the woman he loved and the place he was beginning to think of as home. He was as furious with himself as he was at Maggie. "Damn, I have to learn to control my temper." Distracted, he almost ran a red light as he thought, she really did go behind my back, but all that jealousy bullshit about Jules—she's not interested in him. I'm going to have to watch her every minute, stay close. That's going to be a problem—I can't be there every minute. If anything happens to her—she's the most important thing in my life—she's become the whole reason for everything I'm doing now.

I stood with the dinner burning through the towel, my hand shaking. I was stunned. He's been annoyed at me before, but never this bad. I could not recall hearing him yell at me this loud or in such a nasty tone. The dog was sitting and leaning up against me at this point. We were both shaken.

In my bed that night I cried, remembering our meeting, our funny and tender moments, even our misunderstandings. I remembered him in the kitchen eating all my Christmas cookies, and the dancing to Elvis in our underwear. He is so frustrating at times, so busy being in charge, he never lets anyone else help. I don't want him in jail, or even worse. Why didn't he understand that? Dammit, I'm determined to look and find out what I can. Even if what we have is over, and he never speaks to me again, if I can keep him out of danger, I'll be happy. His safety is more important to me than the relationship.

I got to the office early and telephoned Fred Kelly complaining of slight pain in the old aneurysm area. He got on the line and said, "Mag, Rainey called, said you had lunch together and complained to him. I want you in the Center early tomorrow morning, you hear me? This could be serious. Jules wants to do a few tests. No, don't wait until tomorrow, I'm getting you admitted now, for tonight. Get to the Center either this afternoon or evening, I'll see you there, bye."

He hung up before I had a chance to explain to him that this was an elaborate ruse for Kurt's sake. I was being shoveled into the Center now, whether I wanted to be or not.

I would see more hostility now from Kurt. But, technically, his last words were "do what you want," and I wanted to help him, dammit!

I got out of work, explaining the hospital recommendation. They were more than helpful getting me out the door. I packed my briefcase, no sense in letting quiet time go to waste when I could bill hours.

Chapter 29

Dr. Kelly called my referral into the Center and Rainey's office. I was packed and ready to go by early afternoon. I debated about what to tell Holly. She had spent so much time with me at the Center this summer and fall that I just knew she would blow up if she heard I had more problems. I reached for the telephone.

It rang as I touched it. It was Holly. "Mom, last night I got a strange call from Kurt and he was furious with you. Told me to tell you not to go over to the Center. You don't need any medical treatment, and you are being a fool about this whole thing. He seems pretty bent about Rainey and you flirting with him, seems convinced he's losing you. What's going on and why is he calling me?"

I wasn't exactly sure what I should say to her. "Holly, think of it as a fight between Kurt and me. The other day at lunch, I mentioned a slight problem in my surgical site. Dr. Rainey, the surgeon who did the original work, jumped to the conclusion that the aneurysm may have returned. He wants me in for a day or so for tests. That's all there is to it. But Kurt seems to be of a different opinion. I guess they are going head to head as doctors."

"But Mom, I thought you cared about Kurt. Why aren't you listening to what he says?"

"Long story, Holly. I trust Rainey, and believe me, I'm not flirting with him. He's very skilled, and he was my doctor. Fred Kelly concurs with Rainey. Kurt is jumping to conclusions about Rainey and me, he's jealous over nothing, and I think by now realizes it. Jules and I are friends, but I could never care about anyone like Rainey. Kurt's the only one in my life and always will be. I'll only be there for a day or two—don't even bother to come. I'll be home before you miss me, I promise."

She sounded a little panicky. "But Mom, suppose it's something more?

More surgery? Big or little surgery?"

She was genuinely concerned. I had to put her at ease. "Holly, Rainey is just being super cautious. Kurt's all for giving it more time. Don't fret, I'll call you."

She sounded relieved. "For heaven's sake, don't pick up any more doctors. We have them coming out our ears in this family with Cooper, Ivy, and now Kurt, who I really like, by the way." She was laughing as I finished the conversation with her and hung up. One more obstacle out of my way, now on to the hospital.

By the time I got to the admissions office it was snowing and sleeting outside. I had called and asked about parking. The lady in the admissions office told me where to put my car in the patient's parking lot. I then talked to Nora Feeney, and she also assured me she would gently let the 3rd floor staff know I was not to be disturbed. She would peek in from time to time at night and take my buddy, Mike Krantz, into our confidence. He was working dayshift and would be there for me. We decided not to tell him I was not ill—that would have been too much. Technically, I was there for observation and a test or two and I really could use the tests.

I was told my room would be ready on the third floor east. I took my small night bag and instead of waiting for a nurse, I started for the elevators. I saw Nora exiting with a crowd. She was with a tall girl with a head of curly dark hair. They were laughing. From the bone structure, posture, and timbre of their voices you knew they were mother and daughter. I walked over.

"Thanks for your help, Nora. I really..." I had glanced over at the young woman and was astounded to be looking into the pale eyes of Jules Rainey. There was no mistaking where they came from. Fortunately, these eyes were not cold. There was lightness and innocence in them, complementing her youthful good looks. It was a stunning revelation.

I stammered and finished my thought to Nora. "I really need your help and Mike's and hope this whole thing is over soon."

The young girl patted Nora's shoulder and left with a, "See you at lunch, Mom."

Nora looked at me and explained. "I'm back in today doing paperwork, the eternal hell for all administrators. That was my daughter, Connie. She's starting graduate school in the fall. I'm quite proud of her, Maggie."

She smiled as she watched the young girl disappear out the front door.

"I'm official, Nora, just going upstairs to 3 East."

"You're supposed to be in a wheelchair, or at least accompanied up to your room."

I smiled at her. "Nora, you're just the person to do that. Come on."

I punched the elevator button, and it slid open silently. We were the only passengers. I could not help myself, so I asked, "Just how long were you and Rainey married, Nora?" I kept my eyes straight ahead as I asked this question.

She replied quietly, "It was her eyes, wasn't it? Those pale blue eyes of his." She leaned against the wall as the doors opened and people got on.

We arrived on three, walked to an open seating area just beyond the patient wing, and sat.

"Not long, Maggie. We knew it was a mistake almost right away. The early 80s peace and love era was coming to a close. He was taking a surgical staff job here. I just finished nursing school. We were friends. We thought it would work somehow, but it didn't, right from the start. There were too many differences. He was from a Black family with money who resented me being poor and white. My family was an Irish Boston clan and racist as hell. I was a strict Catholic, and he was a hardheaded atheist. There were other differences too numerous to mention."

She stood and took my little overnight bag. "Let's just say we parted before Connie was born in Boston. He came here. I followed so she would have a father. Unfortunately, he was never a father to her; he barely saw the child. He has always been very, very generous with his money for her, but not his favors. I married Phil. End of story."

"Nora, this is your business and stays that way as far as I'm concerned. Even Kurt doesn't need to know."

"Jules asked Connie to come today for some family business papers to sign. I guess since his parents and brother are gone she's his only heir. They needed to take care of things. I didn't ask. None of my business now that she's an adult."

I looked over at her. "Your story, not mine. None of my business and it stays that way."

She smiled. "Thanks. I appreciate it." She then handed the bag to Mike, asked to speak with him later and I was settled into my room.

So Rainey has a few secrets, too. I guess we all do. Now I was beginning to see part of Nora's animosity toward anyone from a privileged background. I would love to tell Kurt about this but a promise is a promise. I changed and got into the bed.

I kept my cell phone plugged and charging near my bed. I was taking no chances.

Chapter 30

Food was being delivered, I shook my head at the tray lady and had her take it out before she even got all the way in the door. This time I had come prepared with cookies, fruit and dry soup mix. Since I was ambulatory, I could get a drink from the nurse's machine or go to the cafeteria. There were no dietary restrictions.

Nora sailed in later. "I spoke to Kurt a little while ago, Maggie. He was on the floor but he seemed distracted. I guess he'll be here hovering later. Poor man seems not himself today—worried, I guess."

That he was on the floor and did not come in hurt. That she said he was distracted made me feel good and bad at the same time. I was hoping he missed me as much as I missed him. At the same time I was concerned that maybe something had happened again.

I sat on the edge of the bed munching on an apple from my overnight bag. "Anything newsworthy here, Nora? Anything I may need to know?"

After her startling revelations earlier she was back to her old starched self. She surveyed my gown and peignoir set and picked at the towels on my washstand, folding them in what she perceived was a proper way. The peignoir was silk in a pale blue with long sleeves and a soft tie that closed in a bow over my chest and a ruffle on the very bottom. I like the way it floated around my ankles like a cloud.

"The same staff is not here at night. It's almost a complete turnover since you were here in September. I think I'll just stick close to this floor on my shift and help out. That way you will be covered."

I was looking at Nora closely, regarding her as a suspect even though she was helping with this plan of ours. I thought how she could easily pull the trick of marking dosages. Who knows what may be going through her mind. I think part of the reason she disliked Kurt was because he came from a similar background as her first husband. Things that hurt like that can stay with you. I thought she had the steel in her spine to kill. And who knows what she would do to protect her child if she perceived that someone was either intentionally or unintentionally putting the child in danger. Another piece of the puzzle, but where did it fit? What would Kurt know that could possibly cause harm to Nora or her child?

I finished my apple. "Mind if wander up and down the hall a bit and talk to the staff?"

"You're the patient and you're ambulatory, so do what you want. Within reason of course, Maggie." She turned and stiffly walked out.

We'll never be friends, I thought. She makes me uneasy each time I come face to face with her.

I wandered the halls and since it was visiting hours, I made good use of my time. I went up to the cardiac surgery wing and looked up a few of the nurses from last summer. There was only one I recognized and who recognized me. I did look quite different from the dumpy blonde with owl eyeglasses and gray in my hair I had before. He complemented me and we chatted a bit. I tried to draw him out about the problems but he either did not know or felt it not proper to discuss with a patient.

Walking back down the hall to the elevators, I saw the handsome Dr. Packard swing out of the nurse's station ahead of me. He was patting some nurse on her shoulder and laughing. I figured I would go for it. What could happen in the hall?

"Dr. Packard, I believe. I'm Maggie Suit. Someone pointed you out to me as one of the best and brightest residents in this hospital." I figured with his type, flattery would be best way to get acquainted.

His dark eyes looked me up and down and took in the attire. His immediate response was professional distance, but then memory clicked in at the name, I could see recognition. I was also glad the new peignoir was modest.

"Oh, yes, I remember seeing you. You're supposed to be Van Doren's latest conquest, I hear. For a bastard, he certainly can pick good-looking women, I must say." He moved a little closer to me as the complement rolled off his tongue automatically.

I deliberately batted my eyes and thanked him. We started down the hall together. "Someone told me, Vince, you don't mind if I call you that, do you?" I gave it my best shot, eyes batting, voice semi-simpering. It's plain disgusting what I can do when I have to, I thought. "You were in a fight with him. The way I hear it, you were terribly hurt? I hope you're all right now."

I laid my hand on the sleeve of his coat. Oh boy, was I laying it on. I was even making myself sick.

Wonder if he sees through this little act of mine? Egotistical people sometimes can be conned easier than ordinary folks because they think everyone perceives them as wonderful as they imagine themselves to be. He fell for it, I could tell.

"Now why would you want to know about that, Mrs.—?"

I interrupted. "Suit, Vince, Maggie Suit. But call me Maggie, why don't you?" We were in the elevator by now and when he pushed the lobby button, I asked, "Cafeteria, or are you leaving?"

"No, I'm on my way to drop off some papers in the office, but if you would care to meet me in the cafeteria, I'll buy you something cold, Maggie." He smiled.

I settled myself in the cafeteria. Looking around I noticed it was old, and the efforts to make it cheerful were few. The steam tables looked clear and clean and everything was carefully prepared but the overall effect of plastic flowers, outdated posters, brown linoleum floors, and faded yellow paint gave the impression no one really cared about this part of the building. The tables and chairs were old and wobbly. The only real plants on the windowsills were dying of thirst and drooping in their pots.

Vince appeared with two large iced drinks. He managed to brush my hand as he put the drink on my side of the table. "Now, what are you in here for, Maggie? Not another heart problem, I hope? Word has it you're still seeing Van Doren, but from what I see, you don't seem to be too attached to the idea yourself."

I replied to his obvious innuendo, "Don't be too sure about what you hear on the grapevine, Doctor. For all you know, I could be here spying on you right this minute." I had to know about seeing him in the restaurant that afternoon of our accident, so I added in my best perky voice, "But as it happens, I was spying on you earlier this winter at Mama Lucy's Italian place in Olney. I think I saw you there one night at the bar talking to two men. Little far out of town for you, isn't it, Vince?"

He brightened at the mention of the restaurant. "Hey, that's a great place to eat, isn't it? You must have seen me with my old school friends. They're brothers, and own a construction business out in the 'burbs. One lives in Gaithersburg and one in Olney, so I wander out on occasion and visit."

He smiled at me across the table. "As for the spying bit, someone as pretty as you could really get away with it, I'm sure. Were you looking to spy on me tonight, or are you just cruising the halls in boredom?"

"Just bored, having tests in the morning. Nothing serious, but Rainey asked me to come in to make sure my old problem hasn't popped up again."

I leaned forward in a conspiratorial manner. "But tell me, Vince, the nurses were talking the last time I was here about you and Kurt punching one another out. How he got really nasty and broke your nose. It looks fine now, but what caused such a thing to happen? I mean, a broken nose on a face like that would have been a tragedy." I tell lovely lies when forced to. Kurt was right, I could con folks.

"You're lucky you work with the best folks around here, and I can certainly tell there's no aftereffect." I sat back, batted my eyes, shivered in disgust, and sipped the drink slowly.

"Oh, that's between the good doctor and myself. He never knows when to keep his big nose out of other people's business. But from what I hear, he's being paid back in spades. I guess you might say that payback is hell." He smiled, but as he spoke his eyes were cold with unspoken anger. "Now that he's in hot water, I hope he sees how it feels."

Kurt watched from the door of the cafeteria as Maggie and Vince shared a table and conversation. Vince was leaning in smiling at her, talking. I now know how a stalker feels, slinking around, spying on someone, he thought. That asshole, Packard, of all the people she had to latch onto him. He's doing his best to edge me out, I can tell. What an egomaniac! Shit, she's what, ten years older than him? Whatever he's saying, she sure isn't buying it. I know that look of hers. Will the guy never get his goddamn hormones under control? Going to chase lover boy away. This should be fun.

Vince glanced up and stood abruptly. "Look, I gotta go. Things to do." His manner suddenly changed—he became more detached and professional. He walked away, leaving me sitting there.

Suddenly, a shadow appeared over the table. "Mrs. Suit, I believe? Don't you think it's time you got back up to the third floor? They'll be looking for you. Good night."

Kurt turned on his heels and walked out of the cafeteria without so much as a smile or nod, just that cold pronouncement. Oh, this isn't working out at all, he's still angry at me, I thought, as I watched his back disappear.

The light bulb came on then. Kurt was right. Packard did not go into details and none of the staff was going to talk to a mere patient about conflicts, gossip, and staff problems. What the hell was I thinking, coming here to snoop around? I took the elevator up two floors and walked down to my door just as visiting hours were called. I was back in my room reading when I heard a polite tap on the door.

As the ballplayer, Yogi Berra said: "*Déjà vu* all over again." A large handsome man with tousled brown hair, green eyes, and a crooked smile rapped on my door and then came into my room. I looked up at him and hoped he could see how much I loved him.

His demeanor remained professional as he said, "Maggie, I'm just here to get a little current information. We need to update what we have from September."

"Kurt, stop this stuff, hon, of course you know I was here. I met you here. What's with this formal stuff? We're alone. Can I have a hug if I admit that you were right and I was wrong? I'm ready to go home. I'm leaving in the morning as soon as they let me."

"Please, Maggie, let me ask you a few questions for Dr. Rainey. As you already know *he* is your physician, I'm just the resident on duty for this evening."

He sat stiffly down in the chair, took his pen out and started to ask me routine medical history questions. I was also embarrassed to be wearing a blue silk peignoir and asking for hugs like some cheap middle-aged groupie.

I answered as much as I could, but kept looking for any sign that he was just teasing me. My heart was pounding when he took my pulse, my heart valve was clicking so loud it sounded more like a clock. Pulling a stethoscope from the pocket of his lab coat, he stood up and came over to me. I just knew he was going to hold me and laugh at this whole scene. I leaned in to him as he placed the cold circle on my chest.

"Kurt, listen to me, I was talking to Packard just to see how annoyed he still is, or if he was holding a grudge. That guy really has it in for you. He told me he was out visiting some friends when I saw him. I didn't mention you at all. He claims they are old school chums, but you know darn well they didn't look like any school chum types to me, they looked like thugs. Honey, I think you were right this hospital thing is a bad idea."

He remained calm, professional and unperturbed by my comments. He checked my heart sounds front and back, felt my ankles for fluid retention, which I usually had. Asked a few more questions, then got up to leave.

He stopped at the door, turned, and said, "Maggie, I'm sorry about that flirting with Rainey crack, that was uncalled for. I have a bad temper and really lose it at times. My ex can tell you about it, probably one of the reasons why she's my ex. I understand you did this for me, but I didn't want you to put yourself at risk. I made myself very clear about it. I feel you went behind my back. Of course, now I realize why you were so upset the other day at lunch. You felt left out, betrayed, just as I do now. I think this has taught us that we don't know one another as well as we thought we did." He walked partway out the door then said, "I'm glad you're leaving in the morning. We can talk about this another time. I'm very busy here tonight. I have to leave." His tone was firm and deliberate. He left.

I realized what an idiot I was and that I wanted to leave immediately. I wanted him to take me home like he did the first time we wound up at dinner in Georgetown. Somehow, I had to get through to him. I picked up the phone and had the good doctor paged to apologize again. He was right. I was wrong.

Email to Steve: *It's hard to stalk the woman you love and get your damn job done at the same time. I spoke to her, but I kept it neutral, no yelling. I did apologize for my temper and some of things I said that was just plain irrational and downright stupid. But I am going to kick Rainey's ass for doing this and she ain't getting any roses, my friend. She was wrong, too, and knows it, she admitted to me a while ago. Glad I'm not rushing into anything with her. And I'm sure she's way too wise to jump either. I only hope we have something left to work on after the past two days.*

Return email from Steve: *Keep her safe. You did say she was a keeper, hardheaded tough lady, but a keeper.*

Chapter 31

He did not return my call. Instead Rainey showed up. I explained to him what the problem was, and he agreed that since I changed my mind he would arrange for me not to be disturbed. After an x-ray and one small test, he would see about getting me home in the morning.

"I guess I'm not that close to the staff, and I don't see how they interact with patients. Yes, it would not be proper to discuss hospital business with someone in here for treatment. I'm sorry, I didn't think of that myself, Maggie. We'll get you out as soon as we can. Sleep now. We'll work on this in the morning early."

As he turned to leave he remarked, "Maggie, I'll explain this to Kurt. I know it's disturbed your relationship." He slipped out and down the now darkened hallway.

I thought, *disturbed*, hah! It just plain blew it up in my face, that's what it did, Jules Rainey. I watched some TV hospital-style, and fell asleep dreaming of the guy with the green eyes and crooked smile.

Sometime later that evening, a nurse appeared and handed me a pill and water. He took my blood pressure and left.

The next morning, I was still a bit drowsy from the sleeping pill they had given me during the night. I was not sure what time the nurse came in. I did not request it, but I suppose it was part of the regimen I was supposed to be on.

I got ready for my first and last day at the hospital. I was scheduled for some tests for the aneurysm, so I was prepared for the squeak and wobbly wheels as a gurney pulled up outside my door.

A large pleasant man with a round face, glasses and wearing the standard hospital greens with surgical cap and booties arrived, complete with professional smile. "Are you ready for your first trip of the day, Mrs. Suit?"

He seemed pleased and anxious to help me as he pulled the gurney up by my door. "Do you need help?"

"I'm sure I can get up and get on that thing myself. You may have to steady me a bit when I sit down. Thanks."

I climbed off my own bed and moved over to the gurney. It was high and I had to hop to sit up on it. I wobbled a bit and the man helped me. As I lay down he tucked a sheet around me. Then he started to strap my feet.

"Now wait a darn minute, there, I don't need to be tied down. I don't fall that much. Just covering me up is enough. We can do without the restraints, thank you."

He continued to pull them tighter, and I began to panic. He was ignoring my protests. He started pulling the buckles over my arms, even as I fought him. I could see his arms and realized they were covered with coarse red hair.

"Hey, where's your badge? I thought you all had to wear them." A cold feeling in the pit of my stomach was making me sick. I kept moving my arms, struggling, and I managed to keep them apart as he tightened those straps. I had some wiggling room but now was scared, actually terrified. This is the guy—I'm sure of it. How does he know me? Is he really an orderly here, or just a hired someone to do me in? I started to holler for a nurse.

"I lost the badge to another overexcited patient like you this morning, Mrs. Suit. No one is going to question us going down the hall. You can holler all you want, they're used to it here, you know. Nora's been called off the floor, and the other staff don't know you." He was businesslike, abrupt, and efficient in pulling the covers up and getting me out the door.

"Nurse! Nurse! Help! He's taking me and he doesn't have a badge. I don't think he works here. Help me, help me!" I yelled. I wiggled and shouted as we went past the nurse's station. The orderly looked at them, smiled, and with one hand made a crazy motion.

"Hey, I'll sue, he's taking me without permission. Check your records. Help me! Oh God, help me get loose here! This isn't right. He's kidnapping me, please help!" I kept shouting long past the nurse's station. The man stayed quiet and kept pushing me along, smiling.

We were going down the hall. I knew all the hollering wouldn't help. I had to think of something, anything to get myself free. He was pushing me down a long corridor. I knew we were approaching another nurse's station beyond this door. It was still a distance away. I started working my hands free from the straps.

I made noise and started shouting again. More to keep him thinking I was still in a panic. Because now I had a plan—it was crazy and dangerous, but it just might work. The guy was no orderly, or he would have put the sides up on this thing. Thank heaven for his stupidity. I was fighting the straps and by now had my hands free. I kept them under the sheet at my sides, but continued to holler, move and squirm as much as possible. When he changed positions to pull me through, I was going to act. My feet were still tightly buckled. We went through the first set of doors with me yelling and the "orderly" calmly gesturing and smiling at people in the hall. This was the original old wing hospital and the swinging doors do not automatically open when approached.

From cruising the halls last night, I remembered that the next nurse's station was located at the end of the hall, with the doors right there leading to the elevators. I was going to have to act quickly, or face whatever this man had planned. That thought gave me courage. For once in my life, I was glad I was a sturdy female and not some tiny wispy little thing, since the plan hinged on my size. As we neared the station and the double doors, he again stopped, and walked towards my feet to open the swinging door. Closing my eyes, taking a deep breath, I made my move. Throwing off the cover, I worked the straps loose, and quickly heaved my upper body over the side of the gurney with as much force as I could muster. The stretcher, with me on it, went over on its side. I landed right in front of the nurse's desk.

I started hollering again at the top of my lungs. "Help, help! He dropped me. Oh, my back, help me, my back!"

I was lying on the cold tile floor. I fought the tangled sheet, pulled it partially off and started to wiggle my feet. I kept screaming and shouting, "He dropped me. I'm hurt, my back! I'm going to sue this place for hurting my back!! Help! Help!" I kept shouting.

We were near the nurse's station, and I could hear a commotion, then the sound of soft shoes running to the overturned gurney. Help at last. I yanked the cover off completely and realized the flimsy cotton gown and hospital robe were up over my head. The third floor nursing staff was now getting a good look at my rather flamboyant black lace underwear and hairy, bare legs. Oh nuts, no time to worry about modesty. Still strapped to the gurney I continued to yell until I could see several sets of legs and shoes.

A kind but firm voice warned me, "Don't move, ma'am. We're going to help you. We have to get another stretcher and get you on it. If your back is hurt, we want to make sure you're not further injured." Hands unbuckled my feet, the gurney was righted and moved away, and a blanket covered my more intimate parts that had been hanging out for public viewing. Voices asked, "Where's the guy who did this? Is he new? Where'd he go?"

I tried to speak in a normal voice. It was hard to do, as I was shaking so much my teeth were rattling. I knew outside of a few bumps and bruises and possibly sore back muscles, I was not hurt. All my physical therapy and working out this fall was paying off. But I had to keep them with me. I had to keep playing along. Concerned faces, black and white, male and female, now became part of the feet that had showed up to help.

"Listen, the orderly who was taking me down for tests, he didn't have a badge. I'm not sure he even worked here." I was looking around for the man with the red hair but he was gone. I guess in the confusion, he decided to quietly drift into the background.

"Now, sweetie, don't fret about the guy, he probably went for help," one nurse offered in an effort to calm me down.

"You don't understand. I think he was trying to kill me. Listen, my name is Maggie Suit—get Nora Feeney. No, she's not here now, is she, she's night." I was sort of babbling and thinking out loud in my fear. "Please get Dr. Van Doren, he's on duty, or Dr. Rainey, they're my doctors."

I guess I was making some sense, because one of the women left and I heard her talking on the phone, paging Dr. Rainey and Dr. Van Doren to the third floor west nurse's station. A stretcher was placed next to me. Several people reached down and lifted the whole thing and put me back up on the runaway gurney. As soon as I was stable, I started to sit up but was gently pushed back.

"Please don't move, ma'am, we don't know how bad your back is. What's your room number, do you know it? Allan, check her wristband, please, and get the room number and call that station for information. Did you notify Dr. V and Dr. Rainey, Cora?" The efficient nurse snapped out orders to the staff. I was relieved.

I lay there, trying to get my heart and breathing under control. I was safe, but for how long? Would he come back and try again? Where was he taking me? What was he planning to do to me? I stopped thinking about that—I didn't want to go there. I waited in the hall while the staff found my doctors and notified the other unit of my problem.

"Mrs. Suit, what have you been up to?" Dr. Rainey, ever calm and efficient, patted my shoulder and in an automatic gesture felt my wrist. He said, "I understand you caused quite a commotion here, falling off the gurney, hurting your back. We'll have to take you down to x-ray and have you checked out."

He looked at me steadily, and for some reason, I thought I could see a glimmer of glee pass over his usual somber face. I guess the idea of my falling off the gurney, losing my gown and dignity, was almost more than even he could handle. He was actually trying not to laugh. So is this the real Rainey, smiling down at me with a gleam in those pale colorless eyes of his?

"Allan, please help me get Mrs. Suit down to x-ray right away." He turned to me and with all the sincerity he could muster under this scary but hilarious situation said, "I'm going to walk right here with you, Maggie, just so nothing else happens to you on the way down."

He kept pace with the gurney, and I kept looking at him for reassurance. Paranoia was running through my system as high as my adrenalin at this point. I desperately wanted Kurt to show up. This orderly, Allan, and Rainey could be finishing the job that the man with the red hair started. I wanted Kurt. All of a sudden, I was not feeling very safe at all. I was frightened and suspicious of everyone and felt very alone.

Kurt had just finished up in surgery when his beeper went off, and the page was announced. He stripped off his gloves and a nurse handed him the phone. He flew out the door past a startled surgical technician, anesthetist and orderly.

He was calling to her in his head. Hold on, babe, I'm coming! He punched the elevator button—too slow. He turned and took the stairs two at a time. Workmen blocked the second-floor steps. He flew past them, sprinted across the hall, and grabbed an elevator marked UP just as the doors were closing. She's got to be all right; please, God, let her be all right. The nurse was so cool and matter-of-fact about her, it must be okay—has to be. Hurry, hurry, these elevators are so damn slow. All this bullshit of running around, I told her no one would talk to her. And dammit, she tried to apologize last night, but I had to play big silent and dumb, for what? Teach her a lesson? If I'd taken her right home, this never would have happened. Rainey's with her, she's in good hands at least.

Jules and the attendant rolled me to the elevators and the door opened on Kurt. He was wearing his surgical greens, cap, and still had one surgical cover on his shoe as he pushed out of the elevator. Rainey grabbed his arm, "Kurt, everything's fine. I was there. She took a spill in front of the 3 West Station, and they were kind enough to put her back on the gurney. Allan and I are taking her down to x-ray because she was yelling about her back."

Kurt looked at me with such concern and tenderness. I felt I needed to reassure him I was all right.

He leaned over and put his hands on my face. "You sure you are all right, babe? What hurt's you?" He turned to Allan, the orderly, and said, "Never mind, Al, I'll take her from here. She's family, and Dr. Rainey and I can take care of her."

It seemed the accident and page had changed the distant doctor into my

170

man again. I was shaking, but having Kurt near, I was calming down. Allan shrugged his shoulders and left us standing in the hall, the two doctors and the crazy lady on the gurney. I grabbed Kurt's hand and held on tight. "Hon, I think I'm fine. My yelling was just to get free of the guy that did this. Can we just go somewhere before the x-ray stuff? I need to talk to you both."

Rainey leaned over the gurney and whispered, "Did you see who did this?"

They maneuvered me into a waiting elevator. I lay quietly as we went down a floor and through a tunnel, then out to what looked like a suite of offices. I was pushed into a conference room.

Kurt hugged me once we got in the door. I was pleased to stay cuddled in his arms and would have happily forgotten to tell the story, but he let me go and pushed me over to a large coffee urn. "Do you want some coffee or tea? It's sort of cold in here, so keep the blanket around you. Now tell us, what happened, babe?"

He pulled a chair up, grabbed my hand, and held on. Rainey circled the conference table and took a seat across from me. He was tapping a pencil on the pad impatiently. I figured I better make it short and sweet.

Chapter 32

After explaining about the man who fit the description of the killer, my wild ride, and how I knocked the whole thing over, Kurt tightened his grip on my hand. He looked at me and then over to Rainey. "Okay, we have to stop right now. You've had enough! This was a damn dumb stunt you two cooked up and now look what almost happened!"

Turning to me he took my hand, kissed it and said, "No more, Maggie. It's too dangerous and all this was for nothing. The staff won't talk to strangers." He turned to Rainey as he said this, "Why didn't you figure that out, Jules? Or were you so fired up with snooping, you didn't think straight?"

"Oh, hon, you were right, and we were wrong. I realized it last night, and Jules was going to get me out of here early today. Isn't that right?"

He nodded, got up from the chair, and came over toward the conference room door. "Maggie had a close call, and she's right. I should have realized the same thing. Staff doesn't tattle to patients. I'm sorry we let this go so far, Kurt. Accept my apologies." He nodded to us both and quietly exited.

I sat wrapped in the blanket as we watched Rainey leave. I turned and started to tell him something when I was caught up in his arms. He held me tight, locked in a hug that was almost crushing. I leaned into him, the fear and fright I felt melting into his warmth and strength. I could feel his heart beating fast in his chest as I clung to him.

"Maggie, if anything happened to you I don't know what I would have done, believe me, I couldn't handle it." He kissed my forehead and murmured into my hair as he held me.

"I'm sorry I was so angry, but I just knew something would happen. I love you, babe, and I've not been more than 50 feet away from you since you've been here. You might say you had your own personal bodyguard."

We held one another. "This morning I was scheduled in OR, and couldn't break away." His kisses were now moving gently down my hair to my ear as he explained and apologized. He held my hand, and caressed it lightly with his thumb.

He moved away and said, "I hope after you get out of here this afternoon you'll wait up for me."

Our hands touched as he handed me the small cup of water and I downed the freezing liquid in one gulp. He held his small cup of water, looked down and said, "If I keep thinking about tonight, I'd be better off pouring this on myself."

We both laughed, and it seemed to help ease our tensions. The next hurdle we had to face was getting me back upstairs. The gurney I was sitting on had a wobbly wheel. He opted for a wheelchair right outside the admissions office.

I slid off the table, rewrapped the blanket around me and hopped into the chair. We started out for 3 East.

"I gave Rainey Holly's phone number," he said as he pushed me toward the elevator, "and we agree you're being released immediately. She's going to want an explanation of this whole hospitalization thing, and you tell her what you want her to know, I don't care. But for now, I'm going up to your room, we're shutting the door and staying put until she arrives. You're in no shape to drive home. I'll leave my rental here tonight, and bring yours home with me. I have the spare key to your car.

Twisting my head and speaking quietly as he bent forward, his face near mine, I replied with more bravado than I felt, "Why don't you drop me off, tell the nurses no visitors, and get back to work. This has cost you a good couple hours and I'm sure you're behind now. I'm fine, hon, nothing happened and Holly's on her way. Tell you what, when you leave, I'll prop the hard chair under the doorknob like they do in movies, and won't let a soul in until I hear her voice, how's that?"

We arrived on 3 East and he maneuvered me into the room. I got up and declined his offer of help to the bed. Trying to maintain a sense of dignity, but looking at this man I loved more than anything in the world, I said quietly, "Go catch up, then try to get off at a decent hour. You know I'll be waiting for you."

He brushed my lips with his ever so lightly. "Babe, no more snooping around, and promise you'll keep the door shut, or I'm not moving."

"Hey, I promise."

He grabbed the small armless chair, lifted it high in the air over my bed like it was a toy and put it near the door. "Now, when I leave get this jammed up here. I want to hear you do it from the other side. And remember, not even a nurse, we don't know who's pulling these stunts. I'm telling them you're being discharged. I'm rescinding all orders written for you including medications, so no one really should bother you until Holly gets here."

He started for the door, turned and said, "Take care, babe, love you, now let me hear that chair."

Kurt sprinted down the hall and got a *no visitors* sign. I heard him put it up and leave.

I lay down on the bed, pulled the covers up and thought about my close call this morning. One thing I know, this red-haired guy is no nurse, orderly or member of the staff. Putting up the side rails would have been automatic for a professional (and I probably would not be here now, I think). Another piece of the puzzle. How does he get in? Where did he get the uniform? He obviously knew where he was going, so he must have worked here at one time? Doing what? Where? I should call Detective Walters and let him know about this. Maybe Kurt's already done that. My mind was going too fast. I promised Kurt I would not snoop any more, but at least we could add these tiny pieces to our puzzle.

Chapter 33

I must have slept. I woke up when I heard the sound of the lunch trays. Oh good, I thought, I have a perfect excuse not to eat that awful food. But my stomach was reminding me that dinner last night was a long time ago, and these were lunch, not breakfast trays. I got out of bed, went to my case and rummaged around. A package of cheese crackers, some graham crackers, another apple—that should be just fine until tonight.

Tonight, oh yes, Kurt said he would be home tonight, and I wanted it to be a special homecoming. I'll fix a great dinner with candles and some of that nice wine he brought me. I smiled to myself, as I munched the crackers and made plans.

The phone rang and I sat up to answer it. "Holly, did you hear from Rainey? When are you coming to get me?"

"I have to stop by Rockville first, that Hart building. I have some paperwork to drop off. So it will be an hour or two before I get there. Your wooden surgeon friend, and Kurt, both called me to come get you. What's going on? Tests finished so quick?"

"Yes, I'm finished and I can go home. I can't drive right now. Kurt will bring my car home tonight. I can drive him here in the morning, or afternoon, whenever his shift starts."

"Are you all right? I mean did they find anything? I guess not, since you're coming home so soon." Holly sounded pleased.

I pulled the phone over toward the bed covers and said quietly, "Holly, there's been a problem. Not with me, I'm fine, but I need to talk to you when you get here. Let's stop for late lunch on the way home. I'm not eating this hospital garbage, and I'm starved. Don't say anything now, just get here."

"Should I bring reinforcements from the lab?" She was referring to Cooper, who at 6 feet 3 inches can look intimidating, even though he's a

175

gentle, bookish man.

"Not on your life, just you and me, and some decent food will be fine. Cooper can happily play with his rats all day."

Holly's voice dropped an octave to match mine. "Is it serious? I mean is Kurt in trouble or anything?"

"I'll tell you over lunch. Just get here, I'm starving!"

"I'll be there as soon as I can." She hung up.

I popped the first of the cheese crackers in my mouth. A decent lunch would hit the spot. Putting the phone back, I picked up some work and started to reread what I had done. I still needed that glossary of terms and it should be better organized. I got out my red pen. A knock on the door startled me, then I heard Kurt's voice outside.

"It's me, and I have Detective Walters here. Can we come in?"

I jumped off the bed and pulled the chair away from the door handle. From the grim expression on their faces, I knew something else had happened. As long as Kurt's safe, I don't care, I thought as they crowded my shabby little room.

Walters sat in the guest chair, and Kurt and I sat on my bed. He put his arm around me, his expression showed it was going to be serious.

"Gentlemen, I give up, what happened to bring you both to my hideout on a gallop?" I was purposely trying to be flip to see if I could lighten the mood.

Kurt tightened his grip on me and said, "Mags, they found the guy with the red hair."

"Great, maybe he can tell you what's going on. Is he a sicko, or just a stooge for someone else—a hired gun?"

Walters leaned forward and spoke. "We don't know. He's dead. Found out behind the dumpster with a tourniquet wrapped on his upper arm and a shot of something about halfway in. Looks like he was a junkie or ex-junkie going back on the stuff and shot up something that was a little too hot for him to handle. He was a part-timer here, and I thought we had an alibi on him."

He sighed and straightened out, leaning back in the chair. "We're not sure where the stuff came from that killed him, but since this *is* a hospital, one good guess is he got it here."

"Or someone gave it to him to shut him up." Kurt was talking to us in a distracted way.

"Oh good, now you're being blamed for this, I suppose." I sounded defensive, leaning against his warm body on my bed. I looked over at Walters sitting slumped in the chair. "Did you find Kurt's wallet, his driver's license, hospital badge, and tags off his car next to the body, by any chance?"

"No one's blaming me, I was in the OR completely surrounded by a

176

whole surgical team late this morning after I left you. At the last minute, Rainey bowed out and asked me to work with a new resident on a rather routine procedure so, for once, I'm in the clear." He kissed the top of my head in a rather offhanded manner.

"How about you, Mrs. S? Were you out of this room at all after the good doctor stuck you in here with the no visitors sign?"

"Walters, you heard what happened from both men and the nurses at 3 West. Do you really think with that creep running loose around this hospital I was about to go out and wander the halls?"

I shivered as I remembered the trip down the hall then said, "Detective, that Packard's such an obnoxious ass. Did you check him out carefully? I mean, he holds quite a grudge, and it seems from talking to him last night that he's simply delighted with Kurt's predicament. And Kurt and I saw him with two men at a bar the day of our accident. The two men looked just like criminals to me. He told me they were old school friends, some friends! It wouldn't take much for him to set this thing up. Maybe the murder was accidental. Not that it can be dismissed, but he may not have planned it to go that far."

After giving Chet Walters this information on Packard, I straightened my peignoir and noticed Kurt was absently playing with the bow on my right sleeve. He seemed distracted. He was thinking of something, his body was here, but his mind somewhere else.

"Something on your mind, hon?" I asked.

He looked at me and answered slowly, "No, something Walters just said. It flew in and out of my mind, and I can't remember what it was. No matter, I have to get back soon, as I have bodies of my own piled up and waiting."

He dropped my sleeve, smacked his knees with the palms of his hands, and stood up. "When is Holly coming for you? I really want you out of here, now more than ever."

"She's practically on her way. She has one obligation, and she'll be here. Thanks for the bad news, fellas. I'll lock up when you leave."

"I'll wait to hear the chair on the door," a sober-faced Kurt said to me as the two of them walked out.

I did as he asked. He listened, mumbled something, and then the hall was silent. I could hear visitors, soft rubber wheels going up and down outside, but I never thought to look. I must have dozed off trying not to think of this morning but the romantic things I planned for the wonderful evening ahead.

Chapter 34

A sharp knock woke me up. "Mom, it's me. Can I come in? I have Dr. Rainey here with me."

I got off the bed and pulled the chair away. Holly came in, followed closely by Rainey. Holly looked nervous. Her eyes kept darting to Rainey.

"Stop fidgeting, Holly, I'm safe. I suppose, Jules, you've been filling her in on what happened and now she's scared silly. To update you two, Kurt and Walters were just here and told me about the guy with the red hair being dead out by the dumpsters."

I picked up my clothes and went into the bathroom to finish changing. That chore finished, I started folding up the peignoir set. Holly continued to look at me in a strange way.

"I'm here to take both you and Holly home, Maggie. I have taken the afternoon off, and plan to spend some time with you. Now if you don't mind, stop fooling with those clothes, just jam that stuff all in. Holly, help her why don't you?"

He turned to Holly, and she complied so quickly I was amazed. She started sweeping things into the little case—dropping bottles, papers, and my precious report. She whipped open the clothes closet, and checked in there. All this time Rainey was leaning against the shut door, his hands in his pockets, watching us with cool blue eyes. I began to feel a little like I did this morning when he was walking me to x-ray, uneasy and no reason for it.

"He's got a gun in his pocket, Mom," Holly said as she pulled the case shut and turned to stare at this handsome man, who until a few minutes ago, I felt was a friend. I was shocked and scared. My thoughts flew to Kurt.

"Where's Kurt, have you hurt him or taken him, too?"

"Such loyalty, Maggie, I admire it. But, no, I haven't seen him. He's safe, and you will be, too, if you do as I ask. The gun is very small but it can kill just as effectively close up as a larger one. And I think we can safely say you and Holly are going to be close on our way out the door. Now, Holly, get a wheelchair for your mother, rules, you know, and remember what I told you."

She complied and was back with a chair and a nurse in about one minute. Rainey dismissed the nurse with a wave explaining he would personally see to his friend, Maggie, and her lovely daughter.

"Did you say something to the nurse, Holly?" I asked.

"No, Mom, he told me what he would do to you if I did. I acted as natural as I could." Turning to Rainey she said, "You bastard, I'd like to bash your pretty face in right now."

He gave her that famous reptilian smirk that passed for a smile. "Now, Holly, there's no need to be vulgar. I'm sure your mother taught you to be a lady. Grab the wheelchair, and push your beloved momma out the door slowly. Wave nicely, Maggie, as we go past the nurse's station."

I obeyed orders. I somehow knew if he could kill a man this morning, and that poor girl in December, he would have no qualms with my child or me. We were stuck. I was in fear for her life and she in fear of mine. He had us trapped by mutual fear for now.

I could tell Holly's mind was racing. I hoped when we got downstairs we could think of something, or holler, anything to get this over with. Oh God, maybe Walters and his troops were still there with the dead man. Or maybe Kurt is out of surgery by now and looking for me. Something, anything to get us out of Rainey's grip. The gun was small but lethal and scared the hell out of me.

"Pull up to that water fountain, Holly, it's time for your mom's medication. Something mild to put her in a sleepy, cooperative frame of mind. You take one, too, my dear." He gestured to her to take the vial of pills in his hand.

"Now both of you will be easier for me to handle in the car and at home. Thank you for being so cooperative, ladies."

His smile gave me the shivers. It was amazing to think that this man was the person we had thought was his friend. Why was he doing this to us? I must have found out a little too much with my snooping, or he just feels like killing someone again because he's crazy.

I spoke. "Jules, you're supposed to Kurt's friend. Yet all this time you were undermining him, causing these problems. Why? What did he do to you?"

I kept asking questions that got no answers so after a few moments I shut up. I wondered what this handsome snake had done that Kurt knew about. My mind was racing along and coming up with dead ends. All I knew was that I swallowed a pill and maybe it was cyanide, and I would be dead in a moment or two. I fixed my eyes on Holly, thinking at least I would go out looking at my beautiful daughter.

"Now in here, ladies, just for a few minutes until the pills make you two more relaxed and in a better frame of mind." He pointed to a door and Holly carefully pushed the wheelchair inside a small examination room. It had been used recently. There were half-empty coffee cups on the side table, markings, and charts on the small green board on the wall.

Rainey smiled and with more force in his voice said, "Maggie, stay in the chair. You'll be glad you did soon. Holly, if you feel sleepy or faint, just sit down right next to your mother."

She sat down heavily. I could tell the pills were affecting her fast. I felt the effects too, heaviness and drowsiness. I settled into the comfy wheelchair. Just a little nap would not hurt. Rainey was really being rather thoughtful about this whole thing, not cruel at least. Whatever he decided to do could wait until after I took just a little catnap, I figured. I slept.

When I woke up, Holly was gone and Rainey was staring down at me. "I don't see what Kurt sees in you, Maggie. When you sleep you snore, and you certainly do look your age with your hair all messed up like that and no makeup on. He really should find someone more attractive than you. I wonder if he's ever thought of a younger woman, someone completely different."

He was scary and now he was pissing me off. Kurt and I were perfectly content with our ages and faces and snoring and all that comes with loving and being human together. I then remembered something and said, "You mean more like your daughter, Jules?"

"Your brain is good, even if your looks have slipped with age," he replied in a cold voice.

It took a real effort to look up at him as he encouraged me to stand. "You know, Rainey, you're full of shit. I'm just the woman to say it. Your kid needed you, and all you did was throw money at her." I heard myself say drunkenly. "Now, let me give you a piece of advice, buddy boy—" I wiggled my finger at him.

Ignoring my rambling, he interrupted. "Maggie, try to walk in front of me now. We're going out to the parking lot, and I don't want to have to explain your behavior." He hesitated then pushed me back in the wheelchair as he said, "Never mind, this isn't going to work, stay put. I'll wheel you out."

He started pushing me carefully towards some parking lot I could see. In a conversational tone, as if he was discussing the weather he said, "Holly was nice and cooperative and is all snug in the backseat of my car, handcuffed to the seat. You're going to join her now."

With that gun in his pocket scaring me, I tried to concentrate on where he was taking us. It was hard to think straight. We passed two professional-looking men and Rainey smiled and put them off with promises to come talk to them later in the day, but explained first he had to help his friend to her house after minor surgery. They smiled, waved and walked on.

He nodded at a tall good-looking woman with curly brown hair. I tried to signal her but my hands were too heavy.

We stopped at the side of a sleek, silver convertible with the top up. Some kind of sporty sedan type of car. I was much too drunk to figure out the make and model, but somehow knew I really should. However, it was just too much effort now.

With me safely inside and handcuffed to Holly, I had enough sense to check her breathing. I was relieved to find she was curled up peacefully, wrist stretched out with the cuff locked, as Rainey indicated. I was handcuffed to Holly's free hand and my other hand was handcuffed somewhere on the seat. I suppose, I thought to myself, with no hands free we were safe to drive wherever. I was so sleepy at this point. I just drifted off resting on Holly's hip.

I don't know how long I was asleep, but I remember opening my eyes briefly and thought I was in a garage, and Rainey was unlocking Holly's cuff and pulling her out of the car. "I see you're fighting the pills, Maggie, don't do that. Holly will be fine. I'm taking her inside and upstairs. You two will be back together in about 10 minutes, I promise you."

He left with an almost comatose Holly stumbling and mumbling on his arm. I noticed that Rainey was a strong man to maneuver her so easily. He'd need that strength to get me upstairs, I drunkenly giggled to myself.

Chapter 35

He struggled, but got me up the stairs. I was barely able to stumble along and don't remember much after climbing what looked like Mt. Everest. When I woke up and my head started to clear, I realized I was in a small sunny bedroom with cheery yellow wallpaper, old-fashioned white furniture, and a yellow throw on the bed I was napping on. I saw my baby, Holly, asleep on a chair beside the bed. She was facing forward and almost on her side, her mouth was open, her skirt was hiked up, and her shoes off. Her head turned to face me like she was trying to tell me something. She was definitely asleep and the position looked terribly uncomfortable.

We were still handcuffed together. The catch was Rainey had handcuffed me on the bed, pulled my arm through the ironwork at the foot, and handcuffed Holly to the other side. We were, in effect, together on different sides of the white cast iron bed frame.

My foggy brain began to clear. I was still drugged, because the only thing that popped into my mind was the famous Laurel and Hardy line: "Well, Stanley, this is a fine kettle of fish you have gotten us into." I kept picturing Stan the luckless looking dope, scratching under his hat at Ollie all puffed out with indignation. I sort of snorted and giggled at the thought. I need to sober up here.

I had to get Holly up and thinking for us. She was faster, and smarter, and I just knew she would come up with an answer to this mess.

I jiggled the handcuffs. "Holly, wake up, it's Mom, come on, Holly, wake up for heaven's sake, we're in trouble here. Holly!" I hissed and shook my end of the cuffs, which made her arm flop.

"What time is it, Mom? No school today, too sick, have cramps." Holly was waking up but the drug still had hold of her. She was back in school.

"Mom, I'm up, I'm up."

182

"Holly, think clearly now! You're not in school, you're here with me in a locked bedroom God only knows where, with a crazy person outside the door or downstairs. Holly, do you hear me? Do you understand me? Holly, wake up for heaven's sake!" I continued to shake the handcuffs. I was beginning to hurt myself.

She was waking up. I could see her eyes clearing as she sat up. "Oh, Lord, Mother, but I'm stiff. How long was I sleeping, do you know? This is a bad dream isn't it?" She looked around and blinked.

"Guess not. Did you figure out where we are yet? How the hell did you get us into this? What's that guy want with us? I thought doctors were supposed to be so trustworthy and helpful."

She was angry, and scared, too. I gave her the abbreviated story of what happened this fall and now that I knew it was Rainey I wondered, *why*? "I think Kurt will get it too if he tries hard enough. He was sitting on the bed in my room when Walters mentioned the dead guy's alibi and it just hit me now Rainey was it—he claimed the man was working in his office or nearby when it happened. Rainey was this guy's alibi. Kurt must have been trying to remember that. Rainey and this guy must have been working together."

"That's all good, Mom, but now you're telling me we're stuck together with these things on." She shook our mutual hands as she talked. "We have a madman running around this place who killed two people and is getting ready to kill us. We don't even know where we are. No one else probably knows where we are either. What are we supposed to *do now*? Is this candid camera or are you and that nutsy doctor of yours playing me for another patsy? No, not kidnapping and guns, even you're not that crazy."

She looked at me as she said those last words so loud I'm sure Rainey heard it wherever he was in the house. She said quietly, "That monster is probably stirring up a pot of fava beans and humming to himself about dinner. You got us into this so figure a way out, *now!*"

"Hey, I was figuring on you doing that. A way out, I mean. Anyway I'm so scared, I have to pee, and it's all I can do to hold that in and all I can think of now. I wonder if I yell at Rainey, if he'll let me go."

"Now that you mention it, Mom, I could do with a good whiz myself. Start yelling and I will, too, let's see what happens. I don't relish sitting in a puddle here. Someone went to a lot of trouble with this room and I'd hate to mess it up."

She looked around and was actually admiring the pale cream drapes, the chair she was in was yellow silk as was the coverlet on the bed I was attached to. I struggled to sit up.

"Holly, this is no time to admire his decorator. I have to sit up now, move with me on this, I'm getting a cramp. Come closer, good, now I can really yell." Which I proceeded to do. "Rainey! You have two women in here who have to pee. Let's go, Jules, one at a time, or both together, or your sunshine room here will be awash in it. Come on, mister, open up! Rainey, where the hell are you?"

Right behind me, Holly started with an imitation. "Hey, Doc, we need a diaper change. Get up here, mister, we have to go!!"

We stopped to see if we would get a reaction. I heard someone coming up the stairs. Good, we are on the second floor at least. But where? On whose second floor? The damn door was unlocked. He simply opened it gently and walked in.

Completely unflustered, he looked at us and said, "Ladies, one at a time. Remember, I do have the gun here. If either of you try anything the other gets punished, remember that. I'll unlock first one, relock, then the other, do I make myself clear?"

"Yes, yes, Rainey, but hurry up. And me first, I don't have the control after 3 babies that Holly has, so let's go!" I squirmed on the bed.

He did the unlocking and locking routine and we both were greatly relieved of at least that burden. It was embarrassing to pee in from of him, but I kept reminding myself he was a doctor. A murdering bastard, but a doctor all the same. And he did turn his head politely. When it was all over he left us locked in our old position, closing the door and going back downstairs.

"Shame this room has its own bath. I was hoping to get a look at the place, Mom, how about you?"

"Yeah, thought about it. He has some nerve. The man didn't even bother to lock that door."

"Mom, he has all the marbles, so I guess it's his game right now. Come on, we have to do something. What time is it anyway? It's dark outside." She twisted her arm and looked at her watch. "We must have really been out. The last I looked at a clock when we were leaving with Rainey the Ripper it was 3:30."

"I just thought about Kurt and Cooper. You were due home and Kurt and I had a sort of special evening planned since we were making up."

"Don't spell it out for me please. It's bad enough to realize you know about such things, I can't think about it!" She shuddered with disgust.

"Forget my sex life, girl. Listen up, those two men are not going to know where we are, number one. They're going to start calling and finding out we are both gone, number two. Then comes some snooping, and they find out we left with Rainey, number three. I hope Kurt can get to number four, which is

184

calling Walters. I know I saw some doctors in that parking lot when Rainey was pushing me to the car. They'll remember he left with us. Now, if we are at his house maybe Walters, Kurt and Cooper will come crashing in here and save us."

"Or Rainey will serve us for supper. Mom, face it, he's crazy. He's not going let us live until Scooby and Shaggy figure it out and get to the cops. He's in the cellar now probably digging holes six by two, side by side. We've got to help ourselves. Now tell me if I'm wrong, but are those iron flower thingies on the bed wide enough for me to squeeze through? I mean, if I can get my head through, maybe I can pull the rest of me to your side. When kids are born that's the big problem, isn't it, the head? Come on, let's try it."

We maneuvered and twisted until she finally managed to push her head carefully through the iron bars. I was almost crying out with pain at the contortions.

"Stop, stop, I'm dying here, get your head back. It's too painful. It's not going to work, Holly. Your head gets through but I think we need more room to get other parts of you to follow. We need a crowbar or something to pry these things or bend them at least. Even if we could move them a little, it would help."

"Look," she said, pulling her head gingerly back through the bars and giving my wrist some relief, "you lift weights and I'm a workout nut, maybe we can bend this ourselves? I mean, it's an old bed, let's give it a try." She lowered her voice as if Rainey were outside the door.

"We can try, but it looks pretty sturdy to me. The old ones are so much better made than the new ones."

We tried and with huffing and puffing and pulling we simply couldn't budge the bars an inch. We were both exhausted, feeling the effects of the earlier drugs, and frightened but not talking about it. We kept at it and then to make matters worse, the mattress on the bed started sliding off.

We stopped, panting, trying to catch our breath; the mattress was half off the bed by this time. I looked down at where it had started to slide. I saw what I figured was our salvation. "You know, Holly, this happened at home one night with Kurt and me—this mattress thing." I laughed thinking about how funny that was.

"Oh good, reminiscing about your sex life again, no way, stop! I refuse to hear this crap, Mom, I'm warning you."

"Oh, we were in bed reading poetry, as I recall, Keats, Shelley, Kipling—no matter, and the world started to tilt." I gestured to her to come closer as I moved gingerly to a squat on the box spring. I kept working the mattress off the bed while talking to her, she started watching me intently.

"The poetry reading progressed, but I noticed the world kept tilting on its axis and I finally managed to get Kurt's attention."

I kept moving the mattress slowly inch by inch looking at Holly as she watched intently. "'Kurt, dear,' I said to him, 'I think the earth just moved for me.'" I related the story as I continued pushing at the mattress slowly. It slid silently to the floor. She kept watching me. "He looked down at me, from his book, of course, and said, 'No, sweetheart, the mattress fell off our bed.'"

She watched as the coverlet and the bottom of the stately old iron bed started to show just below the box spring. I carefully and quietly moved the spring as far up the bed as I could. Holly was now pushing with me, and grinning. The decorative design curved out at the bottom and the tips were not attached to the bottom rail in the middle of the footboard. There was not much room, but with our combined strength I just knew we would be able to lift the box spring up and over the lip of the bed edge and get the ivy or flowers on one of the bars to bend enough for Holly to make it through to my side. We could not make noise or Rainey would visit us and we didn't want that now.

It was a plan, not a good one, but the only one we had so far. We started quietly doing our workout on the bedpost. There would be pain and possibly some damage to Holly's back involved, but worth it if it worked.

Chapter 36

Kurt smiled to himself as he pulled into the driveway. Maggie promised to be home, and knowing her, she would be planning a special evening for the two of us. She can be quite creative, and I know whatever she has in store will be worth the rush home. He sort of pushed through the whole afternoon thinking about the evening.

Pulling up in front of the house in Maggie's car, he noticed complete darkness. Must be something with candles and body oils, I'll bet. His body heat started rising in anticipation as he jumped up on the porch and in the front door.

"Maggie? Babe, I'm home. Where are you? Upstairs?" Stupid was running around wildly at this point and asking to be let out. No answer.

"I'm letting the dog out, but let me know if you need anything down here before I come up." Quiet, no sound. Just Serge, the cat, on the landing, blinking at the sudden light.

"Maggie, where the devil are you? Come down here this minute, or I'm coming up and spoil your surprise, babe," he called up the stairs and still no answer. He got the dog settled. Taking the steps two at a time, he got to the top landing. Complete darkness and the feeling of emptiness in the house—abandoned.

"Mag, this isn't funny. Where are you?" He started opening doors and turning on lights. No, Maggie. Damn! I just knew she'd be here, it's our big night. She promised me. "Maggie, if I find this is one of your stupid little jokes, I don't appreciate it, sweetheart," he said in a teasing voice.

The phone rang. Kurt snapped on more bedroom lights, crossed the floor, and answered her phone. "Maggie, is that you? Where the hell are you?"

"Cooper here, Kurt. I was just calling to ask you the same thing. Holly was supposed to be home and she's not. Dog was not out. No dinner, lights out. It's like she left this morning and hasn't been back. Think they're together?"

"Hell, if I know, the same thing here. Maggie was due home from the hospital. Holly was to bring her sometime around 3 or 4 o'clock. Coop, I don't like this."

Icicles of fear started in Kurt's stomach and moved up and down his spine. "Cooper, there have been some weird things going on in my life that have spilled over to Maggie. Now I think it's spilled again and taken Holly with it. Get over here as fast as you can. I'm calling a friend of mine on the D.C. police. And if you have a gun, a handgun, bring it."

"Kurt, what the hell is this all about?"

"Dammit, Coop, just get over here and hurry!" He slammed the phone down, pulled his cell phone out, and dialed Walters' home number. No answer. He tried the precinct house, and was told the detective and his partner were both out. No one knew when they were due back.

Kurt started to think and pace while waiting for Cooper. Can't let fear and panic get me. Get a hold of yourself and starting thinking like the cops, cold and logic here.

He pulled the cell phone out and called the hospital's admitting office. Identifying himself, he asked about Mrs. Suit's papers and what time they released her. He was told there was no release, and that she had left unexpectedly without notifying the admissions office.

Who I need here right now is Rainey, Kurt thought. The man is made of ice, and could really handle this better than I can. I'll call down and see if he's still at the Center. See if he knows what's going on or saw Maggie and Holly.

The call proved fruitless. He asked to be transferred to Pat Sewell, the resident on duty in his area. She said Rainey had signed out early before 3 o'clock. She remembered because he motioned something about not feeling well. She was so shocked at Rainey taking off sick, she remembered it.

Kurt was totally frustrated by now. "Pat, give me his home number, do you have it?"

Pat, being sarcastic, replied, "Even if I had it, policy says no numbers, you know that. I can give you his cell number, we all have that."

He tried speed dialing the man's cell number and got no reply. He really must be sick. A first for the reptile, or was he missing, too?

Next, he telephoned the nurse's station on 3 East. No one saw her. As luck would have it, no one was doing a double shift that night either. All they could tell him was what the day people explained to them, that she left with her daughter and Dr. Rainey was with them. He pushed her out in a wheelchair. Her room was empty, but no paperwork on her release was filed. They were concerned as well.

Something was in the back of his head, something about Rainey and this morning. About his schedule and Rainey's. No, Walters' comment about the dead guy. He was so upset now he could not think. Again, something Walters said one time about Rainey's office or area, it kept eluding him. I have to concentrate here. Maybe it will come to me.

Cooper came through the door at that minute, looking like the wrath of God. His tall frame was stiff with anger, and his manner was definitely threatening. "If you've put Holly and Maggie in danger with some stupid scam of yours, I'll never forgive you. I don't know what you want with a gun, but it's in the car. Not loaded, but I brought ammo just in case. Guns mean something very serious, man. What the hell is going on? Where are they?"

Kurt grabbed his jacket and hustled both of them out the door. "Look, I'm as in the dark as you are about where they are. But I'll fill you in on the story that I think may be part of this. I'm heading down to Georgetown and the Center. I think we need to be there to get answers and I may need your help."

They went out to Maggie's little red car and on the way out retrieved Cooper's gun. Cooper, upset and angry, looked over and said, "Van Doren, you can have my help, but if they're hurt or harmed because of you, I can't promise that you won't be hurt or harmed, too. I love Holly and I care about her mom. They're my family. I don't want trouble for them."

He snapped on his seatbelt and looked over as Kurt pulled away. "Now what's this all about and why are Maggie and Holly in danger?" Cooper wanted answers from this man who had so recently become part of Maggie's life.

Bright neon lights splashed colors against store windows as the car weaved and threaded its way through the evening traffic. Kurt spelled out the problems, beginning with the medical mix-up all the way to this morning's death of the part-time engineer at the District Center.

Cooper, sitting in the small car, adjusted the seat as far back as it would go. "I heard about that guy's death on the radio on the way home. Let me get this straight. Maggie almost bought it this morning with this red-haired guy. And you're saying you think this same dead guy killed that nurse, Millie, and sabotaged your car? How about the clinical trial? No way could he have pulled that off."

Coop shifted his weight to look at Kurt. "Come on, now, how could a guy with no medical education and background get on the floor to make a small change on a patient's chart? He probably wouldn't know a chart from a phone book. You're right, he must have been a hired gun for some of this, but there's definitely someone inside doing you harm. Someone with pretty sophisticated medical training, if you ask me. Someone who can retrieve a chart, read and make sense of it, and then add to it. Sounds like Nora, if you ask me." Cooper glanced over at the tense man who was driving faster than he should. "She have the hots for you?"

"I'm not sure, but I think she was what you could say, *open to the suggestion*. Hell, if I know at this point." He glanced at Cooper while saying this then turned his attention back to the road. "I know Rainey's missing, too, and mixed up in this somehow. I'm not sure what to believe. It's more confusing with the women missing. I'm not thinking straight right now. That's why I figured if you came along, two frantic heads would be better than one."

Cooper reached over and gave Kurt's shoulder a push with his hand. "It's better than sitting on our asses and whining about what's happened. Want me to try getting the cop on the phone for you?"

Kurt fished out his cell phone and handed it to Cooper. "It's on the speed dial there. Imagine having so many problems you have your own pet cop on speed dial."

"Coming up on the hospital. Let's go in and see if security knows anything. Then, I'm going to look up Rainey's address, and we can go talk to him, if he's home. I think I can remember where to find it. There are so many damn little streets in Georgetown, you can go nuts looking for a place, or court, or square. We'll find him, and maybe the girls are there. He claimed he was sick and you know women, out taking care of the walking wounded."

Cooper looked at Kurt and laughed. "Maybe Maggie. But Holly, never, she'd step over his body on the way to the door, I swear it. Not that she doesn't have kindness in her, but she hoards it for folks she feels are important to her. And I can tell you right now Rainey ain't one of 'em. She thought he was a creep from the word go."

They parked in the staff lot, and Kurt told the security guard it was his new car. The guy knew him and let it slide. "But next time, Doc, get the sticker on okay?"

The two men were hurrying toward the back entrance. Two men came out with a tall good-looking woman. The trio approached, and when they saw it was Kurt, one of the men called out, "Hey, Van Doren, just the guy we were looking for. We have a situation here with a patient up in the Pavilion, a Mrs. Rochester. She's here for Rainey to do her veins in the morning, and we can't find him."

"Not now, Doyle, on an emergency. This is Dr. Desimone, we're trying to get to Rainey ourselves."

The tall lady, Dr. Weisberger, looked at the men. "If he didn't come back from taking his lady friend home, I would think he is on special duty, shall we say?" She laughed knowingly. "She was a cute little blonde and he did seem very careful of her. She must have had outpatient work and was still quite groggy. Doyle, I didn't know you were looking for him, I would have told you I saw him earlier—oh, after lunch sometime, maybe 2 or 3 o'clock. Hey, I guess even Rainey has hormones."

Kurt overheard this and stopped in his tracks. "Linda, Dr. Weisberger, what time did you say?"

"Let me think, I guess it was about 2. No maybe 3 o'clock because I saw patients on K Street up until 2 or a little after." To her self more than Kurt, she said, "Let's see, I left the office around 2:30 and grabbed a coffee, fat free latte, at the coffee shop near the office. I saw him when I was on my way in and he was leaving. Yup, must have been closer to 3 o'clock or after 3. Why, is it important?"

"Don't know, but your information may help, thanks. And, Linda, you're a good ad for what you do. We have to have lunch sometime and continue our discussion." He shouted to her as he grabbed Cooper and started for the entrance.

Cooper looked at him in shock as they walked toward the entrance. "Well, that's a new twist on that tired old line, let's do lunch, and you look good. And of all times! I thought Maggie was your main squeeze, as my kids say. Or are you one of those love 'em and leave 'em types, with a nurse in every exam room like on TV?"

They entered, and ignoring Cooper's remarks, Kurt went to the reception area and checked to see if Rainey was in the building.

A frustrated Kurt slammed his fist on the counter. "Damn! Just as I figured, not here. We need to find security." They talked to the officer on duty, who knew nothing about the two women.

"Let's get my pocket file, his address is on it, and head over there. I'm pretty sure Rainey's with Maggie, but why? And where's Holly? No one mentioned two women."

They hurried down the long corridor, passing various offices and conference rooms. At the end they caught an elevator to a lower level. It opened onto a basement area with various signs, among them was one marked: Pathology Lab. Another said: Staff Offices.

Cooper, keeping up with Kurt, was determined to find out about this Linda. He glanced over at the worried man. "You just amaze me with your brazenness. Worrying about Maggie and making passes at another woman!"

"You're wrong on that count. I have one woman, Maggie, who's currently in a lot of trouble, and so is Holly. As for Linda, her and her old man, Dick Weisberger, run the biggest surgical practice in this end of town and the Maryland suburbs. The schmoozing is simple. I need a job, she has jobs. They've been looking at me for a while now. Simple as that, old buddy, nothing more." They kept moving rapidly along corridors buried under the hospital.

"Sorry, Kurt, just being protective. Where to now?"

"My crummy office is where, and we're here."

He took out his fob and got them into a small 9 by 12 room painted in a hideous salmon pink with patches of white plaster in several areas. A large watermark on a dropped acoustical ceiling spoke of a recent flood, or one that took place when Noah was in charge—it was hard to tell. The worn gray rug was serviceable and had been recently vacuumed with sweeper tracks still visible.

"They sure spare no expense for you slaves to science, why nothing but the best, I see. This is worse than my office and I thought I had the pits, but I won't trade." Coop glanced around as Kurt thrashed through the top drawer in a beat-up old gray government surplus desk.

"Here, let's go, Cooper. I'll drive, you look up Rainey in this file."

They started back out the door at full tilt when Kurt's cell phone started chirruping. It was in Cooper's pocket. He fished it and handed it to him.

Bleeding from about 20 minor cuts and scratches on her arms and back, Holly cupped the tiny phone to her ear as she tried 911. She could not get 911 to ring. "Damn piece of junk!" She hit the phone with her hand and then she tried Cooper's cell phone. No answer. I gave her Kurt's cell phone number; she dialed and got him on the first ring. "Kurt, it's Holly."

Fearful of Rainey's coming in, the two handcuffed women hid almost completely under the bed as she talked to the men on the phone.

"Holly, is your mom there? Is she all right?"

"She's fine, but shut up and listen carefully, I'm making this quick. I can't get 911 on this damn toy phone, and Rainey the Ripper has us up in some room in his house. He had us handcuffed between a bed, like a Nancy Drew Mystery."

Kurt and Cooper were both listening and started to talk at once. "Holly, we're—"

"Shut the hell up and just *listen*! Don't play hero. Get the cops and get us

192

out of here. We're not sure when and if this crazy fool will blow and kill us both. I got loose with a lot of blood and pain and Mom's help, but we're still sort of afraid to move. Not sure where he's creeping around and to make it worse, we're handcuffed together. But, I found my purse. The bastard left my cell phone in it or did not think I had one. He had it hidden in the bathroom. He figured we couldn't get it. Boy was he wrong. When we set our minds to something nothing stops us, right, Mom?" She said it with pride. "Where are you two anyway?"

"We're headed to Georgetown on our way to Rainey's house. Don't ask. I just figured out most of it. He's the one who gave the red-haired guy, Swenson, an alibi the day of the murder. I started to put it together earlier. I'm not familiar with how to get there. Any help in that direction?"

"Hell no, Mom and I were out like lights while he drove over here, pills of some kind. Get the cops to get you here. For God's sake, don't play hero. We're scared, scratched, tired, and hungry. We can't even use the bathroom or he would hear us move, so *hurry*!" She hung up.

"I didn't catch it all, what did she say?"

"Cooper, we have to get to them and get the cops. Rainey's our man, and he's pulling a kidnap charge on himself now on top of two murders. I know we have to get to the girls."

"What did Holly say? Actually, Kurt, we are little out of it to play hero all alone."

"Didn't plan to, let's get the cops on that phone."

They were passing a dark street and Kurt looked up. "We getting close, it's got to be around here somewhere. Hey, that's the place Maggie and I went to the night she was released, did she ever tell you about that place? What's the name of it, can you see, Coop?"

He rolled his window down to get a better look, the old sign was neon and pink and some of the letters were out. "I think the joint's called Raymond's or Ramundo. Too many letters out for sure."

Kurt was slowing down. "The place is a gay bar. Maggie and I laughed about it all the way to your house that first night. I think we're close to Rainey's house."

Cooper looked at him said, "Once the police get here, we'll just follow the flashing lights."

"Good idea, call them. Hey, I think I found the house." He tossed his cell phone to Cooper and was scrutinizing house and gate numbers as he slowed to a crawl. "Yes, bingo! That's it—39th and St. Isadore Street, right on the corner. I remember it now. I've been here a few times. But at night it looks different."

Cooper was busy speed dialing the detective's number—no answer. He called the main 911 number and explained the situation. He was put on hold.

"I don't believe it. Here I'm reporting a kidnapping and possible double murder, and they put me on hold."

"They figure you for a looney, get some balls, and throw that doctor shit around. It usually works, watch!"

Kurt waited a minute and was transferred to a bored detective in homicide. He spoke sharply. "Look, Officer, I have two sick women in this house in Georgetown. I'm their physician, Dr. Van Doren. The man holding these women is possibly the killer of the two at the District Hospital Center. Now enough of this crap, if you don't send help, I'll have to go in myself and then call Mayor Jenkins and your chief. *Do you understand me?* We have a double kidnapping and possible murderer of two people, *so get off your ass and do something.*"

All you could hear was the detective scribbling and saying, "Yes, Doctor, of course, can you give me—"

Cooper grabbed the cell phone from Kurt. "Officer, the address for Dr. Jules Rainey is at the corner of 39th and St. Isadore Street in Georgetown. Yes, I'm Dr. Desimone, a colleague of Dr. Van Doren's. We're sitting right outside the house now…get here!" He punched the end button, and looked smugly at Kurt. "Sometimes you have to give addresses, it helps." They nervously grinned at one another.

Chapter 37

"We can wait or try to get in, what do you think, Coop?"

Without words the two men climbed out of the little car. Kurt whispered, "Stay behind me and cover my back and do what I do."

Cooper whispered, "Fine with me."

With Kurt in the lead, they started slowly up the brick path toward the small house. The moon was bright, and shadows from the fence, trees and bushes of the small well-kept yard kept the sidewalk dark. They used the shadows for cover, moving quietly as they approached the front steps.

Suddenly a voice from the porch announced, "Good evening, Kurt, who's your friend there? Another relative of Maggie's come to rescue the ladies?"

Rainey moved into the dim light from the side of the wraparound porch. Holding a small pistol, he beckoned them to approach.

Kurt whispered to Cooper, "Did you bring the gun?"

"Oh shit! I thought you did."

Kurt then raised his hands to show he wasn't armed. Cooper followed.

"Jules, I don't know what's going on here, but don't take this out on the girls. They don't know we're here and I know they must be scared."

"Shut up! Stay away from me and the gun. I know how to use it, but prefer not to at least at this point. Get in the house. Remember, if either of you get out of line, I won't hesitate. Then I'll go up and use it on the ladies, too. There are lots of people here tonight, and lots of reasons to keep cool heads. Are we agreed on this?"

"Agreed," the two men said in unison, walking slowly in the front door and down the hallway to a sitting room.

The room was small, but exquisitely furnished. Crystal lamps, ivory silk drapes, prints and paintings adorning the walls in elaborate frames. Red and ivory silk furnishings glimmered in the low lamplight of the room.

In the distance they could hear sirens wailing and knew the police had finally decided to put in an appearance.

"Mom, I think the guys are here and the cops, too. Listen, that's music to my poor scratched ears."

I tiptoed into the bathroom, grabbed the peroxide from the medicine cabinet and some sterile pads. "I think getting you through that twisted bar was worse than when you were born. You have a scratch about a foot long down your whole back. And your poor ears have taken quite a beating. Turn a bit and let me just touch them up with this."

"I have to hand it to you, I never thought you could hold that little iron bar up long enough for me to squeeze through. If you had let go, I think my lung would have been punctured or worse."

"Mothers can do wonderful things for their kids, Holly."

"And on a full bladder, too!" Holly smiled at me as I patted on the peroxide over her ears, and down her back. She flinched as the cold liquid touched her.

"Do you think it's safe to go out now or should we wait? I don't hear a sound—no cops, no men, nothing. I wonder what's going on. Do you think we should go to the top of the stairs and peek?"

"Stay put for heaven's sake! You want to get your head blown off at this stage? If the cops are in control, they'll find us. If Rainey the Ripper's still in charge we'll we find that out soon enough, too. So just stay put!" I hissed at Holly.

Kurt and Cooper were seated side by side on an uncomfortable ornate sofa. The ivory cushions made it appear much more comfy that it actually was.

"Jules, if I sit here all night, my back will be broken. I'll be no good for surgery tomorrow." Kurt was making a stab at conversation, alluding to the next morning, hoping he'd be alive to see it.

Jules Rainey crossed his legs and made himself comfortable in a small armchair near the tiny ornate white fireplace. He pointed the gun squarely at the two men and said, "I suppose you've figured out most of it by now, gentlemen. I have your women upstairs carefully handcuffed and out of harm's way." His formal words were coming out faster than usual.

Kurt stared at the gun in Rainey's hand, as he realized the sirens had gone past the tiny house and were headed in some other direction. No help coming, it seems. Stupid bureaucrats need paperwork to scratch their own asses, he thought.

"Jules," he said quietly, "I simply can't believe you're behind all these

196

problems. I can put you at the nurse's station and doing the chart, but Millie Prentice was someone we both liked and depended on. Who was that man who almost killed my Maggie today, Jules? You'll have to forgive me, but I really would like some answers here before I go off to meet my maker."

Jules leaned forward and favored the men with, for once, was a genuine smile. The kind of smile he had only seen on the man's face a few times. "Kurt, neither you nor your friend here—I'm sorry, I did not get your name." He bent his head toward Cooper inquisitively.

Cooper answered formally, "Desimone, Dr. Cooper Desimone, I work at NIH and Holly, Maggie's daughter and I—"

Rainey waved the gun at him. "Enough, Doctor, I'm glad to meet a colleague, and don't worry, you'll be out of here in a few minutes and so will Maggie, Holly, and Kurt."

He gave Kurt a soft look and Cooper, noticing it, suspected Rainey had some deep feelings for the man. He'd seen that same lovesick look on Maggie's face when Kurt arrived to spend Christmas Eve with them. Cooper glanced at Kurt and realized he was putting it together, too.

"I knew you'd figure out where Maggie was and come looking. If you didn't, I would have left a message for you. But I made no secret of leaving the hospital with the two ladies. People saw me, greeted me, and I, in turn, talked to them, as usual. I didn't harm them except for a small pill to make them drowsy and more cooperative. You see, I wanted you to get here to explain, sort it out, you might say."

Kurt sat on the sofa next to Cooper. His heart was hammering in his chest. He wanted to jump the man, run up to Maggie and make sure she was all right. He glanced at Cooper and could tell he was about in the same place. They could both rush him, and since the gun was small caliber, there was a good chance it would be just a minor wound, but the chances were about even that it could go the other way. And if Rainey prevailed, the consequences to the women after such action had to be considered. Better let him talk, the police would eventually get here. They have to pay attention to our phone call.

Rainey was in control and started his narrative. "Gentlemen, for the past few hours I've sat here and pondered my situation. I want to explain clearly, so you may help the police later."

Jules Rainey was clearly in his element. He was using his best lecturer's voice, something Kurt knew from years working with the man. Now he sits across from me a murderer and Maggie's kidnapper.

"Let me explain. When you and Maggie left the Center that night in September you stopped at a little place for dinner near here. You were both so wrapped up in conversation I don't think at first you realized Raymond's was primarily a bar for gay men. You stuck it out, but I left the back way. I'll bet you probably had a good laugh on your way out."

He shifted the gun and moved slightly in the chair. "Keeping one's sexual preference secret is difficult. I suppose by now it's clear to you. It's what I hid from you and the rest of the world for many years."

He leaned forward, the gun still steady. "Now, you think, is that what this is all about? The accidents, the killing—over a man hiding his sexual preference? In a way it was, but there's more to it than that. You see, Kurt, I come from an era when men of color were readily admitted to medical schools and received degrees, but rarely achieve what I have. Yes, there are men who have done it in science and politics and I'm proud to say I'm one of them. We are the exceptions, not the rule."

Kurt and Cooper stirred slightly but kept their eyes on this man.

"Think how much it cost me to gain it. I could never come out of the closet, as they say in my circle. Most of the people I knew are only friends because I have money, or influence. A lot of people are jealous of my position and some are just homophobic. If they knew my secret, sooner or later, my job at the District Center and my teaching would be usurped. The *theys* of the world would see to it that I left a job that I love and end up working in research, or in some potty little private practice stripping old ladies' varicose veins. Not a nice picture, but true, I'm sure.

"Then there's the matter of my daughter. I have always kept in the background, kept her at a distance. She needs and deserves a happy life. Luckily, I've always been able to provide her all the comforts money could buy. A lot of what I did was to protect her, shield her from the truth about me."

Kurt looked puzzled and said, "I didn't know you had a daughter, Jules, we both have that in common, I see."

"Her name and her family are all in the papers I've prepared for later on. You'll find out all about her soon. She's a lovely young woman." Pride showed in his voice and eyes as he talked about her.

He continued, "So, I sat here this afternoon while your women slept. I pondered what to do with my life. I'm a proud man and prefer going out now, because I don't want the Center, you, or my daughter to be ashamed of me."

Kurt shook his head in disbelief. "Jules, you have it wrong on all counts. People all over the country recognize you for your skills as an educator and surgeon. Hell, I could never have achieved what I have if any other man with less patience had not taken me in hand. I'm the proverbial 'good-time Joe,' the optimist. You *taught* me to use that ability to put people at ease."

Kurt continued to try to talk and reason with Rainey. "Where did you ever get this twisted idea that you would be ostracized for being gay? This isn't the 19th century, or the early 20th for that matter. Intelligent people try to judge individuals on their merit, not the color of their skin or a lifestyle—"

Rainey interrupted, "Enough, Kurt, you can't change my mind about what I'm about to do, you know me well enough. But let me tell you how this spun out of control, out of my hands. I almost never frequent a place like Raymond's. But Red insisted I go out to dinner with him that evening. The place has an excellent menu, it was close, and I was too tired to cook, so I gave in. When you and Maggie walked in, I was stunned. I moved to the back quickly and left. I was not sure you saw me. But working so closely for five years, I was afraid that you caught a glimpse, or gesture, something that you would remember and later put it together.

"I decided that I would try to get you out of town. I planned a harassment campaign using Red. Once you were gone, I'd be out of your mind and any memory of that night at the bar."

There was a knock on the door. A firm official knock and loud words carried into the quiet sitting room.

"Dr. Rainey, this is the police. Can you open up, please? We would like to talk to you about a report we have here."

Chapter 38

Without thinking, Cooper got up, glanced at Rainey, nodded and strode down the hall to the door. "Officer, Dr. Desimone here. We have a situation with Dr. Rainey and a gun. There are four of us in here. If you would just be patient, we're trying to diffuse the situation and will keep you posted, is that all right?" He walked back to the sitting room.

Through the door, a strange voice boomed over a bullhorn.

"Doctor Desimone, is it? We have to treat this whole thing like a hostage situation if you aren't coming out. We'll move back and call for help."

Cooper, back in the sitting room, sat down. Rainey looked at him and said, "Thank you. I appreciate what you just did."

He continued, "But do remember I killed a man today and I caused the death of another a couple of months ago. I know my arrest and the notoriety would cause a media circus."

Looking at Kurt, Jules continued his explanation. "I never planned to hurt you. Just for you to keep having incidents come up that would show you in a bad light; nothing serious, just gossip and finger pointing. I was hoping to get you to quit or transfer. When you stayed, I knew I was going to have to do something more drastic. I picked on Red who's been coming to Raymond's bar for a long time. He was the one of the few who knew me and my profession and he's cared about me for years."

Rainey sat back and crossed his legs, the gun remained steady. "Now about Millie's death and your problem. I've used Red for many little errands in my life—nothing illegal before this started. I asked him and he agreed to the attack on Prentice. He went a little too far, the fact that she died was unfortunate. A tragic accident, but from then on I knew Red's days and mine were numbered."

Kurt was getting impatient with the story, and with Rainey. "What the

200

hell was that so-called accident I had all about? It could have killed us both. That was not a little annoyance."

"No, I'm afraid that was Red working on his own. It's almost impossible to control another human being completely. Red was jealous of you. The accident was simply his own way of trying to get rid of his competition. He was becoming hard to control—as the death of the Prentice woman a couple weeks later showed me."

Kurt snapped at Jules, "What the hell had you planned for Maggie today? She was strapped down and being taken to God knows where when she tipped that gurney. What was that all about? Was that Red or you?"

"I tried one last ploy to get you to resign. I agreed with Maggie's rather flamboyant scheme from the start. It sort of fit perfectly. I could see it might be my one way of getting out from under after I disposed of Red. I figured if Maggie was attacked, they would naturally consider you a suspect, alibi or no alibi. It would go harsh with you at the Center. Too many little things have piled up with you at the heart of them. I would have called for your resignation myself, as I explained at lunch the other day, remember?"

Kurt was annoyed now. He got up in front of Rainey and started pacing. Rainey raised the gun ever so slightly to follow the agitated man's movements.

Kurt stopped, turned and shaking his head said, "Your ego and some kind of perverted attachment to me caused all this? It was just to save your pride, soothe your ego?" He kept pacing and saying this over and over.

As he turned to say something to Cooper he saw the gun go up to Jules' mouth, a noise like a popgun went off. It ruined the small chair.

"Mom, did you hear that funny noise? It's not loud enough to be a gun is it? I mean, could they be popping wine corks down there?"

"What the hell do you think is going on down there, a party? No, it's been a while and I've heard nothing, no Rainey. I know I just heard Kurt's voice a few minutes ago. I think Rainey's holding the men hostage. This is getting really scary. Give me that shoe of yours. I'm going to try the window again. Damn, the paint must be a hundred years old here." I grabbed the chunky fashionable shoe from Holly and started pounding away.

"Mom, they'll hear you downstairs."

"I don't care at this point, we have to do something. Get pounding!"

As Holly and I started to pound on the window, we glanced down and spotted a young woman holding a gun. She saw Holly, went away for a moment, and reappeared with a piece of paper.

WE ARE HERE TO HELP.

I read the note. Holly snorted, "I'm just as concerned about Cooper and Kurt now."

Holly nodded to the trucks behind the figure holding the sign and said, "Hey, look the fire service to our rescue is with that good-looking woman down there."

"That's Tanya Jackson, a detective who works with Detective Walters. That guy that's been snapping at Kurt's heels for weeks."

A ladder was placed just at the window. A young face dressed in a fireman's hat popped up and said, "Ladies, we're going to break the window. We'd like it very much if you would just try to get out and on the ladder as quickly as possible. There's an armed man in the house. The police are treating this as a hostage situation."

The cute fireman looked about 16 years old. Holly and I held up our hands, and she shot back to the young man on the ladder, "Listen, we're handcuffed together here. We can't climb out anywhere until we get these cuffs off. You say the men are hostages, too?"

All thoughts of her own safety gone, Holly turned to me. "We need to help them, Mom. Listen, I'll get one shoe and you the other."

"Please cover yourselves and move away from the window," came word from the fireman.

We moved to the side and held the silk drape in front of us for protection. The window exploded inward. Someone was pounding out the little pieces of glass.

Suddenly, the bedroom door flew open and Cooper and Kurt rushed in. Kurt grabbed me and pulled me into his arms. I was so happy and relieved to see him, I burst into tears. Cooper was holding Holly, she was crying in his chest. We were still holding hands, you might say, linked together made the reunion a bit awkward.

"Maggie, I'm so sorry about this...mess. Oh, babe, are you okay?"

I looked up at his dear face and kissed him soundly. He returned the kiss.

The fireman outside the window turned and shouted, "I'm coming down. Man, they're just making out in here now."

Safe in Kurt's arms I asked, "Have they taken Rainey away yet? Is it safe to leave? I really don't want to see him. He was so nice and then so frightening. I just don't know what I'd do if I have to face him."

"I'd like to kick the slimy creep," sniffed Holly, looking over at what she perceived was a disgusting display of affection between Kurt and her mother.

"No, he's downstairs, but you don't have to face him. He died about 3 minutes ago. He shot himself. There's a long note explaining everything along with estate papers and instructions for someone to pick up later. His lawyer, I think."

A uniformed officer came in with a set of keys on a ring. He kept trying keys until one clicked and we were freed.

Rubbing my sore wrist, I said to Kurt, "He caused it all, didn't he? The whole stupid thing, including the two deaths and now his own. I had some of it figured out, but the why is still eluding me. What a sad sick man he was."

Kurt kissed me again in spite of Holly being there. "We'll explain it all to you later."

I thought about Nora and Connie and said, "I wonder if he was protecting his…"

"Daughter? Yes, how did you know about that, babe? And who and where she's at is anybody's guess."

"Yes, Connie. That's her name. I want to make a quick phone call or two before we do anything else, if you don't mind. It's sort of private, can you lend me your cell phone?"

"Sure. You know who Connie is and where to find her, don't you?" He handed the phone to me as I started for the bathroom.

A few minutes later, I emerged and handed the phone back to Kurt. "I'll explain my part later. Now I just want some food. We've had plenty of rest today."

"Hey, guys, let's eat, then go home," Holly said loud enough for the whole house to hear.

Cooper looked at Kurt then back to Holly. "Can't, sweetheart. We have to make statements and paper work. We'll be at it the rest of the night."

I was not ready for paperwork yet. I looked at the group and wailed, "I have to eat and rest first, is our pet cop here, Walters?"

Kurt nodded.

"Walters are you down there?" I shouted.

"Yes, do you need me?" came the shouted answer up the stairs.

"We're ready for you. But you have to take us to an all-night burger joint first. I haven't eaten since yesterday—no, make that day before yesterday. I need some food!"

He arrived in the doorway and smiled at all of us then sighed and said, "Deal."

We all looked at him, gave a thumbs up, and repeated, "Deal!"

The next day the *Post* and the *Times* carried short stories on their back pages headlined: "Former D.C. Center Employee Found Dead." Underneath, it went on to explain the police had strong evidence that Harold (Red) Swanson was responsible for the death of Nurse Millie Prentice back in December.

In a front-page story, just below the fold, the *Post* reported the death of Jules Rainey, Chief of Cardiovascular Surgery at the D.C. Medical Center. The paper went on to state his education, years of service, research work, and accomplishments. There were flattering comments from the CEO of the Center, and several colleagues. The death was attributed to depression, brought on by ill health, and personal problems. This was the paper's polite way of stating it was a suicide.

Over a late breakfast, Kurt sat and read the stories with a stony face. He pushed the paper aside, got up, put on his old brown suede jacket and went out for a walk in the snow.

I sat at the breakfast table, glanced at the stories, got up, and looked out the back door after him, hands in his pockets, walking alone up towards the woods behind the house.

Stupid was sitting by her food bowl, and as I poured her kibble I shook my head and commented to her, "What an amazing few months we've had, meeting, becoming a family. Whatever is in store for us, old girl, the future can never beat this amazing winter."

I started to toss the paper in the recycle bin when the car and driver section slid to the floor. I picked it up and something caught my eye, an ad that read: TRIUMPH TR4A, 1966. New paint. Dark Green. Extensively refurbished. New interior including black leather seats. Newly finished top. Fitted walnut dash. Independent rear suspension and wire wheels. Duel exhaust. Rebuilt engine. Drives perfect. It gave a price and phone number.

I glanced down at Stupid and said to her, "I think I might have idea for a cure for his depression. The green machine lives!"

Epilogue

The party was huge. The day was typical July weather in Washington, D.C., sunny, hot and humid. Everyone was there, local politicians, hospital administrators, staff and patrons who committed large sums of money toward the trust for the new building. They all turned out for the ribbon-cutting ceremony that hot day over the Fourth of July weekend.

Kurt was the trustee for the whole operation, so we sat up front with the dignitaries all through the speeches and tributes that were part of the program for the opening ceremonies of the Rainey Staff Housing Complex, which was quite an event that Saturday.

"It's hotter than blazes out here and with more hot air coming from the podium I'm ready to faint," I complained quietly into Kurt's coat sleeve.

"Almost over, Mags. Keep your cool for just a bit and then it's inside for the fancy big spenders luncheon," he murmured out of the corner of his mouth.

Speeches over, they found Holly and Cooper walking toward the Center's large reception area set up for the dignitaries' luncheon.

They strolled slowly in hot afternoon sun and Holly leaned forward and murmured into my ear, "What a hoot, Mom, going to a luncheon in honor of a bastard who almost killed us. Makes us kind of hypocrites, doesn't it?"

I shot back at her, "Shut up, you brat, and behave! This is a very important occasion for Kurt and the hospital. They're honoring the man for his contributions to the Center, so get over it." Holly grinned and playfully poked me in the ribs as we walked along.

Settling Holly and Cooper, Kurt, bent over and quietly asked, "Can I see you a minute in the conference room, hon? I have something to discuss with you."

"Sure, let me just grab something to drink first. I'm melting, okay?"

"Deal." He grinned at me.

I inched my way to the drink table and nabbed a glass of ice-cold white wine from the waiter.

I then indicated to Kurt with my wine glass. "You lead, I follow."

We entered a small conference room. Housekeeping had gone all out to get the Center ready for the big day and everything sparkled. Kurt walked in and peeled off his suit coat to get the full effect of the chilled air in the room.

I walked around the table looking at Kurt. "Sure brings back memories. I remember this conference room with you in it that scary morning."

"Mags, be serious now." He walked over and grabbed my arm gently and sat me down in one of the upholstered chairs. "Kind of fitting to be in here with what I have to say."

"Well, get on with it, man, food's out there."

"Remember what I told you, way last September when we first met? I said I wasn't cut out for domesticity. I've tried to convince myself that's true for a long time after my first bad experience. But when this Rainey thing ended I realized we need to be together, we belong together. I know we have to work out some things in time and we have baggage from our earlier lives to deal with, babe."

He took my hands in his. "Margaret McCall Suit, will you do me the honor of making this arrangement permanent? I'm sure when we're ready we'll both know it, but I need to know now if you feel the same way."

"Oh, hon, you know better than to ask." I stood on tiptoes and kissed his dear face and taking his hands I went on, "I agree we aren't quite ready now. You jumped into your first marriage too quickly, and I've spent a lot of years raising my brood and being alone. It's hard for me to give up that independence, even for you, love." I then started to wrap my arms around him but he gently moved them back into my lap.

"Now wait, I want to do this right, I have something here for you. It's the reason I asked you to come in here in the first place." He produced a small blue velvet bag with a gold drawstring. He opened it carefully revealing a white silk lining and removed a diamond ring. It was a rather large pear-shaped diamond surrounded by smaller ones. It sparkled and shimmered in the lights coming through the large windows of the conference room.

I looked at him as he slipped it on the third finger of my left hand. It fit perfectly. I was speechless as tears slipped down my face. "I have this little inscribed ring that is almost a perfect match to this one that was a Christmas present."

Kurt caught me in his arms and we held one another. "This was my mother's ring. I wanted you to have it. I hope you don't mind. It tells the world that we're together and serious about our commitment to one another." After one final moment together, we left the conference room with me pulling him along to the family table.

"Hey, Doc, what were you doing in there giving my mother a physical? What took so long?" Holly glanced at the hand her mother held out.

She grabbed it and exclaimed, "Oh my God, is that a rock or what? That much ice is usually reserved for skating rinks. Mom, hey, I really will be a bridesmaid. Ivy is younger by 12 minutes so she gets to be the flower girl. Oh, we have to get to Ivy and tell her. Have you set a date? We have plans to make!"

Everyone was laughing and talking, and tables around us overheard and started congratulating Kurt and me, as well. I was dragging Kurt now by the hand across the wide floor. Ivy and Cooper followed us.

We met Mayor Jenkins on his way into the party. He started to greet us and say something, but I kept pulling on Kurt, not stopping. Waving to the mayor over my head, I pulled my laughing man across the hot blacktop parking lot to his green machine, as I shouted, "Can't stop now, your honor, we're in a hurry! We're celebrating!"

Printed in the United States
17205LVS00003BA/70-72